I Killed the Monster

I Killed the Monster

ANTONIO CASALE

iUniverse, Inc.
Bloomington

I KILLED THE MONSTER

iUniverse books may be ordered through booksellers or by contacting:

iUniverse
1663 Liberty Drive
Bloomington, IN 47403
www.iuniverse.com
1-800-Authors (1-800-288-4677)

ISBN: 978-1-4620-7118-0 (sc)
ISBN: 978-1-4620-7119-7 (ebk)

Printed in the United States of America

iUniverse rev. date: 11/28/2011

To my father and brothers, Mark and Ireneo, all swallowed, prematurely, by the voracious appetite of the monster.

CONTENTS

ACKNOWLEDGEMENT

This is a novel, although it pretends of being partially autobiographical and based on the personal experience of the protagonist. Any reference to names of people, areas, events are purely fictional or coincidental.

The main purpose is to enlighten men and women of every race and credo, who have been diagnosed with the 'monster,' how to cope with and win over it.

The male protagonist claims that when he was finally rescued from the abysm of miseries, he sought the expertise of a writer to convey his experience in a meaningful literary body. His skilled hand covers the entire span of the book.

THE NEWS

Dear reader, did you ever see a monster? I mean a real monster. It may be visible or invisible, but that does not change its destructive nature. Millions of people have already had the misfortune of being confronted with it. In the terrible clash, some have prevailed, others have been sacrificial lambs. The various results have indicated to us that fear has to be avoided at all costs because it leaves permanent scars in our minds and hearts. This brings us to an ulterior consideration. If you feel that you are a robot, and, therefore, exempted from any monsters' invasion, do not bother reading this book. I am confident that good sense will prevail at the end. By reading it, you may be fortunate enough to be spared the agony of becoming the next innocent victim of the monster's lethal nails. In turn you can help others to fall in its grips. And, so, if by any chance you are going to be attacked by him, I encourage you not to draw any desperate conclusion or succumb to a hysterical behavior or a state of hopelessness. Stop and read this book because it may offer you the opportunity of a lifetime; however, you must get armed with knowledge. Like the Hydra of Erna, the monster is one, but the heads are many. You are called to be the new Theseus.

With these premises, my dear reader, I will introduce you the author, who will give you an accurate web of this creation based on the information provided to him by the protagonist. You will have the honor to meet both of them immediately. Read, now how the author and the protagonist met.

In July of 2009, Chris Saleca was strolling around my house with his wife's puppy, Sweet Princess, when he heard, in his proximity, the rumbling of a motor. He stepped to the side for fear that the animal would be hit. The shrieking sound of the brakes urged him to turn around. A cloud of smoke generated by the creeping tires on the pavement hampered his sight. By the time the visibility was restored, a Maserati stopped briskly a few inches away from his body, but it was enough. Chris, a writer by profession, was not a man who got easily scared; however, in that circumstance, he threw himself instinctively on the ground rolling a few yards until he hit his head against a rock and lost consciousness. He recovered soon after, but as he looked on the right side, he realized that he was dangling on the edge of a precipice which surrounds the whole circle of houses squatted on the summit of the hill. He looked down and almost lost control of the grip. He was cognizant that his survival depended on the remaining strength. He could not let himself go. They would not even find his skin. The puppy began to bark vehemently and got his teeth in the owner's shirt. The driver realized that the seriousness of the case, quickly unbuckled the security belt. Not to waste time, he left the motor running and rushed on the scene. In that handful of seconds that separated him from the unfortunate man, the dog had managed to hold his position. This gave the owner the chance to collect the residue of his energy and, with a feline lateral jerk, gain the flat land. The driver grabbed Chris with both hands and pulled him even further inland. Before he made any attempt to get up, the young man passed his hands over his face to look for any presence of blood. To his surprise, he ascertained that they were stained with blood. He also discovered some abrasions and lacerations on both arms and just below them, a hematoma. He looked at his puppy and said, "Thank you Sweet Princess for saving my life. The dog barked a couple of times to express his joy and, then, began to lick him all over the chin. The driver apologized and offered Chris a ride to the hospital for a check-up, but he declined.

Chris was twenty five years old, tall and slender. The forehead looked like the front of a car with two big blue headlights. The nose still showed the marks from previous fights with other youngsters. The chin was perfect, but his cheeks were exposing forward a bit too much. The head resembled the roof of a straw hut, well sectioned in an orderly fashion. The color was a combination of dark and light streaks at the upper part due to the persistent action of the sun. He spent a couple hours a day in the gym to keep his body in shape. Perhaps, his physical endurance and agility provided him with the extra strength to survive in a dreary situation. Never before, it occurred to him to face death while dangling from a rock.

With Chris' assurance that he was fine, the driver rushed to his car, rolled down the window on his left side and turned off the motor. He went back to Chris with a broad smile and pulled him on his feet. The newcomer took a handkerchief and started to dust off Chris' shirt and pants. "Nice meeting you!" he said.

"Yeah, do you know that you almost killed me?" he shouted.

"My Pupa never hurts anyone."

Chris looked at him with a slight sense of despise and replied with indignation, "Well, if your Pupa or whatever you call it, does not hurt anyone, maybe you are the killer behind the wheel."

The man stretched his right arm and said, "Pupa and I have our deep divergences at times, but we have always smoothed them out. But, allow me to introduce myself. I am Mimi' O' Fabuloso For you, I am only Mimi', but I came here to talk to you about another Pupa."

Chris felt disarmed by his good demeanor and said, "You mean you have a second car like that?

"Well, not all Pupas are the same. I got 'burned' very badly with one of them. I got robbed of my love, freedom and happiness and I was left on the verge of an abyss. That is a big story per se. We will come back to her. Right now, there is another pressing matter to agree upon," he assured him.

"I see" replied Chris convinced to have understood the underlying drama. "As of now, my pressing matter is my health and I have to wash the stains of blood from my face and apply a disinfectant."

The driver got a gallon of water from the trunk, picked up a Neosporin tube with sterilized cotton and provided the necessary aid.

Mimi' was on the threshold of thirty years of age, thin and tall, like an electric pole. His brown eyes seemed like two caves under shiny straight hair. Anyone would have ventured to say that he had polished it with some kind of cream. Likewise, his mustache was lustrous and, after curving laterally, rose up to the nostrils and curled again in front of the cavities. His nose was as straight as a bamboo stick. The lips were prominent and so were the ears. In that respect, he looked like a rabbit. The skin was dark and showed some light depressions on his face. His habiliment taste was ostentatiously refined. He wore a Dolce & Gabbana's white suit with a sport blue shirt. On the small top pocket of the jacket, he had a yellow handkerchief exposed half way in a 'V' formation. The translucent black shoes reflected the glowing hair giving the appearance of a distinguished gentleman even though he walked a bit clumsily.

"Mr. Pipi'," said Chris.

"Ah, wait just a minute," interrupted him brusquely Mimi'. "You are mispronouncing my name and you are changing the meaning too."

Chris could not control a bit of laughter at his mistake. He apologized, and after various unsuccessful attempts to pronounce it correctly, he decided to give up. At the end, he apologized.

This time, Mimi' did not appear disturbed by it. Indeed, he said, "I think you like the name."

-"Well, It is more than that. It sounds full of charisma to me. Again, I did not mean it for disrespect. I was just captivated by the accent."

"In reality, it is not an exotic name, "he tried to explain. "It is very common in Italy and France."

But Chris had no intention of spoiling a meeting with a stranger. They shook hands and started to walk toward the car.

Halfway, Mimi' stopped and said, "My father was a Brazilian soccer player who played with the Milan team in Italy. During those years, he met a girl, who worked for a national television, and they got married. I was born and raised there. I hated school. I caused a lot of problems to the teachers. I ganged up with my peers and played many pranks on them. I was expelled more than once for inappropriate behavior. To keep me away from the wrong crowd, my father bought me a scooter. I jumped at the idea of owning a motorized machine and I ran up and down the hills all day.

One Sunday, the police knocked at my parents' door and said, "Mr. O'Fabuloso, your son is driving an uninspected and unregistered vehicle. In addition, he drives without a license. "My dad reproached me saying, "I told you not to run this scooter without taking driving lessons." Then, he called the officer on the side and talked to him for a few minutes. A week later, a different policeman visited my parents. He complained that I was driving without a protective helmet. Again, my father shouted unthinkable remarks at me."

This is the top part of the hill where Mimi' parked his Maserati.

One Sunday, the police knocked at my parents' door and said, "Mr. O'Fabuloso, your son is driving an uninspected and unregistered vehicle. In addition, he drives without a license. "My dad reproached me saying, "I told you not to run this scooter without taking driving lessons." Then, he called the officer on the side and talked to him for a few minutes. A week later, a different policeman visited my parents. He complained that I was driving without a protective helmet. Again, my father shouted unthinkable remarks at me."

"And your mother?"

"My mother was busy writing checks to lawyers for my mischievous actions."

"Very interesting. Now, I know why you almost killed me."

"Almost."

"The jewels that you wear around your neck and wrist and the sport car you drive clearly indicate that you are a wealthy person."

"Well, my father was entrenched in the 'saudao.' When his career came to sunset, he could not find any job as a trainer and went back to Sao Paolo. I did not see any future in Brazil for me. I suppose that my misbehavior had some impact on his decision. No doubt, my parent's departure left a void in my life." He looked on the ground and added, "Soon after I met an American girl. She was full of spice, until . . ."

At that point, Chris' curiosity grew even more and he asked, "Why are you disclosing your private life to me, a stranger?"

Mimi' gave a profound sigh and said, "It was a way of 'breaking the ice', of getting to know each other. But, let's come to the substance. I wanted to meet you for quite some time. Unfortunately, for a series of events, unimportant to you, I was unable to pay you an impromptu visit. Now that I found you, I am the luckiest man in the world."

". . . And why is that?" Chris inquired with a mixture of surprise and apprehension.

"I found the treasure of Monte Cristo."

"Are you sure that I am the right person? I am dubious . . ."

Mimi' interrupted him with a loud, sonorous laughter, but he closed his mouth rather quickly. His canine teeth were a bit off course, criss-crossing each other. As soon as he regained his composure, he had the sudden perception that Chris was analyzing his teeth. He pointed at them and said, "I have an appointment with the dentist next week. I have decided to straighten them out. At any rate, the purpose of coming here is to propose you a project."

"What are you alluding to?" Chris exclaimed with another touch of curiosity.

Mimi' shook his head a couple of times and said, "You see, people are being stripped every day, literally, from their loved ones. They are dying or about to die simply because they ignore the monster."

"And, what is that?"

"You will find out very soon, "he replied. He snapped the forefingers of the right hand, turned on his heels and went back to his Pupa. He grabbed a briefcase from the passenger's seat and quickly reached Chris. "I thought you were going to show me some cosmetic products. You have the impeccable appearance of the perfect salesman. Am I wrong?"

"It is not a question of being wrong or right," he assured him. I have nothing to sell. I came here to make a deal with you."

"Here we go again with the salesman idea," said Mimi' with emphasis and shook his head.

Mimi's facial expression changed. He became serious. "I almost got killed by a monster a few months ago."

"A monster?"

"Yes! Now you understand why I am here."

All that seemed a riddle to Chris. Mimi' must have had a telepathic mind and said, "You have nothing to fear, nothing to lose."

Christ started to show signs of impatience. He still was unsure about Mimi's proposal. "My friend," he said, "I am afraid that you came to the wrong person. I am not a lawyer. I cannot help you."

Mimi' placed the briefcase on the hood of the car and pressed his fingers on some numbers. The briefcase opened. "This is, according to people, the Pandora's box," he said with an enigmatic look. "In it, I have placed jewels, dollars, financial transactions . . . You name them. Now, I have only one treasure."

"What is that?" responded Chris with increased curiosity. In the briefcase, he had not noticed any gold or silver, so, what could his interlocutor hide in it?

Mimi' attempted a half smile and said, "No, no! Here I have valuable papers."

"Is that all?" exclaimed Chris. "All that noise for a bunch of papers?"

"You ought to know that because of these papers I searched for you everywhere"

"Why is it? I never left this geographical area except for going to Europe."

"That's true, but you are in constant motion. You are like the wind. You are at home and you are never home. You resemble the eel in the sea."

"If you want to stay in business, you have to run, my friend," insisted. "It seems that we are starting to speak the same language," added Mimi'.

"In my life, I learned that if you really want something, you have to fight for it and I am a fighter."

"What are you? A bullfighter? A gladiator?"

"No, I am none of them. I am a successful businessman with a scanty high school education."

"Well, you graduated."

"On paper, yes . . . One day, I saw my father giving an envelope to a teacher. I thought it was a simple letter of appreciation. He never told me what he wrote or what was inside. Bu, I am quite sure that he gave him a gift . . ."

"I understand. Not everybody is fit to be a football player . . ."

"Exactly! But now, let's not lose sight of the previous issue."

"Which is?"

Mimi 'did not respond. He placed the palm of his right hand on his face and rolled it two or three times in a circular motion, as to reshuffle his thoughts. He was about to say something, but he stopped.

Chris, the author, was dangling from the top of this gorge.

Chris was getting impatient and Mimi' decided to continue. "You see . . . I tried to describe my fight with the monster . . ." He did not finish the sentence. He pulled a folder with another bunch of papers from the briefcase with extreme care, as if he were afraid to harm them. "Here, take them! These are yours. It is only the beginning." He paused a moment waiting for Chris 'reaction, which never arrived. He picked up the first set of papers and said, "And this is the end. There was never any communication between these two sets of papers and there will never be unless you build the bridge."

Chris shook his head in a sign of denial. "I am not an engineer. I cannot do it. You are better off searching for a better one."

"I thought we understood each other . . ."

Chris was undecided. He said to him, "May I ask you what prompted you to invite me for this 'project'? There are thousands of prominent writers in the world who could easily create a better artistic composition."

"Terrific comment . . . ! I could have turned my attention to nationally or internationally re-known authors. I read your first two books. They are fantastic."

"Thank you, but that does not mean that I have to write a third."

Mimi' paused a few moments before answering, probably, to catch up breath, "There is no three without two. That's what they say in this part of the country. Aside from that, I have the financial means to support my project, but, you see, I need someone whom I can trust."

Chris thanked him, but Mimi' interrupted him and continued, "I promised to myself that if I survived this gladiatorial battle, bleeding or not, I would try to put my experience at the service of others." Then, he stood silent for a minute or so that seemed an eternity. He laid his right hand on Chris' left shoulder and added, "Please, make sure that you tell the readers that they are free to be ignorant or educated."

Chris frowned and responded, "I concur with you. You are absolutely right! A book can be a source of knowledge or demonic destruction. Their choice depends largely on their culture and attitude."

Mimi' stretched his arms forward and shouted triumphantly, "Holy words!"

Chris stood there not knowing what to say for a while. By then, he realized how anxious his interlocutor was to have the project carried out. A minute passed by without any exchange. With some hesitation, Chris, finally replied, "Your project denotes a noble idea and I admire you, but, in all candors,

I must inform you that I do not have a famous agent or publishing company that advertises for me. I am all alone in a world of vast financial interests, occult deals and schemes. Your book would be only locally popular, at the most. It would never pass through the voracious mouths of unscrupulous editors.'

His words had no effect on Mimi, who said, "Calm down! I am very well aware of it. My only concern is the reader." He put his right hand on his forehead, as if he were searching for something through the computer of his memory, and added, "Just do your job, and I will take care of the rest."

"If you want to take on that responsibility," Chris insisted, "It is entirely up to you. As I stated previously, my fear is that, without good advertisement, the book will not fly."

At that point, Mimi' grabbed a piece of paper from his jacket and handed it to him. Chris read it. It was the title that he wanted for the book. Chris shook his head and said, "It is not what I am talking about. Mimi' ignored Chris' negative attitude and asked him what he thought of the title.

"Enticing as it may be, it will not spur the readers' imaginations. They want something spicy."

He replied, "If people are realistic, this is spicy!"
"Like your Pupa." He accompanied the last word with a smile.
Mimi' dropped down his arms in a gesture of disappointment.

Chris remained pensive for about thirty seconds. His thoughts seemed rivers of doubts. He looked at Mimi' and said, "I beg your indulgence, but if you feel so intensely passionate about your 'project', you should, at least, seek the counsel of a good writer. Your chances for success would be immensely superior. I am only a 'small fish' in a vast ocean."

Mimi' remained unperturbed and cut him short, "Listen! We all have plans. You have yours and I have mine. I am not sure if yours are pure tactic or genuine humility. Your defense is to repeat either side of your position as long as you win your case. In our contemporary society too many novice artists are rising to stardom in a matter of weeks or months. It is common knowledge that when a film producer challenges universal truths or establish new norms to demolish traditions, he sets the stage for a world-wide clamor and success. If they disclaim Jesus' chastity or claim that Leonardo invented an opaque camera to project a self-portray in the Shroud of Turin, or say that Columbus was the Pope's son, the game is over. And, as you very well know, there are writers who resort to subtle sexual innuendos or blatant pornographic language to emerge to notoriety. You ought to know that these writers are not interested in educating society. Their god is the dollar. Their star rises quickly, but their eclipse can also be rapid. Man, you are the only one who can make that decision. For my part, I need someone who is not interested in selling their souls. Is that clear?"

Chris was getting tired of the long tirade. He recollected his strength once more and made an effort to laugh. Mimi' said, "Don't laugh! I am dead serious. Don't let the reader wait any longer."

Chris remained pensive again and said, "Mr. O' Fabuloso I need some time for reflection before I take on this challenge."

"Please, call me' Mimi'. It is much more fashionable. The reader can call me O'Fabuloso." Then, he added, "Is there anything I can do for you to make you change your mind?"

Chris scratched his head and exclaimed, "Can you change that music in your car?"

"Of course, I can." He opened the car and switched to opera. As soon as he reached Chris, he took a check book from his inside jacket, filled a check and signed it. He dethatched it and placed it between Chris' right hand fingers. "You will agree with me that this music is much better than the one from before."

Chris looked at the amount and his eyes opened widely. "With this kind of music, even the most distraught person will listen to it."

"Another piece of music with the same harmony will come at the end of the project."

Chris looked again at the amount with astonishment. He turned at Mimi" and replied, "This is an honorable, but onerous invitation; nonetheless, I like the new music you put on. It is sweeter that any imagination."

"I never had any doubt. Finally, we are speaking the same language," replied Mimi' with a deep sense of satisfaction.

Chris looked toward the car and noticed a camera. What is that?" he inquired.

"A machine," replied Mimi'.

"Is it on?"

"Sure, it is on."

"What is the purpose? Insisted Chris with skepticism.

"It will accompany us throughout our journey," explained Mimi'.

Chris made an attempt to express his disagreement, but Mimi' assured him, ". . . my journey."

As the reader may have gotten a hint of it, Chris succumbed to the sirens' offer, but not before asking for a concession, "I want complete liberty in the structural process."

"You use any technique you deem necessary to give ground to the reader to debate. My only concern is that you do not alter reality and stick to my plan. Write everything I tell you. You take care of the language."

"It is a deal!"

"Magnificent!"

The two shook hands and hugged.

For several straight days, they met on the balcony of Mimi's house. Chris would write everything Mimi' dictated to him in every detail. And, here it is, unabridged, except for some grammatical or syntactical modifications on which they had agreed upon at the onset of the final details.

O' Fabuloso lived in a rich mansion in Cicero, in the outskirts of Syracuse. His house was gigantic. The dimensions were typical for a big family. It was rumored among the neighbors that he had built it (in reality, his wife did it with his blueprints) with the intention to provide space for his future children even after they had married. The envisioned future scenario turned out to be completely erroneous. The brides of his sons never agreed to live with their in-laws. The "castle" was equipped with the most modern sophistications. To open the doors, one had to be acquainted with a specific code. His cars operated in a similar manner. He touched it with the tip of his finger, not someone else, and the door opened. To start the car, he pushed three buttons. In the kitchen, his wife raised her hand and the oven started to heat up. She moved her fingers and the temperature rose or lowered. She whispered to the sink and the water flowed down. She closed her eyes and the water stopped. An electric chair, which rose from the floor by the touch of a button, took those unable to walk everywhere. The bathroom operated by the sound of a voice. The instructions for the newcomers were displayed in cubical letters on a screen. Whenever Mimi' had to shave, the shaving cream bottle would squeeze automatically the cream on the face and an invisible hand guided the razor. If the blade was dull, it would discard the old one in a disposable recycling little bin and put on a new one. It was a wonder world behind any imagination or interpretation. No one ever questioned Mimi' if it were intended to that specific year characterized by health problems, his stormy life or something else. The neighbors respected his privacy. On the front lawn, two enormous rocks flanked the left side of the entrance, while the pathway was made with concrete and the curved lines on the surface gave the illusion of a sequence of blocks. In reality, it resembled the bodily curves of a voluptuous woman. The walls were made of blocks covered with marble. A big waterfall sang its song day and night. In the back garden, he had statues of Greek and Roman goddesses dispersed in the luxurious flora around a thriller swimming pool.

The interior had five rest rooms completely surrounded by glass windows. The kitchen and the dining room shared the same space. A movie size television hanging on the wall above the fireplace, gave the impression of being in a cinema hall. Another room had a spectacular sauna bath, Pompeian style, with all types of girls in transparent clothes. Some malignant neighbor whispered that the couple never used it. The beds were atypical, in the sense that one had to rise on the tiptoes or use a stool to be able to get on them. It is another modern feature that should concern older folks. The interior and exterior colors blended more on the dark side.

In the cellar, he had a gigantic screen in a segregated room with comfortable seats. There, he enjoyed watching movies with his close friends after a party. A sauna bath was available most of the day in a separated gym. The kitchen was a parade of Carrara multicolor marble.

In the past, the house was the meeting place for social events and many friends and relatives gathered especially to taste good food. Lately, the affluence subsided for reasons that will be obvious to the reader as we move along.

This is a view of the bottom of the gorge.

On the designated date and time, Chris parked the car in Mimi's driveway and rang the bell. Mimi' came to the door to welcome him. After a brief exchange of greetings, he introduced him to his older sister. She was an extremely sociable woman. I never heard anyone making a negative comment about her. She must have been a great cook because she kept a large dish of sweets and a bunch of fruits always on the kitchen table. She was young looking, although well in the forties, but disliked with passion to step on the scale. She visited her brother often and loved to cook.

Pupa's real name was Phoenix. She was tall and blond with blue eyes and very short hair, one step from shaving. The forehead was narrow and the hairline, being low, exposed even more its uniqueness. She had dimples that became very prominent whenever she laughed. Her voice was soft and captivating. Her manners were polite.

As a senior student at Syracuse University, she decided to spend the last semester to study art in Florence. Eventually, life events turned her in a different direction. Let us follow her, therefore, during the Italian adventure.

One day, she was taking notes in front of the "Doors of Paradise" across from the Duomo of Florence. Her pen fell on the ground. She wore a V shaped blouse and a snug blue jeans. The crowd was everywhere and pushing was almost a natural occurrence. A young man fell forward almost on top of her. His eyes rested on the V space. Phoenix bent down to pick up the pen. In the process of recuperating her erected posture, she noticed the eyes of the young man staring at her chest. Their faces brushed each other. She blushed and asked, "What are you watching?"

"Actually, I was pressed by the crowd and I fell into the Garden of Eden." He excused himself.

"I was just wondering if you have seen any woman before."

He hesitated a moment to regain his composure from blushing. "Not at that level, miss, I swear it. I am immaculate."

"Very interesting, but not worthy of credibility from what I noticed."

"I happened to be investigating in a moment of disorder. The crowd was unruly."

"Men are all the same!" She said and left.

The young man followed her and caught up at the next traffic light. "My name is Mimi'," he said from behind her.

Phoenix turned around and saw him. She took a deep breath and laughed.

"Yes, it is true. My name is Mimi', Mimi' o Fabuloso,"

"What?" she said in a loud voice. The tourists stopped thinking that something serious happened.

Phoenix covered her mouth with her right hand and could hardly repress the laughter.

"Are you laughing on account of my first or last name?"

She bent down her head slightly and whispered to him, "It's you!"

Mimi' stood in front of her and asked, "You haven't introduced yourself yet. You have such a pretty accent."

"She stretched her right hand and said, "I am an American student here in Florence."
"Can I propose something?" he asked.
"What? Now?"
"It is almost noon. About going to the restaurant in front of us? I see a free table."
She was startled by the sudden invitation. Her lips were moving back and forth, up and down. Finally, she said "Why not?"

Mimi' whispered something in the waiter's ear and put a note in his hands. Ten minutes passed by and the waiter reappeared to inform them that the couple could no longer hold on the table. It had been reserved to another couple who failed to show up on time. The husband had just called to apologize for the inconvenience. It had been all the taxi's fault. He took a long route to charge a higher mileage. Phoenix displayed chagrin about it. "I don't think this restaurant holds a good reputation and I will make sure that it won't," she said.

Mimi' increased the ill humor of his companion, "How is it possible to make such mistakes? It is not my fault if the taxi tried to jip a few dollars extras from the tourists."

Phoenix invited him to leave immediately. She was in no mood to stay a minute longer in a place that evicted her from the table where she was eating. Mimi' looked more compromising. He made a gesture of indulgence and asked her to be a bit more patient. The waiter told them that there was a private eating room available. It cost more, but under the circumstances . . . Phoenix picked up her purse and said, "Let's get out of this place." Mimi' persuaded to stay. It was too tiresome for her to walk to other restaurants. His gentle insistence paid off.

The waiter smiled and said, "You made the right decision. I am sure you will love it." Irritated by his demeanor, Phoenix was ready to strike him with her purse, but she managed to control her feelings.

The three stopped in front of the reserved room. The waiter opened the door and allowed them to pass. "I will comeback shortly," he said. The room was small and it could accommodate only two people. In the middle of it, there was a round table with a vase full of red roses. Mimi' commented with cold sarcasm to the presence of the roses, "Probably, they were sent to the other couple and the waiter made another mistake." Phoenix looked with indignation at them. She turned her attention to the window through which the Arno River was in full view. An interminable human procession was going by. The Communist party had organized a gay parade and used workers with banners and posters proclaiming the rights of each individual to expose his or her own gender proclivity without church or government interferences. Phoenix sat comfortably with her eyes still fixed outside. The ocean of men and women seemed to be endless. Mimi' saw her taken by the scene and said, "In Italy, they love protests and parades. But this is something else."

"To each his own, they say in America."

"I would be ashamed to take to the streets and parade my own homosexuality. What is there to be proud of? Perhaps, some men want to become woman."

"What is wrong with finding satisfaction within the same sex gender?"

"It is very simple. It is against the law of nature. Any rational human being can vouch for it. Secondly, it is against everything written in the Bible. Look, it starts in the Garden of Eden where God creates a female companion for Adam."

"It is a world of "isms.""

"That is true. Man is going behind his earthly boundary lines. He is not an essence. He participates in the continuous flux of human existence. He does not have the power of the Alfa and Omega. He is only a component in the macrocosm of human existence."

"I start to believe that doctors should study more in depth this hormonal dysfunction. If they can discover a medicine that rectifies the hormonal imbalance, the game is over."

"I concur with you one hundred per cent."

Mimi' had just finished his comment that Phoenix's attention was diverted to a card between the roses. Mimi' suggested she open it as long as nobody claimed the ownership. "Maybe," he said, "it is the restaurant's policy to welcome, in a special manner, the clients who dine in a secluded area." Phoenix was reluctant to try it. Mimi' whispered something to her ear. She drew back and protested, "Don't whisper in my ear. You are not my boyfriend. I have just met you for crying aloud." Mimi' apologized. It was his turn to take action. He opened the card and handed it to her. She could not refuse anymore and read it,

"To Phoenix, a companion of my journey that made my heart tremble."

Phoenix remained speechless. She scratched her head and laid her face between both hands. Finally, she said, "I can't believe it! Why did you do all of this? It was you who orchestrated with the waiter the table reservation, the taxi failure to arrive on time . . ." I was about to choke you with my bare hands and twist your neck like a chicken. But now . . ." She took the huge bundle of roses and brought to her heart. She smelled them. The perfume was sweet and penetrating. She laid her head on them.

Mimi' got up and got close to her. He lowered his head and kissed her. "Not yet!" She protested gently raising his head with her arm. The time will decide."

"What is the connection between the time and us?" He inquired

"Everything has to follow its course, just like the water is drawn to the sea by its infallible trajectory."

"You are very philosophical. That is what happens when someone goes to college." He put his fingers through her hair and added, "Each hair is a flower. You are my pupa. I will call you 'Pupa' just like my Maserati."

"Stop talking like that! We just met!"

"I want to start a relationship with you."

"If you want the relationship to grow and be durable, don't expect me to act like other girls."

"I have no qualms with that.´ He decided to change topic which was causing some friction between them. "I will take you to a better restaurant next time," he told her.

"A five star," she said with emphasis.

Mimi' noticed that he struck the right chord and added, "Of course! You are a girl of good taste."

"Thanks for the compliment. It is in my style to save culinary delicacies found only in highest ranked restaurants."

"And that is a woman's prerogative. I am sure you enjoy first quality food," responded Mimi'.

"You are learning," she commented with a light smile on her lips. "A classy woman demands only the best from her man."

This second part of her comment was veiled with vanity, nonetheless, Mimi' enjoyed it. "I don't blame you a bit and I am here to assure that you get the best."

She bent her head backward leaning on his shoulder. "Do you really mean it?" she whispered in his ear.

"That is without question," he replied.

"You are a darling. You are not a pussy cat. Are you?" Mimi' smiled broadly.

Phoenix was starting to feel more and more comfortable with Mimi'. She stared at the empty wine bottle in front of her and said "In vino veritas." With her unsteady hand, she cut a rose from the bunch and put under his nose. "You will feel the full flagrance of a rose. Here, smell it!" she ordered him.

Mimi' took a deep breath. He felt inebriated. He pulled one from the rest and placed it on her bosom.

"Oh, no, no, no! She protested. "It's far too early for that, much too early. Do not press your lucky star. You ought to know by now that luck does not like to be pushed around. It comes and goes as it wishes. It flies like a butterfly."

Mimi' became very apologetic and begged for her indulgence. "I did not mean to offend you." He realized that it became increasingly difficult to interpret her will.

Phoenix was pleased with his apology and stretched back on the chair. "Where in the world did the waiter go? He is taking too long. No wonder this is a cheap restaurant," she said. "His delay means misfortune to me. Open the palm of your left hand," she asked him. "You see?" She continued, "This line seems to be going to the wrong direction. And look at the other one! It is curving too much."

"So, you believe in good luck," he queried.

She did not reply, but she changed the topic, "Do you mind if we approach each other informally? Formality makes you feel a stranger. I am here and you are in a remote area of China. Formality is applicable to other social levels and in some professions . . ."
"I could not agree with you more. And this brings me to ask you a silly question, "How did you get that name, from the city in Arizona?"
She paused for a few moments. She needed extra time to answer rationally. Although her eyes appeared a bit extra bright, she stated very bluntly, "I do not think so. My name has a mythological history behind it; I do not believe you are interested in it."

Mimi' was about to respond when they heard a knocking on the door. The waiter asked permission to enter and brought in a carriage a cornucopia of food. There were all sorts of food delicacies, and array of beverages and brandies. Phoenix's eyes bulged out. She looked at the eggplants a la parmigiana, fresh buffalo mozzarella, parmigiano cheese, slices of St. Daniele's prosciutto, a big piece of provolone, pasta a la carbonara, red and white wine, champagne, mushrooms, roasted squashes and potatoes. Phoenix took a deep breath. She had never seen such a succulent dinner in front of her since she had been in Italy. The waiter bowed and took leave not before assuring them that he would come back later with the expresso and tiramisu'.

Phoenix was hungry. She would not wait any longer. She said, "This is a pharaonic banquet!"
She ate without pause until she could no longer sustain the weight on her stomach. Mimi' unplugged the champagne bottle and poured it into her glass, "To our future," he said. "To our future," she replied. She drank it with passion. Mimi' poured more liquor and criss-crossed hand until their lips got closer. She put one hand on his lips and said, "Be a good boy."

Shortly after, Phoenix took a deep breath, placed the embroidered cloth napkin on the table and exclaimed, "And, now, who is going to pay for this extravaganza? I have a limited budget and cannot afford more than ten euro."

Mimi' stood silent all the while. When it was time to respond, he said, "Being a cheap restaurant, the bill should be relatively low. I am confident that both of us will be able to manage to share the relatively low bill."

She reminded him, "I have just told you how much I can contribute." Wine had slowed down her reflexes and dimmed her hand coordination. Even her vision slightly blurry, "Why didn't you inform me before?" stretching her arms laterally.

"I told you that this is a prestigious restaurant food quality food and low price."

She was not pleased with the answer. She pushed back the rest of the food and said in a low voice, "It is your entire fault! I should not have accepted your invitation."

"Why didn't you stop eating, instead?" he asked her.

"Because it was too late!" she answered in a loud voice.

The emotions were rising on both sides. Mimi's replies, instead of appeasing Phoenix, were increasing her apprehension. He noticed that she was losing her self-control and said, "The worst thing that it can happen is that we both end up behind the bars."

"Maybe you don't care because you have a solid reputation. Perhaps, the good luck is abandoning me."

"Do you think so?" probed Mimi'.

"We are like leaves blown in the wind. We do not have the power to resist it. We must go along with it or it will drag us by force."

"Is that so?"

She covered her eyes with both hands and said, "Would they allow me to take a credit? I will pay them with interest as soon as I go back to America."

"Who has the money, nowadays? Nobody!" responded Mimi' putting on a serious look.

"If bad luck has decided to deliver me in the justice's hands, here I am. I am going to finish my Italian course study in jail."

In that moment, the waiter knocked at the door. He asked politely if they wished anything else. Mimi' replied, "Yes, the bill, please. If you do not mind it, that is." Phoenix hoped that they would never mention the word "bill." "Why did you have to remind him"? Protested Phoenix. We could get out of here pretending to go to the bathroom."

"That is not being honest!"

Mimi' took a deep breath. The waiter handed him the bill. She snapped it out of his hands. The list and quality of the food and beverage consumed was long. Upon reading the price, she fell backward on her chair. "Two, two, thus . . . . euro . . . Oh, my good heavens!" she muttered. "This is the end of me."

The waiter took the other small flat dish with another paper and handed it to her, "This is a two-hundred euro bill for the red roses." He said and placed a package of Perugina chocolates in front of her. She opened her purse and pulled a ten euro bill. She put it back as quickly as she took it. Her face was red hot. Her hands dropped down. She was unable to proffer a word. She looked stunned. Mimi' winked his right eye and the waiter pointed to Phoenix that there was another card underneath the chocolates. Phoenix was devoid of any energy. The waiter opened it. She read it without will, "Don Mimi' O' Fabuloso is an exceptional client. He is always welcome in this restaurant and so does her guest. We are honored to have both of you here. The entire charge is at our expense. Have a happy day!"

Suddenly, the liquor's power seemed to have disappeared from Phoenix' mind or, at least, partially. She looked at Mimi' with immense incredulity and said, "You mean we don't pay? I do not have to pay all that money?"

Mimi' smiled and said, "It is a matter of fact, you don't have to pay a dime, according to the waiter. I told you that this was a cheap restaurant."

Phoenix could not believe it. The only thing that she remembered was that her bill was extremely high, while Mimi's was ridiculously low. She protested, "You owe me an explanation. Why is there such a difference between your bill and mine?

Mimi' did not respond directly to her question. He was enjoying the surprise to the fullest. But, Phoenix was not content. She took him in her arms and whispered to him, "I beg you. Who are you?"

"Why do you want to spoil these moments?" he replied.

She took his hands into hers and added, "You scared me to death, but I will cherish this memory forever."

The door was open. The head waiter approached their table and inquired, "Miss, would you like to know why your partner was hardly charged for anything?

Phoenix straightened her body in an erect position and responded with eagerness, "Yes, why?"

"He is the owner," replied the chief waiter. He made a half bow and withdrew.

For the first time since the time of arrival, Phoenix experienced a wakeup call. She stared at Mimi' for a time that to both of them seemed eternal. When her eyes began to close, she fell in his arms exhausted.

In the following days, Phoenix called Mimi' on a daily basis. The calls became more frequent and pressing when he was unavailable. In school, her classmates noticed a remarkable shift in her study habits. She neglected doing her homework at times and in class she daydreamed. Fortunately for her, the semester was coming to an end.

Mimi' was unable to see Phoenix for business reasons. At the age of thirty, he owned a chain of restaurants throughout the peninsula, but his life took a twist only after his parents' return to Sao Paolo.

Mimi' was left alone in Milan without money, without profession, without a solid education to compete in an aggressive world market, without hope and, even more importantly, without parental guidance. He wanted to enlist in the army, but a newly enacted law, abolished the antiquated recruitment system and replaced it with a new dynamic and effective one, based on special trained units. According to the newly enacted policy, only highly qualified young men and women could serve after winning a national contest. Mimi' realized that he lacked the ingredients to gain a spotlight and looked elsewhere for a job opportunity. He checked his pockets and found a couple of euro. He locked the door and went out.

The Italian soccer fans play every week at what they call "totocalcio." They purchase a card at a coffee shop containing all the A series soccer teams. At the extreme right, there are three boxes where the fan writes 1, 2, or x. Number one stands for victory of the first team. Number two stands for victory of the second team and X stands for a tie. Whoever guesses the results of all the games on the card will win a "Montepremio," which often amounts to millions of euro. In the event that no one claims the prize, the amount keeps on increasing. Like any other player, Mimi' revered the game and was passionately attached to it.

One night, Mimi' dreamed the final scores of all the teams that were going to play that week-end. He woke up during the night and wrote them frantically on the palm of his hands. "The soul of my grandfather visited me and I believed him."

Early in the morning, Mimi' ran to the nearest coffee shop and purchased two cards. He proceeded to sit around a table in the farthest corner and jot down all the numbers he had written. Once he filled up the spots, he handed them to the cashier and paid. He did not trust the pockets of his pants, so, he hid the copies inside the socks.

At home, he removed a cement tile from the floor and placed the copies underneath. During the week, he spent many sleepless nights. He was jobless and survived by accepting the meals provided gratis by a local convent. In the meantime, the landlord sent him an eviction notice for failing to pay the apartments three months in a row. Mimi' would not think of asking for money to his parents. They called him occasionally, but never asked him if he needed any help. Rarely, they asked him about the type of work he was engaged in. He would always reply that he was employed in a computer shop.

On Sunday afternoon, the last soccer game finished and the TV showed all the results. Mimi' lifted up the brick from the floor and picked up the cards. He checked carefully, then, he checked every score. He felt drowsy and massaged his eyes. He wasn't sure whether he had read the results correctly. He got nervous and started to tremble. On the second try, his eyed bulged out. On the third and last try, he fell on the old couch half dead.

Half an hour later, Mimi' regained consciousness. With some efforts, he reached the bathroom and threw cold water on his face. He wiped it and felt refreshed. He headed toward the table and sat. He stretched the card out and reviewed the scores once again. He wanted be absolutely sure that he was not victim of an equivocation.

The blood started to rush to his brains. All of a sudden, he shouted three times, "I don't believe it!

His neighbors heard him and rushed at his door. They thought that something tragic had happened. They got even more suspicious when a couple of minutes passed by and he did not open the door. They pounded more and more on the door and, this time, Mimi' had to open it before they busted it.

"What happened? Don't you feel well?" asked someone. Another added, "We thought you were dieing. Finally, an old lady said, "I suspected that a rubber came to visit you." Everybody laughed. Mimi' could no longer stand silent. "I saw a mouse."

"A mouse?" they replied in unison. They looked at each other. One of them placed the index finger at the temple and rotated it. They disappeared like a lightening.

The TV news agency announced that the prize fifty million euros and nobody claimed it yet. Journalists all over the peninsula hunted the winner. They contacted every coffee shop and one of them did admit that the winning card was sold in his coffee shop, but that no one showed up or called to make any claim.

The search, then, focused around that area, for days, but failed to identify the real winner. Mimi' spent many hours of the day sitting at the bar asking people, "Did they find the winner? If you know it, please, tell me. Maybe, he can afford a small gift."

"If he did not disclose his identity," replied a distinguished man with glasses, "it means that he does not wish to share not even a cent with anyone."

Suddenly, a group of journalists arrived and crammed in the coffee shop to gather information. Even the national TV cameras were visible everywhere in the neighborhood. It was like a Carnival. The streets were crowded with masked people. Most of them thought that the cameras were dispatched to the area to take some of their action and for that reason they improvised dances and made all sorts of gestures to be seen on television. A man, with his face covered, instead of showing up at the coffee shop, he went to the central office of Milan. He approached the cashier and showed him the winning card. The cashier was taken by surprise and almost froze. He looked straight in his eyes to try to recognize him. The masked man bent his head. The cashier asked him if he wished to pay taxes then and there and get a single check or he wished to receive a check every month for the rest of his life. He masked man chose the first option. He had to wait about ten minutes to fill out all the required documents. In the meantime, the cashier alerted the media. When they arrived, it was too late. The unknown winner had vanished in the crowd.

Mimi' arrived home exhausted. He rested for about ten minutes with his legs elevated on a chair and tried to sleep. It was useless. That evening and, for a few more days, he returned to the convent to claim his daily food ratio. One of his companions asked him, "Did you see someone win the mega prize."

"Lucky him! We are still coming here begging."

"The press has not been able to identify him."

"I tell you. Whoever won is not stupid."

"What do you mean? Those who do not win are not intelligent. Do I look like stupid?"

"No, I did not mean that. The winner knows how to disguise himself." Mimi' waited a moment and added, "Most of the time, luck is unfair and the best man does not always win."

A month later, Mimi' moved to a farming area, away from the public eye. He moved with discretion in the neighborhood and tried to maintain a normal lifestyle. He could not stay idle all the time, so, he became a business man and purchased three prestigious restaurants in Italy. He was hardly home and kept on traveling constantly. It was in one of his trips to Florence that he met Phoenix.

On the day following the completion of her classes, Phoenix was exploring the possibility of remaining in Italy for a while longer. Some of her classmates, returned home; others traveled around Europe, but she had other plans. She decided to work in an herb shop near Milan. Mimi' was overly burdened with his work and did not have the time to see her often. Nonetheless, she kept on calling him every single day.

The day after Easter, 'Pasquetta', is a holiday in Italy and people flock to coastal cities, mountains and ski resorts for relaxation and excursions. And, of course, a lot of food! Phoenix decided to visit Portofino, a heavenly paradise spot on the Ligurian Sea. She was enjoying the sun under a big umbrella. Sometimes the sea waves reached her feet and withdrew in the sand. Someone, from behind her, covered her eyes with his hands. Phoenix tried to disengage herself from the intruder, but she couldn't. Finally, the visitor released the pressure and withdrew both hands. Phoenix turned around and screamed, "Why, you, why did you do that to me?" She got up and hugged him. "I wanted to see you for so long," she said sobbing. "I miss you terribly."

"I thought you did not care about me."

"Do you want me to repeat it? Why do you keep torturing me? You made me go through hell in Florence."

"Yeah, but you loved the outcome of the evening. Didn't you?"

"Definitely! It is unforgettable. I will have always that memory in here." And she pointed at her heart.

Mimi' looked at the sea and the beach and said, "So, you came to this heavenly corner of the world."

She pressed him against her and whispered in his ears, "You are my heaven."

She pulled away from his arms and sat. "Come here. Sit next to me. We can share the same chair."

Mimi' followed her request and got close to her. She took his hands in hers and asked him, "Now, tell me how good luck brought you here. I am all ears. Start!"

Mimi' made a couple of movements with his body to find a more suitable position. Once he attained it, he said, "I came here to scout the area . . ."

She interrupted him, "The area or the girls?"

"Actually, I am looking for job opportunities."

"Don't remind me that! At the completion of the semester, as you know, I decided to stay. Students cannot legally work, I know it. One has to survive somehow. So, I found a job in at an herb shop. I love it. The pay is low, but I don't pay taxes. It is "under the table.""

"And if somebody reports you?"

"The worst scenario that I envision is that they will ship me back."

Mimi' pretended not to hear her. His mind was elsewhere. She noticed it and queried, "Why are you so distracted? Why? Don't I make you happy? O.K. I won't bother you anymore with questions, but can you tell me what kind of job you have? Whatever you do, you must be good at that. This is for sure."

Mimi' brushed the hair with his fingers. "I am engaged in business transactions."

"I had the perception that you were some kind of a salesman."

"Let's say that it is part of it."

"That explains why you did not pay the bill in Florence and made me go through a horrific time. You skunk! They were not exchanging favors with you. You own the place."

"It is not that simple to explain to you."

She put his right hand in her mouth and said," I am going to bite it if you don't tell me the truth."

Mimi' pulled his hand away, "Ahi, you have sharp teeth."

"I do not want to see anyone next to you."

"I have just told you that I am very busy."

"With what? You are not telling me anything. How am I supposed to know it?"

Mimi' stood there a while reflecting before he answered, then, he said, "I operate some restaurants in Italy."

Phoenix smiled and said, "Oh, honey, that's marvelous. Why did it take you so long to spell it out? I am so proud of you." She put her hand on his lips and continued, "Don't tell me that you and I cannot repeat the same experience in that restaurant in Florence!"

Mimi' did not respond immediately. He took his time and replied, "Let me say that it is a possibility."

Phoenix unbuttoned his shirt and asked him to lie on the sand. She took a bottle of sunscreen lotion and spread it on his back. "Now, you are going to take some sun next to me." The heat was intense. Nearby the sea waves repeated the same music over and over again. A fresh breeze decided to come in at times and alleviated the heat pressure. Mimi' fell asleep. She took a pillow and placed it under his head.

Phoenix pulled the cellular from her purse and called her boss to inform her that she would not be in to work for the next two days. Mimi' took time out of his busy schedule to spend it with her. At the end of their brief vacation, Mimi' drove her back to Milan in his Maserati. Phoenix' eyes glowed at the sight of the jewel car, "This is just awesome! I never dreamed of riding some day the best car in the world."

"This is my Pupa, just like you. Do you like it?" asked her Mimi' while he was opening the door for her.

"I love it! It is just stupendous! I can't believe it! Look at these gadgets!"

He went on to explain how some new features worked and said, "Someday, it will be yours."

"That will be my lucky day," she said with incredulity.

Mimi' was not well pleased by the reply. He turned to her and said, "My dear, nobody gave me anything. I did it on my own and my God. Only hard work pays off,"

She hung on his neck and whispered, "Don't get upset! I don't want to let you go. I want to live with you forever."

Mimi' was distracted by a passer-by. He returned his attention to Phoenix and said, "I must confess you that I am terribly busy. These two days spent together have put an additional burden on my heavy schedule"

"Why? Didn't you want to be with me?" And, in saying so, she dropped her arms and head.

He tightened her to his chest and said, "Do not mix feelings with business. I was simply explaining to you how difficult it is for me to take time off."

"Someday, I want to be like you if only . . . . will be on my side." She omitted a word, but he understood.

"There is no difference between two intelligent people. Why, then, one is successful and another works in the trench? Something or someone must be hidden somewhere turning the wheel of fortune. Don't ask me why? It is impossible to decipher a mystery."

Mimi' did not respond and she continued," If I will be lucky, I want to be like you, rich and powerful."

"You may, someday."

"Do you really believe it?"

"You can do anything. As I explained to you before, I have a different frame of mind."

"OK. How could you amass such a fortune considering your young age? Unless your parents bequeathed you a gold mine in the Amazon forest, a tin mine in the Atacama Desert or a pearl well at the bottom of the Titicaca lake, I can't think how you could have done it."

Mimi' laughed so hard that he had to cover the mouth with his hand not to show a crooked molar. "Don't be silly," he said. "My parents are not rich and they never gave me a penny," he concluded.

"Wouldn't you be interested to know my profession?" she inquired by showing a lot of humor.

"What a silly question you ask me. It is common knowledge that you are a student. Besides, you have already told me that you are working "under the table." I don't think you should worry about the future. Probably, you will not need to work at all."

She placed the index finger on his bottom lip and said, "I love you. You are my Wheel of Fortune."

He was annoyed at hearing that word again and changed the subject.

Suddenly, the right tire made like a puffing noise. He felt that wheel was touching the asphalt and drove slowly to the side of the street where he parked. He got out to inspect it and noticed, at his chagrin, that the tire was flat. He returned to Phoenix' window and muttered, "Even the best cars can experience problems. "He placed his right hand on the hood and said "Don't worry Pupa. Life is made up of problems, but I will give you back your health."

Phoenix smiled at the word 'Pupa,' but did not say anything.

The days flowed by lazily for Phoenix. A few weeks in the shop were sufficient to give her some sort of authority in the field. During the weekends, to make up for Mimi's long absences, she started to attend the local casino. Her hair was growing longer and this pleased Mimi'. Whenever she arrived, she caught the attention of many people. The first evening, a young man approached her and asked her if he could offer her a drink. She declined it, "No, thank you. I am really looking for a game table."

"This is what you are looking for, I suppose" and he pointed to a nearby table. "Your hair has a special fragrance," he added.

"Very kind of you" she replied. "I suppose one needs a lot of money to even start playing?" she asked.

"At least, one hundred euro . . . But, if you cannot afford it, I can help you, provided that you will be my escort at dinner."

"No, thank you. It is my custom to try my luck on my own."

"That's fine. At any rate, I will be here at your side for any assistance."

The players paused for a moment at the sight of such a beauty. The one who had the most money in front of him, said, "Welcome to the luckiest table in this casino. I am sure that the wheel of fortune will kiss your pretty face."

"In that case, I should sit next to you."

"It will be my pleasure." He got up and helped her to sit. "Play thousand euros on number two," he added.

"Are you crazy? I cannot afford it. I have only one hundred euro."

"Here, take the rest."

"I will accept it only if you will take it back in case of winning."

"It is a deal!"

The dice rolled on the table until late at night for her. The player who had lent her nine hundred euro kept on looking on her body. Phoenix gave him back the money she owed him and excused herself for a while. Everybody saw her going to the ladies room.

One of the players wanted to escort her to make sure she did not play a trick on them, but the rest of them objected. In the meanwhile, they began to bet on who would succeed in taking her out for the evening. A player even proposed to share the winning money with her. The dice kept on rolling. The time was going by. Players were winning and losing, but there was no trace of the beautiful intruder. The young man, who had approached her at the beginning, stopped the game and called the attention on the missing young girl. They all agreed to send an employee female in the rest room to ascertain that she was not feeling sickly. He called a girl on the floor and spoke briefly with her.

The girl returned in thirty seconds and informed the players that the lavatory was empty. They, then, searched all over the casino and in the parking lot. The result was the same. She was no longer there.

"You mean she won fifty thousand euros and we let her escape?"

Another one said, "We lost money and beauty. This is what we deserve for our stupidity."

Yet another said, "I thought she was a smart cookie, maybe too smart!"

The weather was getting humid in Milan, The sky was eternally grey. Phoenix visited another casino.

She was standing around a table. A couple of minutes passed by and she began to incite the players to bet more. At the end of a game, the players looked around to see who was causing so much commotion. The presence of a fascinating young girl made them stop the game. Everybody claimed that he needed time off for relaxation. They did not realize that it was her strategy to get them distracted before she entered in the game herself. One of them asked her if she wished to play. She nodded. Another player made everybody laugh when he said, "I would welcome you next to me. Maybe, you could help my lucky star."

"But, I do not know how to play."

"Do not worry about that! I will teach you," assured her a younger man.

Everybody laughed so hard that it caught the attention of other nearby players nearby who quit their games and joined the table where the girl was.

Phoenix, undaunted by the clamor, insisted, "What are the winning prerequisites?"

The player sitting on her left answered, "Beauty and luck."

"Funny, aren't you?" she replied. "So, if I sit next to you I will win?"

"Listen! With your beauty and my luck we will win all the time."

All the players roared with approval.

"To play is easy, to win is hard" commented an old man.

Phoenix did not pay anymore attention to their flatteries. She was completed involved in the game. She played all the money she won in the other casino. Once in a while, she touched the amulet she kept in her pocket. In one hour she put on a five winning streak. Her nest increased fivefold. She collected her money and got up. The players became concerned about her next move; "You cannot do that to us!" said one. "It is against the game law of the casino to leave when everybody is playing," added another. A Third man added, "It is unprofessional and lady or no lady we will not be complacent. Phoenix excused herself temporarily. Her explanation assuaged their fear and the game resumed.

After five minutes, they queried themselves if the young lady had diarrhea. The oldest among them got suspicious and went to knock at the ladies bathroom. He inquired with an old woman, on her way out, if she saw a young lady inside. She responded that no one else was in the rest room. The man rushed back to the tables and informed the players that the girl was not in the bathroom. The players got upset. They got the immediate collaboration of the main office and he search began very intensely. Each one of the players and guards took on the responsibility to scrutinize every section of the building with the aid of their body guards. One hour passed and they found themselves around the same table, but without any trace of the girl.

PRECAUTIONARY TIMES

Mimi' called Phoenix and told her, "Honey, I am very busy this week. I cannot make it at the restaurant tomorrow."

"Do not feel obligated, my darling. You know how active I am. I never feel neglected by you. Take your time. I have a lot of shopping to do."

"How is the landlord?"

"Don't mention it! Would you like to know the truth?"

"Of course!"

"I missed the rent for the last two months and he wants to evict me from the apartment. I promised him that I would pay in the next few days."

"Do not move from where you are. I am coming to see you right now."

Phoenix remained with the receiver in her right hand for a couple of minutes without being able to find a plausible explanation to that abrupt cessation of the communication. She sat on the couch and waited for him. The bell rang and she descended the stairs to open the door. The scent of roses inundated the entrance. Mimi' placed them on her arms and hugged her tightly. "Easy! The thorns pinch!"

"Do you like them?"

"Of course, I do." She took him by hand and led him upstairs.

The two sat on the couch. She grabbed a bottle of Martini and poured it into a glass. "What about you?" he inquired.

She bent her head on the left side and smiled, "OK. I join you." She filled a small glass and raised it, "To our future!"

"To ours!"

They took a few sips. Mimi' took her hands into his and said, "Look! I am going to be absent for a week or so. Why don't you move to my house? You do not have to pay the rent."

"No, I still have to pay you. It is not fair."

Mimi' placed his hands on her upper arms and said, "Look at me! You do not owe me anything, neither for the rent nor for the food. I feel more relaxed that someone is in the house." He drew some documents from the pocket of the inside jacket and handed them to her. "Here, put them in a safe place. These belong to a small car that I make available to you. Do not misplace them."

She bowed her head and said. "I cannot accept them. I would put too much of a burden on you."

"If you don't quit with excuses I am going to spank you." He was about to do that, when she withdrew and said, "No, stop, stop! Please, don't spank me." And she started to run around the rooms. He pursued her and when he caught her, he tightened her to him and said, "Are you going to accept the deal?"

"Release me and I will accept on one condition."

"What is it?" he inquired with anxiety.

"We have to sleep in separate rooms."

"I have no qualms about it," he responded self assured.

"Secondly . . ."

"Wait a moment!" he interjected. "I thought it was only one condition."

"Let me finish, first." She said to him." The door that separates our bedrooms has to be closed."

"What need is there to keep the door closed?" queried Mimi' with skepticism.

"You are right, my darling. It should be locked from my side."

"Don't you like freedom of movement?" insisted Mimi'.

"A locked door gives me guarantee, protection and sound sleep. Many friends of mine leave the door unlocked. Out there, there are many night vultures, professional predators. "When they arrive, it is too late for remedy."

"I have no real objection. Whatever makes you feel comfortable," assured Mimi'. "If that makes you happy, so be it." Then, he added phlegmatically," But, why do you seek so many precautions? We don't go to church."

"A locked door is symptomatic of guarantee, believing or not in a divinity."

Mimi' looked incredulous at her. Seeing that he had no choice but to submit to her wishes, he replied, "I am busy, anyhow. I have to leave town in a couple of hours."

The two went back to the couch. Phoenix became serious and said, "Listen! I may have all the defects of this world, but my parents imbued in me the concept of honor. If it is threatened, I pack up and go. I attach the maximum value to honor."

"I admire you for it."

"There are times when we are called to make important decisions that may shape up the rest of our life . . ."

"I agree with you, but there is no need to dwell on it for too long."

"You are right. Let us change the subject."

She gently put her hands on his face and continued, "Listen carefully! I am being followed. The landlord did not say a word about it, but her daughter revealed to me that she was approached by two 'finanzieri,' who are interested in my work. You see. Someone must have reported me to the police. They know that I am working illegally and that my permanency permit is about to expire. I don't have any problem with the landlord. I have the money and I am going to pay him this evening. I delay the rent payment because I do not want him to believe that I am rich. My real concern is with the government as you may evince from my student status."

Mimi' reminded her of the agreement they had reached. She hung her arms around his neck and said, "Oh, darling, it is so exquisite of you to help me. But I am having a second thought. Go, find someone who does not cause you any problems with the law or is not going to be a burden to you. Please, let me go. You will be a happy man. Maybe it is better that I call the agency and reserve a flight ticket for next week."

Mimi' understood that the situation was slipping away from his control and said to her, "Can you give me a chance? Can you give yourself a chance? Can you give us a chance?" A few minutes ago, you agreed with me to stay at my house. All of a sudden, you changed your mind and rescind everything we have built around our relationship. There is a way out of the tunnel, just trust me."

"My tunnel is a long and narrow one," she responded in a very enigmatic look.

"Ok. Ok. will you at least give me a couple of weeks of time, so that, I will be able to finish some business?" He begged her.
She nodded and laid her head to rest on his shoulder.

The following Saturday, Phoenix received a message, "A person in my trust will pick you up at seven p.m. and take you to the office of a close friend of mine who will take care of your permanency papers."
At the date and time prescribed, a limo stopped below Phoenix' apartment. The chauffeur rang the bell and waited for her. He helped her to accommodate herself on the front seat and drove her away. Although she was bound to meet a government officer, nonetheless she dressed casually.

Half an hour later, the car stopped at the Grand Hotel. She started to get nervous about the location. The driver noticed her uncomfortable behavior and assured her that she was in the right place.

The bell button, a young man in uniform, escorted her to a corridor flanked by two lines of trumpeters, who at their approach, raised their instruments and put breath into them. At that point, she felt uneasy, almost frightened. She did not know what to make of it. By the time she reached the end of the corridor, the musicians stopped. The escort left her and she was asked to proceed to the main entrance.
The door was decorated with a cornucopia of flowers whose sweet scent spread all way around.

Inside, on the back of the oval room, an orchestra began to release the notes of a bolero. A steward took Phoenix by her right hand and led her through two lines of girls dressed in white. Phoenix was so bewildered at that point that she did not have the strength to ask any question. She was walking through a sea of doubts. Why so much fanfare to meet a lawman? Was that a trap? She did not have the time to rationalize that a little girl approached her with a bouquet of flowers. On top, there was a card with the following words, "To the most beautiful girl." Phoenix smiled, but she was getting all sorts of suspicions and wanted to run away from that scenario. She was on the verge of doing exactly that when another girl offered her a small box rapped in a red paper with a rose on top. The little girl invited her to open it. She opened the box and exclaimed, "Oh, my heavens! I can't believe it!"

A man, dressed in a tuxedo, replied, "You better believe it!"

Phoenix ran toward him, threw her arms around his neck and started to cry, "Oh, my darling, you did it again. This is out of this world!"

Mimi' took Phoenix to a separate room and let sit on the couch, so that, she might regain her composure. She started to sob. He pulled the handkerchief from his pocket and handed it to her. She dried up her tears and looked around. The walls were decorated with flowers and various tables were covered with succulent culinary delicacies. There was also champagne and some bottles of the most prestigious wines of the peninsula. Phoenix closed her eyes and whispered, "I am in a world of fantasy."

"Not yet," responded Mimi'. "The ring that the girl handed to you is the engagement ring and now I propose to marry me."

She was unable to respond. A knot clogged her throat. A soft "yes" exited from her lips. Then, overwhelmed by the events, fainted and fell backward on the sofa.

It took ten minutes before Phoenix regained consciousness, but she was in no mood to go on with the festivities.

"Darling, I need a glass of water. Oh, Mon amour, I have a headache. Oh, my neck nerves are all bundled up. I would like to rest."

"But, you have just finished resting," protested Mimi'. "Let the games begin!"

She looked at him, but did not say a word. He hastened to pour some water in a glass and gently handed it to her. She was staring at the ring covered with gems and exploded in a shout of joy.

"I am glad you like it," he whispered into her ears.

"I like it?" She muttered with astonishment. "It is gorgeous! You do not know how much it means to me."

"What about me?"

The ring means the whole sea and you mean the moon."

"I can't even reach the moon," replied Mimi' a bit disappointed.

"Well, then, you must learn to be an astronaut."

"By that time, I will be old."

"You are too impatient, my darling."

For Mimi', the conversation was turning sour. He had prepared a grandiose feast in her honor, spent thousands of dollars and, yet, he could not even spend a minute of intimacy. He looked at her disgruntled. At that particular moment, as if she had received an energy shot in the arm, she started to sing:

> "I will play
> At every chance
> Of the day.
> I will try my luck,
> In the dark,
> under the light
> of a gambling spot.

Mimi' clapped more to please her than agreeing on the content. "I am happy you are getting in a good mood." In reality, he was not pleased with the last line. She took notice of his humor and slowly reached a bottle of champagne and drank half of it. Mimi' knelt before her and asked her, "My "My sweet champagne" will you marry me?"

Phoenix knelt too and hugged him. "You know I love you, my pussy cat, but for marriage, we have to give a hard look to it."

"I give you a couple of weeks." He picked a red rose from a bouquet that was on the table and placed it in her hair.

"A rose is always a rose," she said with vanity.

"It is the queen of the flowers," he added with a pale smile.

She pulled him toward her and said, "Kiss my ring." After that, she asked him "Will you kiss my feet?"

"No, those no," protested Mimi'.
"I washed them. Are you afraid, Mimi'?"

"It is not that! Why do you want me to kiss the lowest parts of your body? He pulled a bit backward and for a while each one attempted to imitate the sound of many animals until they decided to put an end to it.

The time was flying into the early hours of the morning. "Darling, I must go now," she said by turning all her attention to him. Mimi' felt still a bit inebriated. He dragged her to him and whispered into her ears, "We go to my house now."

Phoenix tried to disengage herself from the bear hug. He was too strong for her. She stood in silence for a while as if she were pondering on her answer. "I will make you happy, but you have to hold on to your side of the agreement."

"Which one?" he queried with anxiety.

"We have to sleep in separate rooms."

He made a last desperate attempt to persuade her that everything was going to be fine and that her fears were unfounded. "There is no reason why you have to feel so defensive. My house is safe."

"We have already agreed on this, remember?"

"I do. What is the point of reminding me?"

"Men are what they are . . ."

Phoenix got up early in the afternoon. She searched all over the house and in the garden, but there was no trace of Mimi'. On top of the main table in the kitchen, she noticed a paper. She unfolded it and read it, "My queen of flowers, relax. I will be back by the week-end. Be careful! Do not drink and drive! I send you a couple kilos of love. Yours, forever, Mimi'."

Phoenix felt relieved. She smelled the card. It had the scent of a famous perfume. She closed her eyes and said, "And I reciprocate with two pounds of kisses."

Some clouds were walking lazily in the sky, but they did not pose any threat. She was still a bit drowsy from the events of the previous night. She filled up a cup of cup of coffee and sipped it. Her mind began to clear and she decided to engage in some routine stretching exercises.

Shortly after, she got into the car and ran to her apartment to pack up her clothes. An unusual noise aroused her attention. It was not the landlord's moving of the heavy armchair from one angle to another of the porch. The purpose behind it was to launch investigative glances around his apartment house to satisfy his daily curiosity and concern. It was an internal noise. When a tenant owed the rent, he took the broom and hit the ceiling with the handle. Phoenix was exceedingly annoyed by it. She completed the packing operation, went downstairs and placed in his hands an envelope. "This is the past and present rent. Thank you and good-by." The landlord was stunned, "What's the rush? Don't you like to stay here anymore?"

"I paid you, didn't I?"

"People beg me for apartments all the time."

"That's your prerogative. As for me, it is over. Good luck!" She banged the door and rolled the suitcase to the parking lot in the back of the building.

The old man opened the window and shouted, "You Americans are all the same. You have no appreciation. You think you own the world! But, I say that if Communism comes back, I may vote for it. Ah, ah, ah!"

AOSTA

The lights of Le Champignon Casino' were glimmering under a blue sky. Inside, the music and the noise were deafening. Most of the adult population was sitting in front of slot machines. The coins fell into the empty space, inside, with a mechanical cadence. People hardly communicated with each other. Apart from the continuous clicking that rendered the words inaudible to the ear of the listener, the real interlocutor was the machine itself. The players were immersed in an intense and continuous interior monologue. Their minds were the theater of dreams, hopes and, often, of disappointments. Yet, they never gave up their quest for the welcoming scrambling of coins that would fall in the bucket for a few minutes without interruption. The only time they got up was for physical needs. They did not have to do that with stomach pranks. The girls in bikini provided constant provisions of food on large trays.

The scene was somewhat similar around the poker tables. The only substantial difference consists in the large amounts of money being played; consequently, the intensity of the mental involvement is far deeper and it is not transferred to the machines. Every player scrutinizes every card, eye, hand or bodily movement of the rival player. A lot mental work goes on here. At the end, one is mentally and energetically drained. The people who stand up may be involved in spying, but hardly anyone says a word. At a poker game, the eyes and the mind do every imaginable programming and send signals to the hands for the final move. Once the players start the game, a world of indifference surrounds them. Their only appetite is gold.

Conversely, on the slot machines, you can insert the coin without looking. After a while, it becomes a mechanical ritual.

The poker master was sliding the cards rhythmically in his hands. That movement lasted only a few seconds. He would assemble and disassemble them and open them and even let them fly. On the way back, they formed a compact pack. And he did it with such dexterity that it was fascinating just to watch him. He gave you the sensation of being in a world of magic.

In a world of intrigues, it was not difficult to imagine that many occult operations went on. Disguised in the crowd, the controller checked every move of the master player. A young lady was watching from behind him. An older man lost balance and pushed her. She grabbed on the man in front of her and regained her posture. In the meantime, a player got up and left. He had lost a considerable amount of money. The young lady opened her way through the crowd and filled his spot.

The sight of a beautiful girl did not pass unobserved. The players got distracted temporarily, but quickly returned their attention to the game. This time beauty did not prevail over their interests. One may also speculate that the word had gone around the casinos about Phoenix's latest tricks.

That evening, aces and jacks dictated the fortune and misfortune. Like whimsy children, they changed luck almost constantly. Phoenix ran through high and low tides. A young girl stopped to serve drinks. Phoenix gulped a couple glasses without looking at them. She lost three games in a row. She could not understand how the master player made the queen appear with impeccable regularity when she bet the highest price on the jack. She began to peruse the cards. To search for some inscrutable minutia that could give her leverage on other players. Even the controller got concerned about it. His eyes encroached with hers. She got up. It was rumored that some dirty work was going on. At that point, the controller intervened and assured everyone about the honorability of the casino and the honesty of the master player.

It was two o' clock in the morning when Phoenix decided to quit. Her fellow players bid her "good bye" with a smirk. She did not bother looking back. Someone tried to console her on her way out, but she did not hear anything. The loss had been staggering. The charm that she usually kept with her was somewhere in the suitcase.

At home, Phoenix dropped exhausted on her bed and slept uninterrupted through the night 'til late morning. The pendulum marked the twelve hours. She moved her eyes lazily around the room and closed them again. Half an hour passed. She made a slight attempt to sit, but fell backward against the wall and, finally, on the pillow. The ideas in her mind were bobbling after the concussion and realized how imprudent she had been at the casino. She looked at herself in the mirror and said, "You are a dummy! How could you be so irresponsible to carry in your pocket a fortune and, then, lose it?" She brought both hands on her face in a gesture of demise and added, "And, now, what? What can I tell Mimi'? No, I will not dare to mention a single word. It would jeopardize our marriage, stupid!" Suddenly, she put the index finger on her chest to touch the collar and exclaimed in dismay, "The charm! Where is the charm? That is why luck turned away from me! It is my entire fault! I should have known better. I was too impulsive. I should have checked it before I left."

Victory at the Casino

The Casino's financial debacle tortured Phoenix on a daily basis. She confided to a friend model, "I feel like being in the womb of my mother during the gestation period or as nude as in the day she engendered me".

Her friend shook her head to express her dismay. Phoenix stood there silent waiting for a reply that took too long to arrive. Finally, it dawned on her friend the underlying meaning of that statement and said, "Do not despair Phoenix. Luck is like the wind. You never know in which direction it blows. Look at me! The model business is a dirty one. Not every aspirant achieves success. You need a lot of hard work, patience and passion. This is the basic tenet of every profession."

"I disagree with you. The last time the wind blew toward me, it took me to hell."

"Why is that?" replied the model with curiosity.

"Luck is the center piece of our existence. You can be the best in the business, but if you are plagued with drawbacks, the evidence is that your wheel of fortune dislikes you."

"I am not sure if I would put so much emphasis on chance. If you are gifted with qualities and strive to reach your goal, at the end, you will get there."

"It is my entire fault. I forgot to carry with me something very special."

"I guess so! You let your honey gala venting . . ."

Phoenix smiled. Maybe, she did not feel like going over a sour note. Her friend took advantage of the pause to remind her that she should get to work on the wedding plans, "Hurry up! Hasten your nuptial date and you will be floating again."

"Or I may sink." The model laughed so hard and for a long time that even Phoenix joined her.

By the third day of the week, Mimi' did not call. The phone rang on the fourth day and Mimi' found his girlfriend in a depressive mood. She did her best to hide the cause of it. He tried to console, "I know. It is my entire entire fault! I am away for too long. But, I promise you. Tomorrow, I will be home and we can finalize our wedding details. I love you and I will see you soon."

Phoenix responded softly, "I love you too."

It was sunset when Mimi' parked the car in the garage. He walked up a few steps and entered into the living room. Phoenix opened the door. Mimi' yelled, "Surprise! She hugged him. He had his right hand behind his back. He pulled it on the front and handed to her a bouquet of red roses. She kissed him and said, "I missed you so much!"

He grabbed a little box in his jacket and said, "Close your eyes now!"

She did. Then he added, "Now, you can open them!" The sight of a ring covered with sapphires and diamonds made her face shine. She remained speechless for a while. Her head was hanging on his shoulders. "This is just fabulous!" She whispered in his ear. But, you already gave me one."

"A beautiful girl deserves a magnificent ring like this and more. Will you marry me now?" He asked her with a big smile on his face.

She smiled too. "You have already asked me. But, as long as you repeat the same petition, I repeat my answer, "Yes, I'd love to marry you."

From that day on, Phoenix invested most of her time in the wedding plans. The tremendous loss at the casino had temporarily stopped obsessing her. She elaborated a long list of food, wines and an open bar throughout the whole reception. She also ordered a huge three-level sponge cake soaked in rum. There was a large assortment of Italian delicacies, among which, emerged the 'tiramisu'. Mimi' added a list of many prominent local businessmen. He hired a popular television orchestra, "Heritage," along with a world renowned Neapolitan vocalist who had debuted at the San Carlo Theater in Naples five years earlier. At the top of the "cake" he invited a special flamengo dancer from Seville. Phoenix voiced some perplexities to the lavish banquet, but when she heard that the American counsel and the Bishop of Milan would attend the wedding, she felt overwhelmed. Mimi' assured her that the financial burden was well under control. She had to lay back and relax. His assurances did not allay her state of nervousness. Mimi' expected her to be excited, but not worried. He did business with a Brazilian bank "A Banca Brasileira." He went there and opened a checking account for her in the vicinity of one-hundred thousand dollars. The news brought much relief and satisfaction to Phoenix. The huge sum in her name also gave her a sense of authority and confidence from Mimi'.

Two weeks prior to the wedding ceremony, Mimi' was out of town and told her that he would return late at night. Phoenix was walking up and down the stairs. She was restless. It was hot and humid. She went to the garden. The flowers stretched their dry petals to the sun. She watered them. She looked at the sky. There was not a cloud. Suddenly, the wind got impatient. It picked up the leaves on the ground and made them fly in all directions. Even the straw hats of some passers-by were blown off and they travelled up to the next intersection, like in a vortex formation, when the wind subsided, the people working in the gardens tried to collect them. Their effort was frustrated by a new wave of wind. It snatched them from their hands and scattered them all over again. The game went on for a while. Even a group of passengers, waiting at a bus stop, participated in what came to be humorous event. They formed a human wall trying to trap a bunch of leaves. A few leaves ended their flight in the peoples' hats; others continued the crazy flight, until the wind got satisfied and stopped its race as rapidly as it started it. The abrupt end of the race gave everybody a chance to breathe a sigh of relief.

Phoenix returned inside and climbed the steps of the stairs two by two. She paused a few seconds upstairs to catch up the breath. She was puffing in the middle of the corridor revolving her eyeballs in every direction. Obviously, she was searching for something. The telephone rang, but she ignored it. The caller delivered the message and the answer-machine picked it up. She positioned herself with the stomach on the rail and slid down. She almost hit her head against a chandelier. It was still early. She sank on the couch and fell asleep

It was late when she woke up. She got upset at herself for oversleeping. She jumped up and rushed to the bathroom to throw some water on her face. Her purse lay on the table. She grabbed it and headed for the door. In the car, she gave occasional glances to the vehicles passing her. None of them was familiar. That gave her a deeper sense of assurance. The traffic was particularly intense and chaotic downtown. She ran through a couple of yellow lights. A police officer noticed her erratic driving and pursued her. The lights of his car started blinking. She did not have any intention of breaking the law, but did not want to waste time either. She was unsure on the next move: stop at the side of the street or slip away. Fortunately, the police car had a flat tire and stopped right in the middle of the street. She had no other option but to run away.

On the highway, there was no traffic light and Phoenix could speed at will. She passed every vehicle ahead of her. She spotted again a police car with the blinking lights. This time, it was not approaching her from behind, but from the opposite direction; however, for precautionary reason, she took her foot off the gas pedal and the speed returned to its limit. The officer made a switch under a bridge and halted a car from Florida. Phoenix gave a sigh of relief and resumed, undeterred, the race to her destination.

At midnight, she was walking down the isle of the casino. Everybody's attention was converged on the first table. Slowly, she opened her way to it. About five feet away from the desired location, a young man was playing a game. No one pushed him, but he claimed that someone was doing exactly that. He turned around and saw a gorgeous girl. Presuming that the push originated from her, he got up and hung both arms around her waist. The grip was getting tighter. Phoenix gave him an elbow. The man fell backward and dragged others along with him. The last one crashed on the table. In a matter of a few seconds cards and money flew all over the tables, chairs and floor. The players slipped off their chairs like bowling pins. The ladies screamed. The games were stopped momentarily on other tables. Shortly after, a good number of personnel and body guards rushed to the scene. One of them ordered everyone to stay still until they brought under control the cards and the money. As soon as order was restored, two big men put their hands under the arms of the young man and carried him away. His protests were to no avail. Nobody found out what happened to him. Not even the newspapers reported the incident.

In a matter of minutes, the games were reopened and Phoenix sat like a princess on her throne. Occasionally, she gave a glance to the watch. The time was going by fast. At the end of the first game, the master player drew all the money toward him. Phoenix was astonished. She brought her hand to the pocket and could not find the lucky charm. A curse slipped off her lips. She got up and left. The game watchers tried to slow down her exit, but she pushed them away. They did not pursue her because she went broke. Outside, it was dark, pitch dark.

Phoenix arrived home half an hour before Mimi'. She went to her room, locked the door and threw herself on the bed without taking off the shoes.

The sun woke up early and spread its rays all way around the city. At the breakfast, Mimi' was relating to Phoenix that the government was trying to close the noose on internet gambling.

"People search for fortune, especially if they come from low classes."

"No doubt, but the online poker room operations are plagued with abuses."

"You just have to be careful."

"How? Thievery and scams are being dumped on the gamblers almost constantly."

"You have to protect yourself."

"You do not understand professional fraudulent engineers. No protection is valid against them."

"Get a charm and you stop being a victim," assured him Phoenix.

Mimi' laughed. "The online gambling is a street of non return. It is like a blindfolded person. He does not know where he is headed."

THE WEDDING

Mimi' realized that the topic was being fastidious to Phoenix and changed subject. "Can you imagine? Two more days and we will be husband and wife."

"You are a lucky man," she responded with a smirk.

"I suppose I do not deserve you," replied sadly Mimi'.

"Do not say that, darling. You offend me now. Do you promise me that you will never again make that silly comment?"

"I promise," he said. Then he added, "I think that it is proper to discuss the confession issue. Tomorrow, we have to be in church at six o' clock."

"What is there to discuss?" she responded somewhat surprised. "You do not have anything to confess."

Mimi' did not respond immediately. He remained pensive for a while. He knew he was walking on a land mine. "I attend Mass on Christmas and Easter, but this does not mean . . ."

To dispel any doubt from his mind, she said, "You are absolutely right. For you Catholics, confession is a "sine qua non" of your religious life. I just do not like the idea of confessing my sins to a man."

He did not respond. She kept on her rational idea. "If you break John's window, do you pay the damage to John or to Nick?"

Mimi' shook his head. "OK. I see your point. I do not know much about religion, but the Church has received the mandate directly from Christ." Think in this way. If you go over the speed limit on a highway, you break the state law. Do you expect the governor to fine you or the police that he appointed? He paused a few seconds and continued, "Perhaps, it would help you if the confessor would be a woman?"

"You know, I never gave a thought to it. Maybe, in that case, like anybody else, I would feel more relaxed. Nonetheless, it would not change my position"

Mimi' was taking his sweet time to reply. It was not his field of action. Finally, he said, "I think you are right. I would feel more comfortable, too. But, that's me. I am not sure about others."

"Nobody wants to reveal his intimate feelings of guilt to another person," she argued.

"Let me see if I can be the devil's advocate. We open our hearts and minds with our friends."

"Sometimes . . . But, another person? I have my doubts," she responded with firmness."

Mimi' fell into a deep silence. Phoenix shook him up, "O.K. I tell you. I am going to do it for you. Personally, I have no desire to let another person to know my private business."

"The Church was created to continue the work of Jesus. Remember? They have the authority to do so."

Phoenix frowned, "We have spoken at length about it. Let's put an end to this issue." Then, she brought both hands to the temples and exclaimed, "Ahi, we have to pick up my parents at the airport in two hours, remember? Hurry up!"

"For heaven sake! Let's get going!"

The wedding took place in the Duomo of Milan. Cardinal Manzorosso officiated the ceremony. As a Baptist, Phoenix needed a special dispensation. The middle isle was decorated with red roses, while the altar had white and pink flowers. All the pews were occupied by journalists, while the photographers moved up and down the aisles. The main doors were kept open to allow the crowd to listen, at least, to what was going on inside the church. The most aggressive tried to push their way in.

At the altar, there was something extraordinarily bright that nobody could ignore. In place of the necklace that Mimi' had bought to her, Phoenix wore an amulet.

Phoenix' family was strictly Baptist, but for the sake of their daughter's happiness went along with her decision to marry in a

Catholic church. Phoenix followed her parents' footsteps until the age of fifteen when her religious activity waned. It occurred, especially, when her boyfriend gave her a charm as a good luck. For a while, she kept it around her right wrist, but when she realized that it possessed some magic power around the poker table, she became extremely jealous of it. In one occasion, she confided to her friends, "My present, my future and my success depend on this."

Mimi' warned her that the ostentatious display of that object during the wedding ceremony would irritate the Cardinal, but she scoffed at his objection and went ahead with her plan. At the exchange of the rings and the final kiss the crowd broke in a sonorous and prolonged applause. At the completion of the rite, the square in front of the Duomo became the theater of innumerable fistfights. A helicopter dropped thousands of euros for about ten minutes.

Escorted by the police, the wedding party moved for the sumptuous reception to the most prestigious hall of the casino "Il Campione," the B section. All the guests attended it, including the vice-ambassador from the US and the Bishop of Milan. Some American tourists gathered at the front to wish them well, but were kept away by the guards.

Inside, everything had been elaborated in every minutia. A giant vase of red roses occupied the central part of the hall. The band was positioned behind the dancing perimeter and everyone wore a red foulard. The tablecloths were red and so the napkins. The floor was mostly covered by oriental rugs with a variety of colors interspersed among them, but in which the red prevailed. On the bride and groom table, even the champagne and wine bottles had red labels. Not to mention a gigantic cake whose exterior was red chocolate. Among the guests, was a notable local politician who remained ecstatic before such ostentatious display of red. After a minute of hesitancy, he approached a colleague and confided to him, "This is, by far, the best wedding reception I have ever attended."

"But, we have just arrived, my dear comrade."

"The signs of a good day are visible in the morning, they say here."

"We are all acquainted with this proverb, but I judge a reception by the food and drinks. To this moment, I have yet drunk or eaten anything; therefore, I reserve my final comment at the end."

"I do not adhere to that philosophy. Food or beverages are not the point of my contention," he replied a bit disturbed and left. His interlocutor remained shocked by the abrupt disruption of the conversation and wondered where his comrade went.

The gentleman readily headed for the hall, where there was more space and less noise. He pulled the cellular from his jacket pocket and dialed a number by memory. He waited until the voice of a young woman from the other line responded, "Hello, headquarter of the New Democratic Party,"

"Janet, it is I. Do I disturb?"

"Not at all, doctor Lunatico. How is the reception? Are you having fun?"

"Fantastic! I never saw such an exquisite food and elegance in my whole life."

The secretary broke into a roaring laughter. When her humor subsided, she apologized, "I am sorry, doctor, but I could not repress my joy for you."

"Why is it?"

"You never went to a wedding reception in your political career."

"Well, let's not go behind the boundary line, now. Let us say that I dislike confusion."

"I am not sure about that, doctor, but nobody invited you."

He pulled the cellular away from the ear and was about to close the conversation. On the other end, the same feminine voice kept on saying, "Are you still there? Can you hear me?"

"I am not deaf, yet," he responded with bitterness.

"I was just kidding, doctor. Do not mind me. I wish I were in your place."

He did not appreciate her behavior, but what was brewing in his mind was far more important than the secretary silliness. He decided that he would not respond to her inappropriate demeanor at a critical time. He repressed his rage and said, "I have an important idea to submit to your discretion."

"You do not mean that you are surrounded by pretty girls . . ."

"Nothing of that," he replied half annoyed.

"It is a bit anomalous that you would ignore feminine beauty."

"Wishful thinking . . . With this big nose, I assure you that nobody looks at me."

She covered the phone with her hand and broke down in another sonorous laughter.

Her silence, made him suspicious of something, "What is going on? Can you tell me?"

"I was thinking that I am not a lucky woman. You got to be born to be lucky."

He tried to console her by saying, "You still have time to find your prince."

"Is the Bishop there?"

He covered the cellular with his hand and said, "What's wrong with this lady today! Who cares about the Bishop?" Then, he responded, "Yes, he is."

"Oh, good! Phoenix must be happy and honored by his presence. I am so happy for her!"

At that point, he lost control of his patience and whispered, "Stop lying to your teeth! You know that this is a farce. She is putting on the act for her husband's sake."

"That's ridiculous!"

"You should know by now that my comments are based on facts."

"I cannot believe it."

"You better believe it! But, let's go back to my central reason for the call. I would like to ask you if we still have in the attic the old sign of the hammer and sickle." He did not wait for a reply this time and continued, "I have a terrific idea. We could hang that sign on the wall behind the bride and groom. It would be eternally attractive. It could help us win the next elections. This place is crowded. You can call the cameramen and tomorrow it will make the headlines on every national paper."

The secretary got serious. "It is highly inappropriate to advertise our old symbol in a festival of love. It could cause deleterious repercussions for us."

"It would not be if you consider that the decorations in this hall are red. It looks stupendous!"

"I must respectfully disagree with it, doctor. If you do that, it will haunt you for the rest of your life."

The doctor did not reply. He closed the cellular and returned to the reception hall. The same colleague queried about his whereabouts. He replied, "I should have known better. She never agrees with me. The Party needs fresh forces capable of injecting new lymph into the system. A Static condition is the antithesis of movement."

The other person looked at him puzzled, but did not ask for a clarification. He handed him a beer and joined a group of guests nearby.

There was food galore on the tables. The best TV chefs where hired for the occasion. A steady line of drinkers was standing in front of a wall. Five faucets had been installed in the mouth of Bacchus' statue to let go five different types of wine. It was an inexhaustible torrent of the white and red spirit.

On another wall, a fountain gave out three different types of beer under the watchful eye of Moretti, the Italian beer magnate.

In the middle of the hall, a man spat from his mouth waves of fire. It looked like more a volcano than a human being. A dozen of professional belly dancers, originally from Turkey moved flawlessly around him. Their soft bodies flowed marvelously with their elastic movement to the sound of the music.

The guests were divided in two groups: one was dedicated to Bacchus, while the other to Venus, whose statue occupied the very center of the hall.

Three empty wine bottles were standing in front of Mimi'. One of the maids of honor got close to him and whispered in his ear, "I am sure you are having good time tonight." He waived another bottle of wine above his head and shouted, "Hurrah!"

The reception ended around midnight and Mimi' needed help to make it to the elevator and to his room. Phoenix thanked the helpers, closed the doors, took off her husband's shoes and clothes and covered him with a sheet. Mimi' began to snore. She changed her dress and opened slowly the door. She threw a glance in both directions and when she was sure that the hall was deserted, she left. Three minutes later, she was in the adjoining building playing in full swing.

The perfume she had still on from the wedding gown spread around inebriating the players who made some delicate comments. She ignored them. She knew very well that someone tried to distract her. Most of the by-standers stood behind her. She bet heavily on a king, but when the ace showed up, she lost all her money. She got up and left without saying a word. The rest of the players followed her as far as they could. They looked at each other, but no one said a word. There was a short pause, then, the game resumed.

Mimi' was still sound asleep when his wife returned. She opened the gift envelopes and made money distribution among them, leaving aside a certain amount that she placed in her purse.

Three months passed by and Phoenix visited the gynecologist. At the end, the doctor announced to her the happy news.

Unfortunately, Phoenix' status in Italy was approaching inexorably. The VISA had expired and the police sent her a note that she was no longer residing legally in the country. They gave her three days to pack up and leave. Mimi' walked almost constantly up and down the stairs of their house. He could not stand still. Phoenix hugged him and said, "I know that you love me immensely, but I want to spare you the agony of contacting some political personalities for my sake."

"I do anything for you, my dear."

"I know it, but it would be better for us if we move to America. I want my children to be American born."

The announcement surprised Mimi'. He always wanted his children to be born and raised on the Italian soil, but now, he was on the defensive and to avoid any argument, he said, "Whatever you desire my dear. I will join you as soon as I will be able to take care of my business."

She pressed him against her heart and said, "I knew you would understand me." In that instant, her eyes moved slowly to the fireplace where she noticed the charm. She shivered. Her husband asked her if there were anything wrong. She touched her head and replied, "It is only my head."

PHOENIX BACK AT US

At Mimi' request, Phoenix received a couple of weeks of extension on her Visa. During that period, she had ample time to pack up. She even anticipated the departure by one day.

Initially, Phoenix rented a condo in the vicinity of the university. Her parents had been living in the suburban area. One of her sisters purchased a house in a new development where once cows and horses graced peacefully. Birds and deer moved freely in the surrounding woods. Real estate companies soon bought corn fields and farms with all sorts of agricultural product still on them . . . Aggressive construction soon sprawled around, and the idyllic, bucolic scenes disappeared forever.

By the time Phoenix decided to build a house near her relatives, there was only one area available, next to a marshland. Cicero, this is the name of the village, is a few miles from Onondoga Lake shores. In the past decades, the area where Phoenix decided to build a house was infested with mosquitoes. This is not to say that the little terrible animals have been wiped out. Every summer, a helicopter flew over the houses and sprayed tons of disinfectant. Fortunately, the problem does not exist in winter. The bitter cold and the ice keep dormant the mosquitoes.

A decade earlier, about thirty minutes from Phoenix' new house, the Onondoga Indians broke ground on a huge parcel of land. They got permission from the state of New York to build a gigantic casino that would rival with those in Las Vegas or Atlantic Ciity. To lure in old folks, the management has buses available at different times of the day in various locations in the urban and suburban centers. Free transportation and food galore at the resort attract thousands of visitors every week. Most of them enjoy playing at the coin machines. Others pause at the poker tables. Only a handful goes there with the purpose of having a Mardi Gras at the buffet. At that time, Phoenix was not tempted by the buffet with the spectacular array of Asiatic and European culinary delicacies. She had only one objective in mind. At the beginning, she made some tentative approaches to be on her own, with the passing time, she preferred company with some lady neighbors. Eventually, she became a steady customer at the casino until the time of her first born delivery.

Mimi' remained in Italy a while longer to take care of his business. Two days before he flew to New York from Malpensa Airport, the stock market plummeted to a dramatically low minimum of what it was seven years earlier. He made it by the skin of his teeth to complete the last transaction with potential customers, even though the prices were no longer the same. During that week, the stock market on the major capitals of the world trembled and, later, collapsed. The most inexperienced investors lost their life time savings. The car industry laid off thousands of workers and most of the unions disappeared. Politicians from both sides of the aisle blamed unscrupulous bankers who claimed bankruptcy. The replica of another Great Depression was looming in the background. From all over the country and from every social sector cries for federal help rose to heaven. And Washington intervened massively to avert a major catastrophe. It loaned billions of dollars to banks and industries to reshape their ranks and put people back to work.

In Europe, the euro held its position. Indeed, it gained almost forty per cent over the dollar. With this scenario, Marchionne, the prime delegate of Fiat in Italy, launched an aggressive policy and bought fifty-one per cent of Chrysler. After a few months, the economy began to revive. The federal government had done its part, but the world economy took a heavy loss.

Mimi' made a lot of profit from the monetary exchange. It worked out well for him. He paid cash for the luxurious house. He also struck a deal with the Cicero town board. He paid the house taxes for the remaining of his lifetime. He also acquired ten old cars from the twenties and other property. He placed it in saving accounts and in his private safe at home. His financial resources were very stable and, so, he decided to quit working.

Phoenix waited impatiently for her husband's arrival at Hancock International Airport. The sky was overcast. It had rained steadily in the previous two weeks. It was not unusual to see a long sunny, dry weather to alternate with a wet one that seems to last forever. The lawns were soaked with water and the broccoli, along the grass, were growing at a rapid pace. The farmers were getting restless.

As the couple stepped out of the car at their mansion, Phoenix face looked radiant. "I have great news to give you, "she exclaimed. Mimi' did not seem to have heard her. "Why, you do not wish to hear it?" she said in an anxious tone.

"No, no, not at all" he replied quickly to assuage her nervousness. "I did not want to interrupt you. It is all."

She took him by hand and led him inside the living room. "I am expecting a baby," she said in a burst of joy.

"Oh, darling! What wonderful news! I love you. I love you. I love you!" and hugged her.

"Be careful, not to press too hard," she cautioned him.

She took his right hand and placed it on her womb. "Can you feel him?"

"Wow, he is jumping" and both laughed. At that point, he got serious and queried her, "Wait a second! How do you know that it is he?"

"You silly! The doctor, who else?"

Phoenix took him for a tour of the house. Everything was built according to your blueprints. In the bedroom, he jumped on a bed with his shoes and clothe. Phoenix hollered at him" don't do that! You mess up the bed with your shoes." Mimi' did not hear her. He fell asleep like a log. Phoenix could not believe her eyes. She made a phone call and departed."

Not too long after Mimi's arrival, Phoenix gave birth to a boy. Mimi' was a proud father and spent most of his free time with the newly born. Even his wife's frequent escapade had played an irrelevant role. It was going to be Christmas the following month and on that day he planned to baptize the baby and plan a grandiose party. On the back of a huge painting hanging on the wall of the living room, he had hidden his safe box. He took all the precautions that no one was observing him. He locked the doors and pulled down the curtains on the windows. He pulled the painting from the wall, decoded the code on the box and, voila', it was empty. Hundreds of thousands of dollars were missing . . . He queried his wife, "Honey bunch, where is the money from the safe?"

His question caused her a fit. She began to yell, "What do you think I am doing with the money? I have a child to support and the food and the house and the cars!"

He tried to calm her down. "I think I asked you a legitimate question. There is no need to get uptight," he explained to her.

"For a few thousand dollars you are causing a pandemonium," she screamed.

"It is not just a few thousands, but a few hundreds of thousand, "he corrected her.

"Don't worry; you will get your money back."

"How? When?"

"You are so selfish! It is unbelievable!"

Mimi' scratched his head, "something must be done about it," he said.

Phoenix made absolutely sure to have with her the lucky charm whenever she returned to the casino. And, lucky she was in a couple of occasions. In fact, she was able to put back in the safe half of the amount she had taken. Her husband never found out how his wife earned that money.

The following year, Phoenix was pregnant again. During the gestation period, she paid rare visits to the Oneida Casino.

"I need a ventilator," she said to her husband.

"Where, my dear?" responded her husband in astonishment.

"In the family room," she replied staring at the empty space outside.

"We have already one in the kitchen."

"In the kitchen, not in the living-room, 'my lemon juice' . . ."

He shook his head at the new compliment. "It is a spacious room, my dear. There is also a door that leads to the terrace and the breeze that enters from there is terrific. On the left, there is another door that connects the kitchen with the garage. The cool wind blowing in from the street is a blessing. Not to count the open windows . . . I feel chilly, at times."

"And, I feel hot!"

"But, we have the air condition throughout the house, a fan in the kitchen, a fan in the garage, and two fans in the cellar . . . How many more do you want?"

"Why are you getting so itchy?"

Mimi' did not reply. He went outside, sat on the steps and covered his face with both hands.

It was five o' clock on a stormy Saturday, when he met with a business agent to open a boutique with the newest fashion from Italy. In his car, he said, "I do not need any money, but if my wife continue to blow our savings with the same speed, I have to claim bankruptcy. Oh, my heavens, this house is becoming a trap for all of us."

Phoenix got busy too. Every night, her friends gathered at her house to play cards. They would leave as soon as she gave signs of tiredness. Their departure gave her time to meditate after the nurse put to bed her first child. Two weeks before the childbirth, she made a quick visit to the Casino. In the middle of a game, she fainted. Her friend considered that symptomatic of the imminent delivery and rushed her to the hospital. Unfortunately, it was a false alarm. She felt so frustrated that she vowed not to leave the house until the actual pre-birth symptoms commenced. Back home, she reminded her friends of her uncomfortableness. Alarmed, one of them asked her, "Do you want me to call the ambulance?"

"No, I did not mean that, silly. I miss the poker game to no end."

"If you feel so passionately dedicated to that activity, I can call for a poker game in your delivery room."

Phoenix laughed. In doing so, she exposed a brilliant, white denture. "I am bad, really bad," she exclaimed. "But, you have to realize that my husband has been coming home late every evening. What am I supposed to do, play the fiddle?"

"He is in business. What do you expect?"

"I expect him to give me his love every single day, not his complaints."

"Is that all you want?"

"Almost . . ."

With the arrival of the second child, Phoenix hired a second nanny. One evening, she visited a neighbor who objected to that idea. She replied, "I want to give my children the best care. Furthermore, I need some relaxation time. My house has converted into a jail for me."

"I don't blame you. You have the right to have some fun. Look at you! You have gained some weight. Shake it off. Shake it all off."

"Take it easy! Give me time. My husband does not care about my look."

"That's what you think! Men have the tendency to look elsewhere when their woman is not too appealing."

"Once, he used to be very caring. Now . . ."

Her friend lifted the index finger of her right hand and said, "I have an idea."

"What?

"Why don't we make a quick visit to the casino? Maybe, he gets jealous."

"I welcome your suggestion, but there is nothing new in it."

"What do you mean?" she inquired with curiosity.

"I go to the casino for the sake of it. I like it, not because of him."

"Would you like to ask him, too?"

"Not a chance."

That evening, the two ladies took off for the pre-established location. They were half way when it daunted on Phoenix that something was missing. "For pete's sake! I forgot my charm!"

"Why is that? For good luck? You do not need it."

"Like hack I don't! I have the premonition that it is going to be a bleak night." She bent her head downward and rubbed her eyes.

"Do not start being that negative. I have enough problems in to my private life . . . Let us buy a pound of enthusiasm."

Phoenix laughed at the suggestion, "If we could only buy it . . ." She resorted again to a gloomy attitude and added, "Look, I am being realistic. Each time I go to the casino without it, I lose big and the worst part of it is that my husband has begun to smell red."

"Without what?" Responded her friend with inquisitiveness.

"The charm, you idiot!"

"O.K. do you want a piece of advice? Forget it! It is a piece of junk."

Phoenix did not reply. Her mind was elsewhere running behind dreams.

Unlike other Saturdays, Mimi' came back home earlier the night his wife went to the casino. The nanny informed him that his wife had gone out. He did not make a big deal out of it and got busy with some financial documents where he thought could bring order. In the midst of his work, he picked up the cellular from his pocket and was about to press some numbers, but renounced to it. Mimi' had two security boxed where he kept the money and other assets. He turned a lock counterclockwise once and clockwise twice and stopped on number three. The safety opened and the two hundred and fifty thousand dollars were not there. He felt immediately enraged. He shuffled his hair with both hands. His immediate impulse was to call his wife as he tried before. Now, he had an extra reason to call her. The blood was rushing to his head. He sank in the high chair and stood there pensive for an hour or so.

At midnight, he heard a click in the door knob. Phoenix stepped in silently not to wake up the children. She took off her shoes and went straight to her bedroom. The sight of her husband immobile with the eyes looking toward the ceiling made her shiver. "What is the matter, honey? You never come home this early. Is it something wrong?" she inquired.

"You tell me!" he replied by straightening his body in an erect position and staring at her.

"Tell you what?" She replied pretending not to know anything.

Mimi' jumped on his feet and said with anger, "You know exactly what I am aiming at. We have already touched this subject before. My patience is getting thinner and thinner. I can no longer bear this ordeal. Two hundred and fifty thousand dollars have disappeared from the safety box."

"Are you the only owner of the money? She responded calmly.

"Answer me!" he shouted.

"Don't you ever raise your voice at me again, buster!"

The children started to cry. "You see what you have done? You scarred the children. Shame on you!"

Mimi' was ready to strike her with a bunch of papers, but he held it half way."

"Try it!" She told him defiantly.

"The business empire that I construed, it is my creation, my, work, my sweat. I did everything on my own. Nobody helped me. The comfort of this house, the cars, and the business are here because of me. Do you understand? I did it all on my own."

"I know. You do not need anybody anymore. You just came from Mount Olympus."

"You bet. I did!"

"You are pitiful."

Mimi' threw the papers on the floor and began to weep.

A month passed by and Mimi' returned to the box. This time, one-hundred thousand dollar was missing. She saw him making some calculations and said, "If you are looking for the money, I lent it to my parents. They needed it for sudden transactions. They will pay me back."

Mimi' did not approve of it. "I do not think it is fair to give away a bundle of money without my consent."

"Oh, my charm, where is it. I cannot find it anymore."

"The charm? What is the rapport between the charm and the subject of our discussion?"

She puffed a heavy cloud of breath out of her lungs and said, "There is . . . There is."

"If this is case, I suggest you to go back to your parents and return when you have the money."

"You don't trust me! You have no faith in me, you creep! I will leave and you have to beg me to come back." She ran upstairs, packed up a suitcase, picked up her purse and descended the stairs. Brought the material in the car and came back. "I thought you were all set," asked Mimi'.

"Not quite, "she replied with disdain. "I have one more thing undone." She grabbed the child, slammed the door and left.

Mimi' ran after her. "Where is the other child?"

"With my mother . . ."

"You cannot do this. I will not allow you to take anyone of them away from me."

"Don't touch me; otherwise I will call the police on you."

Mimi' remained with his arms outstretched, his mind numbed. She stepped on the gas and left a dark mountain of smoke behind her.

Mimi' sought legal advice from his lawyer. On the way out from his office, he stopped at an undisclosed location and, thereafter, he went to the bank where he made some changes on his accounts.

On Palm Sunday, Phoenix showed up at the door with her two children. As soon as they saw their daddy, they hugged him and kissed him. He said no word to her. The children started to run all over the house. Phoenix alerted her husband, "Mimi', watch them. They may fall off the stairs."

Mimi' had no intention of conversing with her, but he replied, "I'll keep an eye on them."

She threw her personal bag on the couch and said in a loud voice, "I am going to take a shower. Be careful that they won't get hurt."

"I will . . ."

"And, do not let them cry either, otherwise you will hear from me."

Mimi' launched a stern look at her.

It was ten o' clock on a Monday when Mimi' stepped in the urologist's office. He had been making frequent visits to the bathroom and thought was wise to see a specialist.

"Good morning, Doctor Spilorch."

"Good morning, Mr. O' Fabulosa."

"Excuse me doctor. My name ends with "o" at the end".

"I am so sorry," replied the doctor in a genuine tone. And, what brings you here, young man?"

"Doctor, I experience stomach pains quite often during the day. At times, even during night."

"Do you have three meals a day?

"Generally speaking, yes, with a snack in between."

"OK. Now, undress from the waist up and lay on this table."

The doctor pressed his hands on the stomach and adjacent areas asking the ritual question, "Does it hurt you here?"

When the doctor pressed between the stomach and the liver, the patient said, "Here, it hurts a bit." He did not wait for the doctor to continue and asked him, "What do you think it is, doctor?"

"I have a pretty good idea of what it may be, but before I make a final pronouncement, I like to hear from the radiology department. You may dress. The nurse will schedule an appointment for you with the radiologist. She will also set up one with me."

Mimi' was about to ask additional questions, but the doctor was quick to leave the office. Mimi' was a bundle of nerves and felt dejected.

In the afternoon, Mimi' was back at the doctor's office. "That was fast," said the doctor. "Technology is impressive nowadays. It has progressed by lips and bounds."

"It surely did."

"Mr. O' Fabulos," continued the doctor. Mimi' was about to correct him again, but refrained his impulse. "I have good news for you."

Mimi' felt a momentary relief. "I don't have anything doctor?"

"Let me rephrase it: Yes and no."

At that point, the patient felt disconcerted. He thought that the doctor was talking in riddles, but allowed him additional time for further explanations.

"As I was saying, the good news is that you do not have an ulcer."

The answer was still inconclusive for Mimi', and he started to manifest symptoms of nervousness.

"However, you have a minor problem," added the doctor.

"What is it? The patient asked with impatience.

"There an area of irritation that appears to be gastritis, the antechamber of ulcer."

"I don't like that," responded disconsolate Mimi'.

"There is no reason to fear. It can be brought under control. The main ingredient is peace of mind and calm. From now on, you must not stress yourself."

When he heard that, Mimi' shivered.

"I am going to prescribe you some pills. Take one in the morning and one before bedtime. Repeat this ritual for a month and report to me immediately after for further check up."

"Excuse me doctor, what causes the infection?" inquired Mimi'"

"It is not an infection. Avoid spicy and fried food for the time being." He was closing the folder, but stopped. He turned around and added, "Stress is the major component of this condition . . ."

"That figures!" exclaimed Mimi' between his teeth. The doctor did not hear him.

Before leaving, the doctor asked, "Is there anything else I should know or you would like to inquire about?"

"How do I lower tension?"

"Start to laugh and joke."

The nurse approached the doctor and whispered something in his ears. "Oh, yes," he said, "Before I check the lower part of your body, go with the nurse. You have to give her a urine sample." The nurse reminded Mimi' to secure tightly the bottle cap and to place it on the window next to the toilet.

Two minutes passed by and Mimi' was back in the doctor's office. The nurse told him to lower his pants and to bend next to the table. The doctor slipped a pair of plastic gloves on his hands and smeared the tip of the index finger with Vaseline. Mimi' closed his eyes and muttered, "I will ever get out of here. Once you are in the doctors' hands, you remain for a lifetime and good by banana." The doctor was waiting patiently, but Mimi' expected the nurse to leave. Her presence was a reason for embarrassment to him. To his chagrin, she stayed and he had to comply with the doctor's request.

The doctor pressed the prostate. Mimi' almost screamed. The doctor withdrew the finger, unfolded the gloves and disposed them in the garbage can. "I want to draw blood before you leave. We do that in the front office. You do not have to set up any appointment or go anyplace else."

Mimi' felt oppressed by the new disposition and protested, "I came here for a stomach pain and, now I have to go through a whole series of tests?"

"In my office, we do not take anything for granted, Mr. . . ."

"O 'Fabuloso,'" helped him Mimi'.

Mimi' returned the same week to find out the blood results. He sat on the chair and waited. Outside the sky was gloomy. A knock at the door shook him from his thoughts. The doctor opened a file and said, "Your PSA is 4.5. What would you like to do at this point?"

"What do you mean?"

"When the PSA reaches the level of four, it is symptomatic of the presence of cancerous cells in the blood. At this point, I suggest you have a biopsy."

Mimi' trembled. That medical term was new to him. The doctor explained to him that he would take extracts of tissues from the prostate and send them to the lab for test. The reader should know that these testing went on for about twenty years. So, if later, you still hear talking about them, it is not that the author is repeating the same thing.

Back at home, Mimi' felt hunger pangs and asked his wife, "Do we have anything to eat?"

"My darling, why don't we celebrate by going Chinese?"

"I may have prostate cancer and you want me to celebrate?"

"Don't be so pessimistic. Nowadays, nobody dies."

"Maybe, you ought to try to die to understand the meaning of death."

"You are so funny. Come on! Let's go Chinese," she insisted.

"That's not quality food, my dear."

"Yeah, but I love it. We will go to a Chinese buffet."

"I don't believe it!" Mimi' said in a disconsolate tone. "What is going on with you lately?"

"Why? You flare up because I want to go to Chinese?"

"As far as I am concerned, you can go Japanese, or Russian, but that's not the issue."

"I tell you. You are a hard man to get along."

Mimi' felt his brains were busting. She anticipated the bleak scenario and left. When she returned, it was two o' clock in the morning.

In his office, Dr. Spilorch was waiting for Mimi', who was slightly late due to a traffic jam. Mimi' was getting visibly nervous. The doctor read the report from the lab test. "For now, you are a lucky man.," he began. "But, let me give you a piece of advice. Do not lower your guard. Have a check up every six months. You are on the threshold of no man's land. If the PSA does not lower, you may have to have another biopsy when you come back."

Mimi' was jubilant and even though he was still upset by his wife's latest behavior, he tried to converse with her. It was no time to indulge in acrimonious and bitter quarrels. "Is lunch ready?"

"What am I your slave?" she replied in a defiant manner.

Mimi' had an outburst of anger and threw pots and pans on the floor. She grabbed her purse and left again.

It was three o' clock the following morning when Phoenix opened silently the door of a fourth bedroom. She let herself fall on the bed. She was exhausted. She slammed the purse on the pillow. The casino had not been benevolent with her that night. A poker player revealed to a friend that she had lost sixty-five thousand dollars.

Mimi' had left the same amount in the safe from last time clean up. The box was empty once again.

She woke up late. Mimi' approached her in this way, "Enough is enough! I do not care anymore what you do or where you go. You are driving me on the brink of a mental and financial collapse. I was forced to open a small business downtown, but I can't keep up with it. It is getting worse and worse. If we continue like this we may lose our shirt. When you need something, you ask me."

"It is all your fault!" she replied.

"How?"

"You never wanted to come with me. You are a ball of egoism. On the outward, you play saint. Inward, you are a jackal, a snake full of poison."

"Unfortunately, your description of me is inaccurate, not to say false. If you insist with this kind of behavior, we may start the legal process for the separation. I do not know how long it is going to take, but . . ."

"Is that what you want? But I am not going to leave. This is also my house."

"Did you ever work a day in your married life? Did you carry a checking or savings account when you got married?"

"I had five-hundred dollars," she cried.

"And, I suppose that with that amount you built this mansion."

Phoenix screams reverberated throughout the house and reached some neighbors' ears too. A couple of them rushed over to inquire if they could do anything. Phoenix replied, "Yes, mind your pretty business."

Mimi' tired of the altercations, walked to his bedroom. In the hall, he stumbled on an object. He lifted up the foot and realized that it was a charm. He took it to the garage and shattered it with a sledge hammer. The small pieces ended up in the garbage. Phoenix was unaware of it. She searched for it, but found no trace of it. The failure made threw her in a state of disarray. Her friend invited her for another evening of great fun. At the casino, Phoenix would find her piece of mind. For the first time, she was in no mood. She had also squandered a fortune.

MIMI' HOUSE

My dear reader, before we embark on the prologue of the second part of this exciting story, let me alert you on a couple of literary elements. While, Chris, the author, modified the language, not the facts, in the first section, from now on, he will be even more rigorous. In fact, he will record what is being said and transcribe it here correcting only minor orthographical errors. He will ask brief questions or make short comments only to render the reading flow more palatable. It is, therefore, autobiographical in a sense.

Mimi' welcomed Chris (the author) with enthusiasm and open arms. He did not know what to do to please his guest. Chris accepted only a cappuccino with a baba' and a cornetto. Phoenix took the time to show him the house and His briefed him up on the amenities of the location. Chris marveled at the stupendous view. He could see, in front of him, the entire span of Onondaga Lake and parts of the city of Syracuse. He also remained speechless at the vastness of the mansion and luxurious garden with fountains and statues. At the end of the tour, she politely asked permission to leave and withdrew in her bedroom to put on a pair of shorts and a light blouse. Her husband and the author were left alone to carry on their project.

The two sat in the leaving room across from the terrace. In the meantime, Phoenix walked on the terrace and found a comfortable position on the lounge chair. Chris turned, for a moment, his attention toward her and noticed that she stretched her legs under the beating sun. Evidently, she enjoyed sunbathing, especially, in the morning. Her husband was trying to recollect his thoughts when his wife yelled, "Mimi', come here and open the umbrella all the way! It is too hard for me."

Mimí rushed over the deck, lowered his head on one side of his wife's face and whispered, "As you know, I have an honorable guest here. We are busy."

"Why do you have to be so miserable all the time," she rebutted him promptly.

"Can't you get up and do it yourself?"

"I am in the middle of something. Why do I have to wait forever when I ask you for something?"

"Stop complaining and apply the cream on my legs."

The clock was ticking. Two minutes passed by and his wife's voice resounded once again through the hall, "Honey bunch, can you come here to apply the rest of the cream on my legs? What you applied before is already dry."

"Anything under the sun gets dry after a while," he reminded her. "I can't spend all day massaging your legs."

"Oh, you are not romantic at all! You are not a gentleman."

Mimi' looked at Chris with embarrassment and decided to postpone the recording to a later date. Chris acquiesced and left in a hurry.

Chris returned the following week. Mimí was about to start his story. He was interrupted by the telephone rang. He picked up. He knew quite well that his wife would not get up. The feminine voice, on the other side of the line, was so loud that Chris was able to hear her. Magnolia, a family friend, expressed an urgent request to Mimí. O'Fabuloso replied, "I come right away!" The conversation came abruptly to an end, at least temporarily. Phoenix, as her custom required, was enjoying her ritual daily sunbathing. She spread her arms, closed her eyes and turned her head toward Mimi', "When I ask you something, I have to wait light years before you do it. On the contrary, if someone else asks you a favor, you run like a rabbit. I should have married another man. I would have lived a queenly life."

Her husband excused himself with Chris and assured him that he would return promptly. Phoenix, still dissatisfied with the feelings she had just discharged, and continued, "Husbands! Some of them are good for nothing! They cannot survive without a woman."

Chris tried to fill in for Mimi's temporary absence, and said, "Mrs. O'Fabuloso . . ." She interrupted me quickly, "I beg your pardon, sir! I am 'Mrs. O'Fabulosa', if you know what I mean."

"And I beg your indulgence, madam! I did not realize that you changed your last name," Chris responded with a touch of irony.

"I hope you are not one of those who still lives in a patriarchal society," she responded sternly.

Chris was about to answer, when her husband showed up. He stumbled against a pair of shoes, which, by the way, were scattered everywhere. His prompt instinct was to hold his hand on a chair, but he still lost his balance and fell on the table and chairs causing a loud noise. Chris jumped on his feet, ready to help him. The old maid heard a noise and, from the kitchen, rushed to the living room. Looking at Mimi', she said, "Are you all right? You scarred me to death."

"Everything is OK," he replied.

His wife shouted from far away, "Don't bother. He gets drunk from the morning."

The assistant corrected her, "Mr. O'Fabuloso does not drink."

"Don't be silly! I mean that he gets drunk without drinking. He needs me on his side at all times."

Mimí remained pensive for a while, then, he asked his wife if she took the daily medicine. She answered, "It is all you worry about."

Under those circumstances, it became extremely difficult to concentrate. Mimi' suggested Chris to move to his office, but he opted for the porch. It was a gorgeous sunny morning and Chris did not wish to spoil either with Phoenix or among house walls. He loved open air and took every opportunity to walk or run.

Outside, Chris saw a scene, quite unusual. About ten people were waiting in line to talk to Mimi'. Once again, he apologized and went to exchange a few words with each one of them. Chris was able to capture the main idea. All of them were requesting different forms of aid. Chris scratched his eyes. He could not figure out how in the world Mimi' was able to sustain that relentless pressure, both financial and psychological. Apparently, Mimi' did not seem to mind it. At the end of the meeting with those people Mimi' came back to Chris, who expressed his concern about carrying on a reasonable and exhaustive report on his life story, not to mention a conversation. He explained to Mimi' that, although he got paid, it was a terrible nuisance to be interrupted frequently, Mimi' agreed wholeheartedly and they decided, from then on, to meet in the most remote corner of his vast luxurious garden with a biblical name "The Garden of Eden.". I destroyed the original tape, which was practically inaudible and he started all over again. And, now, I close with the preliminaries. The story is about to begin. I, Chris, will join him occasionally in the conversation only to let it flow smoothly.

DOCTORS WON'T TELL YOU

Mimi' took a couple days off to attend a conference on health and nutrition in California. Phoenix did not accompany him as she thought it was a waste of time. Mimi' was happy because he did not have to argue with her on every issue. His primary objective was to learn something that he could apply to his conditions, and, thus, reverse the course of the events. His hope was almost limitless. He was battling against a nasty enemy and a cruel time.

He sat on the front row holding a pen and a bunch of papers. He did not want to miss anything important and took notes at every opportunity. The topic was "What the Doctors will not Tell You" and the main speaker was a legend in nutrition, Dr. Maria Anna.

The speaker made a long, laudatory introduction focusing on the lecturer international academic achievements and the pioneer work she did in the field of preventive medicine. The doctor took the podium and began, "Have you ever ignored stop signs or yellow lights? Have you ever seen a police officer with a flashing blinking light on his car while pursuing a motorist who had committed a law infraction? Or, have you read the obituary this morning, leaned to the person next to you and said, "I am glad it is not me." Of course, this comment is not a revelation. Last week I attended a wake. The defunct brother t was sitting next to me. My beloved wife expressed him her sympathy. His response was quick and shocking, 'It is better that my brother died rather than me."

Someone from the audience interrupted her, "He made that comment?"

"He certainly did. But let me add something before I forget it, at times, I lose the centrality of my thoughts if you know what I mean. It is evident that we live a life of false assumptions. We think that the incurable habits, the unsolvable problems, the invisible enemies lie elsewhere and never in our backyard. We boast being untouchable or, at least, until we can afford pretending we are immune from misfortunes or mortality.

"What is your point?" asked someone sitting next to Mimi'.

"I am coming to it. In the realm of health, responsibility does not always allow us to prevent tragic events or unfortunate situations. We may be careful at the food and beverages and, yet, get sick. If this is the scenario, isn't better to disregard all the warnings and precautions and face everyday life without worry? I am not suggesting that every move we make has to be surrounded by unwarranted apprehension. It would be ridiculous following that course. What I am proposing is the opposite. We should conduct ourselves to act in a normal manner, which is with responsibility. The wife of a close relative of my wife is in the sixties. He is overweight, has high blood pressure and diabetes, but, no, he will not go to the doctor. My wife has reminded him repeatedly that one of these days he will have a stroke or drop dead. He shrugged his shoulders and boasted that he is immune from any illness."

I said to Mimi', "I, too, have a relative who suffers with hemicranias. Every year, with mechanical accuracy, she experiences periods of depression. Every one of us has tried to persuade her to see a psychiatrist. She hates doctors and medicine. I cannot tell the reader how many troubles she created for herself to the extent that her family and friends avoid her.

The other day, a popular sport figure was diagnosed with advanced rare disease. The doctor's prognosis gave him a couple of years of life. We should all realize that a regular physical and, in some cases, a mental checkup is a 'sine qua non' of our health responsibilities if we wish to reduce or annul altogether the chances of life-threatening consequences. Let me be clearer. When a disease is discovered in its early stage, the chances for success are high. Conversely, if we neglect to diagnose an ailment, we may find ourselves on a trip of no return."

"Splendid observation!" Mimi' said.

THE FOOD

The eminent doctor continued, "One of the most common and urgent riddles that a victim of cancer, or other disease, has to solve, pertains to food and drinks. What type and to what extent a patient is allowed to take? Does either one or both have any relevance in the prevention or recovery process of an illness or is just a myth? There is no clear cut position on this matter. In some respects, doctors are similar to politicians or philosophers. They differ only in terms of the approach. The reason is simple. Medicine is a one way discipline. Doctors are trained to attain strictly to fact-findings, to proofs, to clinical tests. They are not trained, sufficiently, in herbal or nutritional benefits. No wonder patients are dissatisfied many times with all sorts of pills to take on a daily basis. Hence, the suspicion that the majority of the medical field is in tacit agreements with pharmaceutical companies is widespread and gains momentum day by day. They may be just rumors, but people are skeptical and it would be interesting to create a bipartisan commission to investigate the problem. This may never occur because the politicking and the secret deals are so deeply rooted in the profession that it has become a 'modus operandi.' We are genuinely impelled to reflect, however, on the opposite approach of the European doctors. Whenever they prescribe medicine to a patient, they associate food to pills. For them, diet is 'a sine qua non' not only of preventive medicine, but of accelerating the healing process. This position is valid for well established infirmities or in the post surgery period. In some cases, doctors recommend to abstain from certain food or liquor altogether.

This is an intriguing and important subject that I refuse to let it go so easily. I have exhausted energy, time and mind trying to find out what is the proper diet for prostrate, but to no avail. Dr. Piselli used to forbid his patients dairy foods, a thesis which has been confirmed by subsequent studies mentioned also in the cancer brochure available in my urologist's office.

Ulterior questions that I posed to colleague urologists invariably received contradictory and bizarre replies. 'Eat and drink whatever you wish,' one of them told me. Another shook his head as to acknowledge his ignorance or the general medical ignorance in the matter. Yet, a nurse explained that caffeine and alcohol should be taken in moderate quantities. How can we remain indifferent to such diversity of opinions? But, more objectively, how can some doctors ignore or disclaim food and beverage relevance in the course of a healing process? In studies conducted up to 2011, researchers discovered that coffee is good for prostate.

It is common knowledge that vitamins, proteins, minerals, and so on, are indispensible for a healthy body. Each organs needs them in equal amount to ensure their adequate functioning that will provide a strengthening of the immune defense system and a quality life. I suppose that every house maid knows how to make good soup. If they use just chicken, the soup will be acceptable, but not delicious. However, if they add other ingredients such as, onions, carrots, celery, oregano, a couple of potatoes, etc., the soup will be extra delicious. Conversely, if the body lacks all the ingredients, (vitamins, minerals, proteins, etc.) some organs either get weak and open the way to infirmities and diseases or will not respond to a speedy recovery after a surgery or serious illness. To ignore these fundamental truths and rely exclusively on pills and surgeries is an offense to patients and doctors' profession . . . It is a mockery of the authority invested in them. It is an affront to the medical profession itself. The patient ought to be informed about a preventive diet alongside a preventive medicine long before the infirmity. They have to inform the patient in the inceptive stage and not when it has degenerated in a grave and irreversible condition.

Mimi' raised his hand for a question. His neighbor cautioned him, "Be careful on what you are saying," He appeared undisturbed and started; "You seem to be unconvinced. If you are skeptical, "The people looked at each other. They did not understand anything. He perceived the skepticism and added," I will remind you of another case. Bruno Capisani, an opera singer of La Scala of Milan came to Syracuse for his routine annual vacation. He looked in great shape. I asked him how he accounted for his youthful skin, he responded, 'Never mind the skin. The doctor prescribed me vitamin pills for the prevention of prostate cancer.' I was almost stunned! In this country, preventive medicine is unheard. It is a forbidden fruit."

"That is exactly what I have been trying to focus on," the doctor replied, "I will give you one more piece of information that will make doctors scared to death and they will ignore it. If they are not interested, then, I will address my one million dollar suggestion to the male gender. I would like to tell the ladies that they are not excluded for obvious reasons. It has been proved that eating a slice of watermelon a day or pink grapefruit will reduce by 83% prostate cancer. Did the doctors pass on you this information?

To prove even more my point, I will remind the audience that since earliest times, people have always clamored for wine's great benefits. There have been disputes over which color is more congenial for a particular food. Red wine, for instance, should be served with meat, while white wine should go with fish; yet, nobody, at least in the old world, doubted the nutritional value of wine. Not until a friend of mine requested an appointment with Dr. Ricci's nurse. She told him almost the opposite. She recommended him to abstain from wine, spicy food and coffee. She favored only a tiny bit of them and only occasionally. These words of caution, however, are in conflict with recent clinical studies which have concluded that wine and a couple of cups of espresso coffee, daily are, indeed, beneficial to the body. Coffee is diuretic and, it has many benefits, chief among them, it staves off Alzheimer disease and keeps the mind alert, but it is advisable in the morning up to three o'clock in the afternoon. You see. We have great doctors here, but there are too many interests.

One old man from the last row got up and asked to be heard. His request was accorded. "As you have just heard, spicy food is deleterious to prostate, however, my wife (This is the first time that she passed to me the information heard on TV.) That hot pepper is, indeed, healthy for prostate. And, would you like to hear another fact? My neighbor has been eating spicy food since she was a child, yet, she hardly gets sick." The whole audience roared in delirium.

The speaker cautioned the audience to turn off their cellular at the inception of the conference. In the excitement, Mimi' forgot to follow the instruction and his phone rang. He got up and ran to the bathroom. "Hello!"

"Hello, darling, how are you doing?

"I forgot to turn off the cellular and I ran out of the conference."

"Did you run out of time? Is that what you said?"

"No, out of the conference . . . It is in full swing."

"I did not hear you well. Did you get anything out of it?"

"It is still going on. The doctor is fantastic."

Phoenix turned to her friend and whispered to her," Play the other card."

Mimi' said, "Honey, I hear a lot noise in the background. What is it?"

"It is just music. Well, enjoy yourself. See you soon."

"Enjoy myself?" repeated Mimi' after he closed the cellular. He heard someone laughing from one of the toilets, then another and another . . . He looked around and did not see anybody. He put the cellular back in his pocket and rejoined the conference.

The guest speaker waited until the rumor subsided and continued, "Equally important is the discourse on wine. Tests conducted at the Campobasso Catholic University's Lab, in June of 2009, have discovered that wine reduces the side effects of radiation on a breast cancer patient. Moreover, wine, regardless of the color, strengthens the liver and the heart. The doctors emphasized that the positive contributor to health is not the alcohol but poliphenol, which is hidden in the skin of the grape. The news caught by surprise a colleague oncologist, who quickly dismissed the veracity of the discovery, and requested the name of the lab where the tests were conducted. Of course, I provided him the original transcript and the translation of some excerpts. "This sounds interesting," he commented and never mentioned again.

"It certainly is!" emphasized the doctor at the conference. "I have seen many doctors in this country in a fifty year span of time; yet, no one has ever suggested or prescribed a patient to take or abstain from certain foods. They are not interested. They do not care. They have been inducted into the field of scientific medicine, where there is no 'if' or 'but'. Nonetheless, food has been and continues to be the source of many medical discoveries. The latest news comes from Galapagos Islands, in the Pacific Ocean. They claim to have found something in a local food that can stretch human life for ten years. Any well informed individual will confirm that plants and fruits from the Amazon region provide the basic ingredients of many medicines.

Blueberries are great anti-toxicant, add to prostate health and are good for memory and eyes. The eye surgeon, every year, expects my wife and me to have a checkup. Not once he mentioned the benefits from blueberries. That is an anathema!

Pomegranates are equally powerful anti-toxicant and reduce diabetes and cholesterol . . . Similar properties are shared by strawberries, cherries and kiwis. Does your doctor suggest you to eat them? Unless you hear on TV or read it on a newspaper or magazine, you stand a little chance to learn from them . . . If you experience cramps in the legs, why shouldn't you know that you are lacking potassium and, therefore, you need to eat bananas or potatoes, rather than take pills? If someone suffers from cardiac complications, you would expect the doctors to inform you about the benefit that fish (salmon, sardines, trout . . .) for their content of Omega 3 it is common knowledge among men with prostate problems that Saw Palmetto reduces the PSA. Oncologists do not accept it and the first prescription they give you is to stop taking it. They claim that herbs camouflage the real blood reading. This position contradicts a medical doctor from Columbia University in New York who is a pioneer in experimenting herbs and other drugs. The list is long with super oxidant like ginseng, noni, garlic, yams, and so on."

A young lady raised her hand and got up, "In this country, we lack a nutritional education from kindergarten on. That is why most of the Americans are obese and health complications.

The general attitude toward medicine is well known, 'I got to die anyhow, so what if I take pills for the various maladies.' The truth is that we do not need all these pills. They are killing us. In most of the cases, we can do without them. We need to stick to health diets and exercises. Mobility and quality food are the two basic components for our well being. So, I commend you for "the fresh air" that you are bringing in this stale atmosphere."

Everybody applauded. The speaker thanked the girl and told her that she admired her for her clear vision about good living. He sipped water from a bottle and continued, "Before I conclude, I wish to underline one more note about prevention. One morning, at LA University, a dear friend of mine looked at a colleague from India me one morning at LA University and told her that she looked sick. Her colleague tried to avoid the question, but, they knew each other from a long time and I could not hide the truth. She revealed to her a 'bombshell.' She had just been diagnosed with ovarian cancer. My friend bent over my shoulder and said with nonce lance 'That's nothing!'

I wanted to scream from the agony that I was bearing inside me. I suppressed any ulterior comment. Non content of my silence, she muttered, "My ex-husband had the same thing, but, as soon as the cancer appeared on the first developmental stage, he underwent some therapies and the cancer was stopped at its insurgency.'

Ever since I have been reflecting on it, some doubts have surged in me. My colleague brought up an incontrovertible point that if followed up and ascertained, it would uncover fundamental malaise of most doctors. The question to ask would be simple. Why don't we take regular check up? It is our responsibility to see a doctor on a regular basis. This second reflection is this, why is there so much obstinacy on the part of most doctors to use preventive approaches patients from physical and mental suffering and, many times, from death? Diet is extremely important as it is a life devoid of stress. Add up a pinch of good humor and physical activity and you are on the way to good health.

"Are you suggesting that there are different modalities in approaching a problem or that there is rivalry among them? Don't they share their experiences?" A journalist asked.

"I am not suggesting anything, except what I said. It is up to each of you to read through the lines."

The journalist decided that it was improper to insist and allowed the speaker to focus on another aspect of prevention. "People ought to know that detection of the disease in its early stage doesn't necessarily exclude the patient's active participation in the decision making . . . He or she has to decide on the right procedure and research a meticulous preparation to follow in order to ensure the final success. This point is so widely disregarded, first by doctors and, later, by the patients that many poor souls arrive at the deadline worse than before. For this reason, therefore, I consider this topic the basis for my future lectures.

It has been statistically proven that one man out of three is a candidate for prostate cancer. I did not make researches on breast cancer data, but I do know that it is very high. As I mentioned earlier, we are victims of daily tension. The reduction of stress is synonymous to good, preventive medicine. Those people whose jobs are stressful are more prone to succumb to disease. My son, Marco, works in a hospital. A co-worker doctor, who conducted numerous autopsies in the past, told him that every man has prostate tumor cells. It would be interesting to find out why some men remain immune to cancer, while it develops in others.

Without doubt, some men or women are indestructible. Regardless of the diet, exercises or temperament, they are immune from any disease because they are genetically driven. A lady, who used to live near me, is ninety-nine years old. She has never seen a dentist and her teeth are spotless. A dear friend, a centenarian, has never been sick or taken pills. Her energies are extremely uncommon in a human being of her age. She is known for being very temperamental and whimsy and longevity is, most likely, due to the genetic make-up in her body. She had four sisters and all lived close to be centenarian.

There are also people who are utterly predisposed to all sorts of health problems. They are careful with the food intake, do not drink coffee or liquor, go to the gym every day and, yet, at the first breeze they catch a cold. The only logical explanation that we can offer is that their immune system is run down or they are genetically weak. In such cases, quality food can deter, but not eliminate the more serious consequences.

"Doctor, talk to us about stress," asked Mimi'

"Stress is definitely a wild beast and we should learn to tame it. We have some remedies available. Our job and family makes pressing demands on us. Withdrawing from the daily routine can be an excellent palliative. Sports, such as fishing or golf, can be a formidable antidote, and, so, reading, knitting, socializing or watching humorous programs that make you laugh. There is nothing more appalling than a sad, catastrophic environment. Run away from it!"

"Do you have any other suggestion?" interjected one lady sitting in the middle aisle.

"As I said, exercises, before and after cancer treatment or can avert, reduce or eliminate an impending danger. It all depends from all the pertinent components assembled together. They can make a tremendous difference in 95% of the cases even when cancer is predestined, so to speak, to follow its course. Of course, if you argue with your husband (or wife) or with your boss on the job very often, your chances of success are nil. I have seen it repeatedly and I emphasize it. People with a scarce sense of humor, women or men lacking self-control and those embalmed in egotism are the first victims."

Mimi' shook his head and covered his face, but refrained from making any comment.

"We do not need a psychologist or psychiatrist to tell us that stress is a killer." The doctor added. "We feel it in many unhealthy conditions. Stress debilitates the immune system and facilitates the development of a tumor. Controlling stress is of paramount importance in the fight against wild animals that hide in us."

Mimi' raised his hand again and said, "How can we avoid stress if a wife stresses you up?

"In that case, you may have to change your wife," responded the doctor with a touch of humor.

The audience jumped on its feet and began to whistle. It took a few minutes before the custodians could bring the uproar under control.

The doctor finished by saying, "I was kidding, but let us be realistic. With the current job scarcity, high taxes, the urge for immediate gratification and environmental deterioration, it is almost impossible to stay calm. One must reach a compromise between the demands and individual capabilities. It also depends from individual characteristics, likes and dislikes. Prayer is a powerful preventive medicine hardly being practiced with conviction by anyone who is stricken by a tumor. But, you must believe in it and clear your heart from impurities to be really effective. I have to confirm that I am no longer a superstitious person. Indeed, I dislike passionately human beings, who rely on man-made artifacts, as if they controlled our lives. It is so irrational to me that I don't even take the time to discuss it anymore. Of whatever credo you are, prayer is a stabilizing agent and can help psychologically end emotionally, thus it creates a new positive 'environment' in yourself."

A professor in the middle aisle took up the floor and stated, "Doctor, as long as you mentioned the power of prayer, can you elaborate a bit more. You cannot leave like this suspended in our minds." Everybody agreed.

The doctor replied, "The time is up, but I do not want to disappoint you. Periodically, I have heard Catholics cherishing St. Anthony's power to let recover lost items. Let us not get confused with words. 'Power' is an attribute of God. We pray to the saints to intercede for us. I must say that, inwardly, I almost mocked those people who made miraculous claims, until I tried to see on my own how effective is the power of prayer. I had lost a wallet. I searched everywhere and I could not find it. Every jacket, pants and suit in the closet was searched very meticulously. Every place where I had kept the wallet in the past was scrutinized. The result was always negative. When everything was lost, I asked myself what would it be the cost for begging St. Anthony to help me find it. Surely enough, I repeated the same prayer and I found it. Was it a fortuitous case? Maybe . . . I thought about it. The doubt lingered in my mind for a long time until another desperate case occurred. I lost the visa card along with the insurance cards. I scouted every corner of my clothes and house, but to no avail. I did not wish to bother St. Anthony a second time on the same subject. Well, I did. I had no other alternative. With great gratitude, I found my lost cards. I marveled even more on a third and fourth occasion with the same results. There are people, out there, skeptical, as I was. To them, I can only say, 'Try it!' Nonetheless, we should learn one truth, one lesson. It is fine to ask help to saints (to God), but it is ungrateful to not appreciate it and return to them.

This leads us to make an ulterior indispensable consideration. Probably, the most preventive medicine against cancer is love. It is not a mystery that we consume most of our energies in material things."

Mimi' could not repress his anger, "That is what I argue about all the time!" The audience voiced opposition to his continuous interruptions and he did not interfere anymore.

"We want a mega TV screen, a new car; we shop for new clothes every week; we want to go on vacation in the most exotic places in the world; we insist in going to the restaurant on week-ends, and not only, and we are obsessed with parties. We leave no time for love.""Isn't this ambiguous?" One of the panelists inquired.

"No! I am referring to genuine love, durable love, not temporary. Visiting the sick, helping the poor, giving without expecting anything in return and doing something for the church or other charitable institutions will undoubtedly make us better human beings and less predisposed to cancer. They enhance our moral status, shape up a positive attitude and provide a healthy feeling to both body and mind. Most of us overlook the power of love in preventive medicine."

"I was right," replied an old lady. Mimi' looked at her, but made no comment.

The doctor closed the file and said, "Tied to love is prayer and I spoke about it a little while ago. We have tremendous instruments available and, yet, we do not use them or do not know how to use them well. We underestimate their importance and significance. St. Augustine prayed with his friends for an entire night on behalf of a local dignitary victim of a mortal disease. The following morning the patient got up and began to serve them. I could go on offering innumerable examples where prayers solved the most desperate cases, but my objective is not to moralize. The reader needs only to know that there are various valid alternatives as preventive medicine."

"Is this an inseparable rule?" I interrupted him again.

"As a rule of thumb, yes, but, then, there are always exceptions. Listen! As the sun gives life to the universe with its rays, so, divine love showers human beings with favors. It is a genuine source of immeasurable benefits. It is all around us and we must search for it. And, now, go and be healthy!"

A tall man, in the fifties, stood, took off his glasses and placed them in the hands of a woman sitting next to him. He looked straight in the eyes of the speaker and said, "Can you elaborate on the relationship between pharmaceutical companies and the grants they receive from the government and other sources? In my view, whether we speak of corporate or governmental funding someone is biasing someone else and the consumer becomes the predestinate sacrificial lamb."

"You hit the nail, sir," responded the lecturer with a broad grin. "To make medical or biochemical researches, we need money. You may organize a telethon or similar TV fund promotions, but the real amount that reaches the actual work is minimal. Statistically speaking (and this is common knowledge), the pharmaceutical industry provides almost half of financial assistance to studies and much more than that to FDA for testing. "The speaker pointed the index finger toward the audience in a circulatory type of movement and added," If anyone of you decides to open a store, do you invest the money for profit or for generosity? You do not find a single Good Samaritan in any business. Corporations are alive because they are financially centered. Having that in mind, (and he brought the finger to the right temple), think! Would you produce the best, healthiest, most organic food in the world if the market is scarce or would you produce food that gave you the highest return even though it may only fill your stomach?"

"What you are saying is this," intervened a man with a long beard. "Research money goes where there is a greater expectation of revenue."

"You got it! And this explains why we are poor in vaccines. The pharmaceutical companies do not want you to die. They want to prolong your life as much as possible. Be assured on this."

"They are not going to triple or quadruple their profits if they provide vaccines," answered the same man.

"Bravo! If they invest on preventative medicine, they defeat their purpose. But also this must be clear," emphasized the lecturer opening a book a reading a couple of lines. "If you fund me, you dictate the terms, otherwise, you will not give me the business the next time."

"If this is case," protested a gentleman from the last row, "Our taxes should be much lower, then."

"You are partially right. You cannot have the government and corporations funding the same testing institution. There would be conflict of interest."

"Do you actually believe that a university would bend their integrity rules to please the funding corporation?" asked a woman journalist.

The speaker paused a moment and scratched his chin. "Well, it is a question of credibility that is at stake. Let's put it this way. Most of the time, we do anything for money. With trillions of dollars in debt, the government is not going to fund lavishly anymore. My friends! Let me end it, here, with this observation. Whether the funds take origin from the government or pharmaceutical companies, politics and lobbyism will always play a central role. It is up to us to change the rules of the game."

The whole audience gave him a standing ovation for an uninterrupted ten minutes. He bowed repeatedly and waved, 'good-by.' Mimi', surpassed everybody else in shouting, 'Bravo! Bravo!'

Mimi' came back from the Californian conference deeply troubled. He had acquired an unprecedented wealth of knowledge on health, but he feared for his own because it was getting too late. Phoenix was radiant with joy in seeing him. She had been able to transgress her own vow and go back to the casino once more. For once, she was serious and asked her husband what he had learned, "What did you get out of it?

"I heard things never heard before."

"For instance . . . ?"

"This female renowned doctor spoke at length about the importance of food as preventive medicine."

"That's a bit abnormal nowadays to hear that talk from "the horse's mouth."

"She was terrific!"

"Did she say anything else that caught your attention?"

"She said many things. Chris was with me and he wrote every detail of the conference."

"Do you remember a couple of things in particular?"

"Really, three ideas got stuck besides food: stress, prayer and love."

"Prayer and love? She sounds like a priest rather than a doctor."

"Certainly, priests remind us often about the power of prayer and love, but they are not the only ones.

Many professionals are starting to acknowledge the tremendous role that the two play in our earthly lives, besides the heavenly."

"You sound like a changed person," responded his wife with surprise.

"Change, at times, is inevitable. We all have to change for the better. A pond with stagnant water attracts mosquitoes."

"I begin to suspect that this author you are talking every day is feeding in you distorted ideas about life."

"Actually, I am the one who talks. He records, then, goes home and transcribes the language by polishing it. He asks a question once in a while . . ."

"I hope that something good is going to come out of this book, otherwise I will crack your head."

"Here we go again! You should have been there in my place," said a disconsolate Mimi'.

"Why, me?"

Mimi' conferred again with Chris on the strategy to pursue and met in the Garden of Eden. The maid brought a lot of food delicacies, but Mimi' was very selective. Chris said, "Well, if you don't eat, somebody has to."

Mimi' decided to go on and finish his story. "I have to do it, maybe not for my sake, but for those who will experience my ordeal in the future," he said in a low voice.

"Now, you can narrate your ordeal in the first person."

THE TENTACLES STARTED
LONG AGO

(From now on, Mimi' addresses in the first person the roots of his problems.)

"On January 15, 2009, as I told you before, I went for the six months prostate check-up. A few weeks later, I was diagnosed with cancer. You may imagine how devastated I felt. The whole world collapsed! Had I known what I learned at the California conference, probably, the beast's tentacle would not have found fertile ground in me. Moreover, I should have taken the advice of the man who advertised a concussion of herbs on TV. He assured me that he would have brought down the PSA to 1.6 in six months. I did not have anything to lose, but I did not get lured in.

For more than twenty years, I had troubles with the prostrate. A friend of mine urged me to see Dr. Piselli, who was considered a guru in the field. His office was across University College, downtown Syracuse. The idea of exposing one's private organs, not to mention the rectal exam, for both men and women represents a psychic degeneration. In my case, it terrified me. It took months of mental preparation before I finally called up doctor Piselli's office. Lucky me! I was told that the doctor was about to retire and did not take any new patients.

Another friend, suggested me to get an appointment with Dr. Paul Ricci, a young and excellent urologist, who shared with him the same offices. Sometimes, people get confused with his homonym,

Gino Ricci, who became nationally popular for making a pair of shoes to President Clinton during his visit in Syracuse.

At the first visit, Dr. Ricci was kind and polite and tried to alleviate my fears even when my PSA was 2.00. I had no knowledge of the PSA and what it meant. I was fifty-years old and by telling you my story, I hope I can spare many of you the agony of going through the same experience. I cannot describe the grim feeling that I developed just by waiting in the office and the uncomfortable and nervous state I was in.

The following year, for reasons that I still ignore, I switched to Dr. Alforundu Gallos. He was originally from India and had a thick accent. Most of the time, I could not understand him and I had to ask him to repeat. But, what really scared me was the sign hanging on his office door. It generated in me the urge of running away. They were technical, medical terms that sounded notes of fear. Now that I am a "veteran soldier," I reminisce with disdain to those days. I repudiate all the trepidation, internal and external that I displayed. Looking retrospectively at my first experience with that doctor, I cannot forgive myself for my uneasiness. It was a disaster. I don't recall the PSA. I even ignored its meaning. At that point, the doctor seemed to be concerned more about my urine infection. How in the world did that happen? With his proverbial serenity, he hardly explained anything. He sat behind the desk and wrote a prescription and discharged me without offering any explanation. When I read the prescription, I realized that it was an antibiotic. I thought that in a matter of a week the infection would disappear. Wishful thinking! I was stunned when month after month the doctor kept on prescribing me the same antibiotic. The infection would not let up its grip. It was so obstinate that it took seven months for the penicillin to eradicate it."

"That's unheard of," I exclaimed with surprise.

"You should have been in my shoes! I begged him to inform me about the source of the problem. He gave me a vague and unsatisfactory reply. I returned home more dejected than ever. Had I known what I know today, I would have taken care of that infection without penicillin and in a matter of two weeks.

In a matter of a year, another urine infection developed and it cost me three months of antibiotic. I became frantic about it. Subsequent to that, the doctor changed his office location and I was tempted to quit him. I was not strong enough, I admit it, and that awareness caused in me a sense of hopelessness, of impotency, of inferiority.

Prior to Christmas, I was subjected to a clamorous mistake that almost paralyzed my brains. The PSA count was about two points. I tried to find out the rationale behind this continuous rising. I made an attempt to search for an alternative, what to eat or drink, but, once again, he displayed his typical disinterest. While I was dressing, the only suggestion that he made was to be cautious with spicy food. He had just finished when he smiled and added, 'I eat some of it, at times.'

I sat in the waiting room until he called me to his office. He shuffled a few papers lying in disorder all over the desk and informed me that I had been diagnosed with prostate cancer. I left the building speechless.

On my way home, I was absent minded. An alter ego drove for me. I thought that the end was approaching. Probably, I had six months to live. My heart sank to the lowest level and even now I wonder how I even reached my destination.

I do not recall the dynamics of my conversation with my wife. While I was in a state of mental turmoil, the phone rang. On the other side I heard the raucous, heavily accented voice of the doctor, 'Mr. O' Fabuloso, I am sorry! I made a mistake. I gave you the wrong response. I got mixed up with another patient.' I jumped in the air by the joy, but at the same time I wanted to sue him or throw him in jail. At the distance of so many years, I will never know how much mental and physical damage his mistake caused in me. The saying that 'the client is always right' does not apply to every profession or situation.

Fortunately, Dr. Alforundu Gallos retired before I was really tempted to desert him. A Syrian doctor replaced him, but somehow, I became so suspicious of that man that I could not explain it. The truth was that I felt very uncomfortable in his presence. Finally, I got bold and took the irrevocable decision to quit him. For once, I showed courage, but the game was not over yet. His secretary kept on sending me bills for about two or three years. I called her and told her that she had been making a mistake all way along. She denied it insisting that I was still his patient. I had only one alternative. I called Pomco, the insurance company, and revealed to the secretary that

that doctor was charging them non-existent visits. The employee replied, 'It is up to you to call the doctor's office if you wish to rectify the error.' I remained with my eyes closed and my mouth open for a few minutes!

As the time went by, I made innumerable researches to locate Dr. Ricci's office and made an appointment with him again. In a way, I felt relieved.

The urine test, once again, resulted positive. My fears re-emerged, but the good news was that the infection disappeared after a couple of weeks. But, that did not solve my problems. The PSA level had increased to 3.02. In the successive years it bounced back and forth, but, fortunately, below four. On each occasion, I raised the finger toward the sky and said full of Christian pride, 'It is the Lord.' The doctor would repeat my comment, at times, in an ironic way. My illusions began to dwindle. The PSA reached 4. The successive test rose to 5.50. The doctor asked me if I wanted to take a biopsy. With all the fears that gripped me, I accepted.

"Did you inquire about the biopsy danger," I (Chris) queried.

"Of course, I did! Some people claimed that it has a negligent impact on the individual's health; others indicated that it was somehow uncomfortable. I even contacted Frank, a gentleman whom I read about him on the internet. He sold herbs. He told me that in six months the PSA would be reduced at 1.5. I was encouraged by the news, but, when he explained to me that I had to take those herbs for the rest of my life, and pay two hundred dollars every two months, I declined the offer. In closing, he said, 'That'll be the day when I let a doctor cut me!' I already gave a glimpse of him before.

Dear reader, I think about his words every so often and I realize how easy it is for someone who is healthy to make a boisterous comment. It is easy to talk when you have knowledge, money, family assistance and a patient partner!

The biopsy was not a horrific procedure. The doctor introduced a mechanical device in the rectum and snapped a piece of tissue. There were times when it hurt and when it did not. What bothered me the most was the blood in the urine that kept on showing up in the following days. The doctor had warned me about it, but he also assured me that such an inconvenience was going to disappear in a matter of a week. And, it did!

As I had prayed and hoped for, the results were negative, but that was the beginning of a long and arduous trial. From then on, I had to report to him every six months for check-up.

One year, the PSA level from 6.2 descended to 3.09. How it happened, I will delve into it later.

In the meantime, the bladder kept on behaving on suspicious notes. Once, the doctor ordered me to take a urine test twice in a row because the first time the results were positive. Although the second test produced no evidence of bacteria, it shook my confidence again in winning the battle. One day, a friend came to do some work at my house. At some point, our conversation shifted on bladder infection. His healing methodology provided an interesting source. He recounted how an Italian friar responded to a man who presented him his concerns. The monk pointed at a bundle of onions hanging on the wall of his convent and said, "That does it." The man followed his advice and got cured.

A few years ago, in Syracuse, the same friend heard a lady complaining about the same problem. She was particularly annoyed by the pills that her doctor prescribed her to take on a daily basis, yet, her condition never showed symptoms of improvement. The story of the monk produced a profound impact on her. She had finally found the source of inspiration that would cause in her a remarkable change. For ten days consecutively, she ate onions galore. With her astonishment and satisfaction, she never again experienced any bladder infection. My friend reader, take note of this!

I am not so sure if the lady was a credulous person, but her relatives can back up their testimony by the doctor's medical tests. Since then, I started to make an abundant use of onions in the salads and my bladder never again has shown any trace of infection. By the way, I do not pretend to be what I am not, a nutritional educator or a doctor. But I did not want this to go by unnoticed by the reader either. It may spare them uncountable suffering, waste of time and money.

Even though Phoenix lived in another world, I have been giving her every morning some of the food and beverages, I learned about. Her sugar count, blood pressure and cholesterol have been drastically reduced. She could get rid of this medicine in the near future; unfortunately, she does not get involved in physical activities.

Many years ago, when the first symptoms of prostatic irregularities emerged, I turned to technology and, so, I explored the internet. I read many accounts of people whose PSA ran as high as 200 and by taking certain herb extracts, they brought it under control, which means below 4.00. One of the juices they took was Noni. Another, which they accounted as being the primary source of the drastic reduction of the PSA, was taken out of the market. No one has ever been able to explain the reason for the disappearance from the shelves after a year later its appearance. In the meantime, I drank a tablespoon of Noni juice once a day instead of three times. One year prior to the discovery of the tumor, I dropped it because it frustrated me doing the same thing every day, a part from the fact that a bottle is expensive." "Do you think that by not taking the proper amount of Noni juice you accelerated the development of cancer?" I (Chris) asked Mimí with curiosity.

"I will never have an answer, but only speculations. I only know that I resisted for about twenty years before I capitulated."

"Was it worth the effort?" I insisted.

"I don't know. I questioned myself many times. The money that I invested, the time, the energy . . . and I still failed. Maybe, it would have worked with another individual with a different personality. And, on this I will return later, but I hoped and prayed that a revolutionary medicine would be discovered. Hey! I did not take into account the pharmacological interests!" he replied, shaking his head and staring at the empty space. Then, he added, "Without doubt, my wife was caught In the midst of this entire ordeal. She must have been affected, at least, marginally, at the beginning. I ignore the impact that it had on her morale. She had to deal with her problems . . . Initially she showed some interest. As my condition deteriorated, she distanced herself even more leaving me in high sea at the mercy of an imminent tempest.

I let him continue his story.

MY FIRST ENCOUNTER WITH THE MONSTER

On January of 2009, I went for my regular check-up. Dr. Ricci had untimely retired. He still looked very young and healthy the last time I saw him . . . Evidently, He was one of the few wise professional to retire on time despite the huge financial profit he was making. Money did not overpower him to the point that he continued until he dropped dead. For that reason, I owe him much respect.

He was replaced by Dr. Thorny, a relatively new to the field of urology. He was young, tall and skinny with a dark complexion. I must admit that his perennial serious look was not conducive to a balmy relationship. You can analyze a person's demeanor in two ways. The individual may be very professional to the point of being fastidious, or he may have a lot of problems in his private life. He just did not sprinkle trust. The nurse must have read my mind because at one point she suggested me to listen to the doctor and not to the herbalist because he had attended a medical school.

The rectal check-up was not encouraging. As he touched the prostate, he exclaimed, 'Whoo'. He discarded the plastic glove-It had the roughness of the gloves women use to wash dishes—and informed me that the PSA reading was 6.7. I could not believe it! I always relied on God's help and on the juice and berries. I must confess to you that I felt betrayed! I could not proffer a single word for the next minute or so. He reminded me that the last biopsy was done ten years earlier and that it was a good idea to re-do it. I nodded, but I was not thinking rationally. To go through those grueling tests that, aside from being painful, showed my most private, gave me a sense of profound humiliation and resignation. I had always thought that God was on my side. Now, I felt alone and abandoned. Internally, I was cold, utterly cold.

The day of biopsy was also a gloomy one. The doctor tried to distract me by informing me that the procedure was visible on the computer. The nurse, a wonderful human being, did her best to console me during the procedure. My dear reader, I do not wish it not even to the animals what I went through. I am not exaggerating. It was an agony the entire time of the test! I looked at the device he held in his hand and I got scared. The prostate was large and the passage of that instrument caused intense pain. I was about to faint. I called on the Blessed Mother; I mentioned the name of Jesus; I called on the saints. I got no response. Each time he extracted a tissue it was like pulling a nail. He cut twelve tissues in all. Even now that I recount that event, I feel shivering throughout my spine and I am going to cut it short because my mind gets numbed when I think about it. What made the whole scenario even more horrible was pulling out the device. What a horrendous experience. The pain returned in all its devastating intensity. I realized in that moment that not all the biopsy processes are the same. The first time that I had it done, it was relatively easy and painless. In reality, the size of the prostate determines, partially, a smooth or a painful operation.

When it was over, I felt immensely relieved. I asked him how the tissues he had extracted and the whole prostate looked to him. He replied that everything looked fine. With his assurance, my home return trip was a mixture of pain and hope. Unfortunately, I ignored the devastating consequences that might lie ahead. I did not know, for instance, and, no one does, if the tumor cells fell into the body bloodstream or if they escaped though the urinary canal. This was the major threat. This was the danger that Frank, the herb vendor from the computer, alerted me to.

For two long and extenuating weeks I bled through the urine and I began to get scared. The brochure states that if a patient bleeds for a month, he has to call the doctor because it may preannounce a problematic situation. Thanks to Divine Mercy, the bleeding stopped when I started to envision a gloomier scenario and Phoenix was far away from my world.

On Wednesday, two days prior to Good Friday, I met the Monster in all its magnitude, and I was astonished. I entered the urologist's office with a good dose of optimism, but that optimism faded quickly away. The doctor, with his traditional serious countenance, asked me to sit down and showed me a chart. I was not interested in the chart. He understood and said, "Mr. O' Fabuloso, I am sorry. You have cancer. Out of thirteen tissues that I extracted, one is cancerous. Nonetheless, signs of cancerous cells are spreading around the area." This meant that in the future there were definite chances for the cancer to spread.

I remained motionless and speechless. The doctor stared at me and asked what I wished to do on the basis of the finding. I broke the silence and said in a soft, monotonous voice. 'It is the will of God.'

"It's right," he replied without adding any word of consolation or encouragement. I felt being all alone in the middle of a desert facing a lion with my bare hands. The saints, the Blessed Mother, Jesus, God and the Holy Spirit were out of my mind in that moment. My mental process was frozen. I lost the ability to think rationally. For the first time, I realized the drama that millions of people lived before me in hospitals, prisons and concentration camps. I was powerless! Finally, I woke up from that torpor and asked, 'What are my options?'

"We do not advise the removal of prostate at a certain age," he responded emphatically.

I was not seventy years old yet and I did not comprehend the logic of his comment. I inquired about other options.

"The second one,' he said, 'would be radiation. And the third is a laissez-faire attitude. It is a "wait and see" approach. We do know that, at a late stage, cancer follows a slow course.

Generally, it takes ten to fifteen years for that type of cancer to spread in its entire dimension. The third possibility is the 'seeds" implant." All of that sounded 'Chinese' to me and I begged him to be more explicit about my case.

He looked straight in my eyes and stated, "Luckily, your cancer is developing slowly and is at the first stage."

"Which means . . . ?

"It means that you can wait and see how it behaves."

"Doctor, I searched on the internet for some information and I read that there is a vaccine being evaluated by the FDA." I expected a positive reply. Instead, he froze once again my hopes.

"It is true, but it would not be good for you. It is for those who do not have cancer. The vaccine blocks the growth of the cancer."

His interpretation was erroneous! The vaccine blocks the cancerous cells from developing. The only and real problem is time. We do not know how long it will take to experiment its validity.

In 2006, a German doctor announced the discovery of the enzyme that causes prostate cancer. He conducted the experiments on mice. He was able to isolate the enzyme and noticed that the remaining cancerous cells died. He said that he would conduct experiments on men very shortly. In a matter of a year, he would give out the results.

Simultaneously, in the US, a doctor conducted similar experiments and he assured that tests on men would begin immediately and that he would announce the results in six months.

We are in 2010 and I have not read a single line on the newspapers or heard a single word on television from either doctor! It is my firm conviction that it will be a long time before a vaccine can be available to the public. I am more prone to believe that the pharmaceutical companies have to reach some kind of compromise. I hope for the sake of all men that a serious governmental investigation be conducted over these experiments.

A while back, I stopped to visit a friend on his job. He is over seventy. He recounted his own experience with prostate cancer. 'The prostate was like a hard ball. Cancer had taken over it.

I opted for radiation because I asked the doctor what he would have done in my place and he responded that radiation would have been his choice.'

"How many sessions did you have?" I asked him.

"Thirty six!"

"Can you recall if you encountered any difficulty?"

"None whatsoever . . . ! Some patients claimed stomach pains, diarrhea or other side effects. I did not feel anything."

"Are you kidding?"

"No, I don't."

"If that is the case, it is not bad."

"Well, you have to realize that radiation kills also the good cells around to the focal area."

"How long were you in the radiation room?"

"Not too long, only ten minutes or so . . ."

I departed thinking more about the consequences of radiation than anything else. A couple of weeks later, I returned. I wanted to find out more. "How are you doing?"

"Fine, the cancer is shot to death. Boom! It is gone forever!"

"But it can come back."

"We all have cancer in our bodies. It develops in some and not in others."

"So, you passed the test with flying colors."

"Absolutely! I did not have any problem. One day, I went to the bathroom and, suddenly, I found myself in a lake of blood from the front and from the back."

"Are you OK now?"

"Oh, yes, I have no problem."

I left with more riddles in my head than ever before. The image of the blood bothered me to no end.

Back in the urologist office, I was still numbed, trying to decide on my options. I asked the doctor, "If you were in my place, what would you do?"

"Good question,' he replied. He remained pensive for a few seconds and added, 'I would go for radiation. At any rate, Mr. O' Fabuloso, I will send you to Dr. Matamonstruos. He is a good oncologist."

"Where is he located?" I inquired.

"In the city center, approximately, ten minutes from your house. Now, stop at the reception and they will arrange an appointment for you."

THE AFTERMATH OF THE NEWS—THE SOCIAL ENVIRONMENT

Following the bad news, I became almost inapproachable. I closed myself in an obsessive isolation and I did not wish to talk to anyone. For a while, I lived the life of a hermit. My wife passed the information to my children and they called me to inquire about the gravity of my condition. She also revealed the news to some close friends. I did not want anyone to know it, not for fear that they would consider me an outcast, but because I wanted to live my problem in silence. The least thing that I hoped for was peoples' pity.

I must confess that I was deeply disappointed. I did not expect to be overwhelmed with love signs. We live in a culture of disaffection. We do not converse not even with our neighbor. We see friends and relatives at a wedding or at a funeral. Let us say that I was prepared for it. What bothered me the most was their passive attitude. I felt disconcerted! When one of their family's members was sick, I was always on the front line. It was my Christian duty to visit the sick, the lonely and the forgotten. Now that it was my turn, I hardly received a word of consolation, of encouragement, a pat on the shoulder, a card, nothing. As a human being and as a Christian, I repeat, I felt offended. I asked myself how people can be so egocentric. We try to pursue happiness in material things and, when the pleasures of life are over, we remain with empty hands. We have a myopic sight about the real values in our life. Not finding any rational explanation, I resorted to my only anchor of safety, my faith in God. Let me say that I this point I tried to reconstrue my relationship with God. Earlier on, I remarked how of a devastating blow such relations received when I found out about cancer. I deeply reflected on it and I concluded that God did not cause me that condition, but it is a hormonal abnormality that we men of all color and race share. I do not exclude that we accelerate the process with wrong choices. And, so, I hope to have changed for the better, and, this time, for good. At this stage of my life, I refuse to hate, to be envious or jealous, but I am not proud of how my relative and friends behaved."

"Mimí, did you feel betrayed by God?" I interrupted him to let him pause a bit.

"As I pointed out previously, yes, I felt abandoned by the heaven in the darkest moments of my life; however, it lasted only for a short while. Upon a subsequent reflection, I realized that my faith was stronger than doubt and I readily submitted myself to the will of God. One sentence

In the New Testament I found a source of hope. Jesus says that it is useless to have fear. Instead, we must put your trust in Him. I do not recall if I read it in the Bible or in a newspaper or heard it on television. The fact of the matter is that my whole approach to the Monster changed instantly. Since then, no one and nothing mattered anymore, except the Lord. In a religious context, I had offended the Lord innumerable times and I deserved the punishment. But, later, I discarded this self-afflicting rationalization. God is not here to punish us, but to save us. We, somehow, cause on ourselves, with our dubious choices all sorts of disastrous situations. If the problem is behind our control, we cannot blame us.

No one can ever imagine how I spent the first night after I was diagnosed with cancer. In fact, I did not sleep at all! My mind was like an ocean in tempest. I tossed back and forth, left and right, never finding a stable and comfortable position, never finding a time to close the eyes. I was coming to terms with life's unpredictable and inevitable realities.

We are born and we have to die, therefore, I felt that my time was coming. For a while, I abstained from carrying out even the most common manual labor around the house. I did not care anymore about the garden, the school, and so on.

Not all thoughts were depressive. One really boosted my courage. The Lord seemed to tell me, 'Do not feel dejected. You have to undergo this test. You still have a lot of work to do for me.' On this vein, I acquired a sudden enthusiasm. I felt regenerated and I started gardening again.

Before I made a decision on the three options, I did every attempt to consult with someone who had previous experience."

"Mimí, it must have been easy, I suppose, to find someone," I interjected.

"Not really. I called my daughter-in law's father, who had been experiencing some difficulties with prostate. He suggested me to talk to the American Cancer Society. I listened without conviction. I did not think that it could help me. Maybe, attending the monthly meeting of ex-cancer individuals, it could have been more helpful. At the end, he asked me if I belonged to any church. Sincerely, I was stunned by that inquiry. My Catholic traditions were quite known in our family and also in Syracuse. Six years of Rosary International could not have passed under the rug in a blinking of an eye. Although I was not pleased with that question, I shortened the conversation. I expected that he would rephrase his thought, but thinking over it, I concluded that not all fingers of the hand are equal and that he meant no harm.

Among family and friends, a few demonstrated a genuine interest in my well being. Others, probably, did not know how to express it and I forced myself to understand their position. My eldest living brother had the prostate surgically removed about ten years ago. He was the target person who could advise me in the event that I, too, made that decision. His narration of the events, however, was not too comforting. He had terrible memories and, in one instance, he feared for his life. But, it was not until my odyssey began that I found out that in addition to the removal, he needed chemo. Aside this, he always reminded me that I was an athlete and that I should not have been apprehensive about. It was going to be tribulation at the initial stage, but things would eventually turn for the better later. He recommended me to drink plenty of water and to stay calm. Either for fear or because I could trust him, I was almost on a daily contact with him.

My older sister, Mary, was among the toughest, yet the most encouraging. She alerted me on the radiations side effects, but inspired me to go on dauntlessly because she foresaw for me a successful conclusion. She claimed that she could foretell the future with the cards. At that point, I stopped her and impounded on her to refrain from such nonsense. The controversy ended right there. She laughed, but insisted that I would come out of it with flying colors. I can't tell you, my readers, how much both my brother and sisters meant to me in that period of trial. I will always treasure their words of encouragement.

A second sister, Ann, and her husband also kept in close contact with me. They often called and offered me all their sympathy. A week did not go by without hearing from them. Their commitment to my cause was, perhaps, deeper because they had to deal with a disabled son all their life. I suppose that it spurred more empathy for me. At times, I did not call them not to rehearse the same subject. They had their own problems and I did not wish to impose on them to hear one even more serious.

Angelo D., in Syracuse, was the only friend who kept in touch with me. He suggested that I talk with an acquaintance of his from Bridgeport, who had opted for the 'seeds.' I was eager to strike a conversation with him and, so, I called him. I was lucky to find him at home because the appointment with Dr. Matamonstruos was getting very close.

I cannot forget John even though I never met him. He was a real gentleman. For half an hour he explained to me that although his PSA was below 4, the biopsy showed that the cancer had reached an aggressive stage. In fact, Dr. Matamonstruos urged him to decide which option to take because it was dangerous to wait longer. John opted for the 'seeds.'

Recently, the number of patients opting for 'seeds' has been growing progressively. The technique is very simple. The patient goes to the hospital for one day, actually for one afternoon or morning. The entire operation lasts from three to four hours. The patient lies with the stomach down and the surgeon injects three steal tiny wires in the prostate. Honestly, I do not understand why it took them that long, when my same operation lasted about three minutes. The rods are radioactively charged and the patient cannot be in contact with pregnant women or children for a three year period.

According to John, he did not suffer at all during the injection period. He experienced a tremendous hard time when he tried to urinate. He pushed and pushed but nothing came out.

He was relieved after five minutes when, he finally, released water and, since then, he has not felt any pain.

In a sexual perspective, the 'seeds' represent the best alternative. The patient loses absolutely no rhythm.

The other two procedures have a partial potentiality to suffer from.

It all depends from the age. If the individual is relatively young, maybe, he should consider the 'seed' option. If he feels indifferent to the conjugal rapports, then, either alternative can be acceptable.

I cannot tell you, my friend reader, how valuable was John's own experience to me. It relaxed me and gave me hope. He even offered his time whenever I wished to call him for additional information.

Angelo D. insisted that I should go for a second opinion. Besides being a close friend he is also a very intelligent and professional man. I have been very adamant in making changes in the middle of the river. His suggestion was very valid, unfortunately, time was pressing. A couple days prior to Dr. Matamonstruos' appointment, I became daring and went to a radiology office downtown. I told the secretary that I needed a second opinion. She was very polite and asked me the name of my urologist. When she informed me that he was part of the team of her office, I was astonished. Without proffering a single word, I turned around and took the road for home.

A second opinion is good, but it has its limitations. It is not that simple to see another specialist in a restricted amount of time. Sometimes, it takes many months to schedule an appointment and before they consent, they 'bombard' you with a barrage of questions related to the family doctor's approval and clinical history. What makes it even more complicated is the human element. Some of the doctors may not like the idea that a patient under his care wishes to sees another one. It may send him a message of mistrust. Fortunately, this thinking may apply to a segment of the medical profession.

Before leaving his office, the urologist handed me a brochure on cancer and told me to go back to his office in two weeks after conferring with Dr. Matamonstruos.

On my way out, I noticed two or three nurses walking nervously to different directions. I stopped a moment and I thought, 'At least, Damocles' sword does not hang on their neck. I am the one whose life is in jeopardy.' For the first time, I envied them, not for their professional duties, but by their crazy running around because that meant to be healthy and I was envious of their health. I stood in the middle of the hall motionless, like a drug addict, then, I moved sluggishly. A nurse looked at me with suspicion and asked me if I were OK. I did not respond. I passed by the secretary's desk. I closed my eyes for an instant and I realized that I had to make an appointment with Dr. Matamonstruos.

The nurse was busy with the computer and I had to wait. During that span of time, I was assailed by the most sinister thoughts. One prevailed above all. I had to call the funeral home and start to make arrangements before it was too late. I am old fashioned. I do not want any of my children to face the financial problems related to my funeral.

I was almost collapsing under the barrage of those ideas when the nurse handed me the appointment card and the papers pertinent to the next medical conference. I made an effort to show a faint smile and walked in the waiting room. There were women and men of all ages, but mostly adults starting from the late fifties. I gave a rapid glance around and, for once; I did not feel alone. Those poor souls were sharing with me the same destiny. A sense of social and human cohesiveness overpowered me. In this valley of tears, no one is an island. We are water from different tributaries ending in the same ocean.

I pressed the elevator button. I did not even notice the people riding down with me. On the first floor, before the exit, at the right, there is a pool. At the bottom, all sorts of coins were strewn everywhere. It reminded me of the Trevi Fountain in Rome. I did not have the will to ponder on the abysmal difference.

The door closed behind me and my eyes came in contact with the light and the blue sky. I felt like paralyzed. I could not walk. It was sunny, but inside me it was polar cold. I was a free man, but a prisoner of a foreign force inside my body. A cool breeze brushed my face and I woke up from my laden apprehension. I struggled to reach the car, to find the ignition key and to start the vehicle."

"Why didn't you rest until you were in a better condition," I asked him Mimí.

"I could not," he responded. "I moved like an automated machine, like a robot with uncontrollable human feelings. The return trip depended more on my driving experience than on my knowledge.

My wife was reading in the garage and did not have much to say. The dog was waiting for me. I picked her up and went to the back yard. She stared at me and wagged her tail excitedly. Somehow, she could feel the drama I was living in and made her most to show her love for me. I caressed her head and she kissed me over and over again. My eyes were full of tears. I hugged her for a time that seemed endless. Her blue eyes searched for an answer that I could not give. A strange heat emerged from her body and spread all over me. In that symbiotic hug of love, for the first time, I realized the invaluable animal friendship and fidelity. The electrical vibration that I received from that closeness gave me reason to believe that even animals can accomplish unpredictable objectives."

"Dogs are man's best friends," I reminded Mimi'.

"In fact, she kept on whining and brushing her paws against my arms. She wanted to talk to me, console and encourage me. I took her head in between my hands and wanted to reply, but I did not have the strength. I could only hug her. Each time I laid down my face, she would leak it. I could no longer bear that immense demonstration of affection and got busy in other domestic activities.

But I must take the liberty to say a few words on behalf of the animals. When I see animal cruelty or read about it, I feel disappointed about human nature. Animals have feelings and emotions as we do. To deprive them of food, of a decent living space or to abuse them, would be equitable to the lowest manifestation of man's inhumanity. Sometimes, I say that those who do not love animals are incapable of loving people. Let us take example from St, Francis of Assisi.

The loyalty and love that animals return to man, in exchange of food and shelter, are behind any description. The psychological benefits they provide to the owners are recognizable even in professional fields. When you come back from work or from a long journey, they wag the tail in sign of joy and they bark with happiness. Does your husband, wife, child . . . ever display such a closeness and heart vibration? Think about next time you want to deprive an animal of his freedom rights.

Lately, I have gathered stories about dogs' faithfulness that skims reality. In Italy, a dog went to the railroad station to wait for his owner. One day, the owner died, but the dog kept on walking to the train station waiting for him. After a month, he realized that the owner had died and went to the cemetery where he laid on his tomb and refused to eat. A good soul picked him up and took him under his protection.

Let me go back to my story. My eyes are getting watery.

Needless to say, I spent a sleepless night. I shivered each time my mind went over the tortuous and unpredictable challenge that was waiting for me. No one who has never been subjected to this physical and mental torture can understand the full significance of my condition and feelings. The world was rotating around me at a light speed. It was impossible for me to stop it or even attempt to slow it down. I was spinning in its vortex and could not think rationally anymore.

Many times, in my youth, I dreamed of becoming a miracle man at the service of the Lord. Soon, I realized that we do not become "miracle makers." Still, I wanted to convert as many people as possible to the cause of God. I was consoled by the fact that, at least, we are free to dream even when we do not readily realize that we do not possess the potential for operating miracles. God chooses whomever and whenever He wants. Even now, standing in front of the statue of the Blessed Mother, in the midst of the Rosary, I nourish such imprudent thoughts, but, at least, I can say that I enjoy dreaming about wonderful events for the sake of the human race and for the glory of Jesus. This time, however, I was praying for the grace of God to free my mind from the 'snake'. Unfortunately, my hopes were quickly dashed and I stood there, in the middle of nowhere, all alone, against a terrible enemy.

I decided to go through hell, not unlike Dante who was guided by Virgil in a fact-finding adventure, but determined to get 'burned' and get out of it once and for all. I kept the appointment with the nurse at the radiology department without knowing what to expect. She was very gracious and explained to me the procedure in taking some prostate pictures. I can't find the appropriate words to describe my humiliation when she asked me to lower my pants. Nonetheless, I realized that it was no time to dwell on morality anymore and I conformed to her request.

The X-rays procedure ran smoothly, so to speak, for fifteen minutes. As most of you already know, X-rays are like candies. Especially, if we abuse them, besides causing cavities, they can cause significant damage to the body. With great surprise, the nurse ordered me to gulp a big glass of water in her presence and, then, she told me to rush to Manlius Radiotherapy, which was about twenty minutes away, for additional radiography. It was imperative that I arrived on time because they were waiting for me. I protested for more than one reason. First of all, I had not been advised earlier. Secondly, I ignored the exact location. And, thirdly, the water from the sink was cold. She explained to me that the office was a block after a reading glass company and I should not have any difficulty in locating it. If I did not get there on time, I would have lost the appointment and the glass of water I drank was worthless.

I shook my head in dismay, but I could not argue with her. The pressure was increasing and

I made the best, in those circumstances, to maintain as much calm as possible. I dressed up in a hurry and rushed to the fountain to drink the glass of water. In this instance, the reader can vouch for me. Isn't water in the buildings icy cold? How could I possibly have been able to drink it in a hurry? I was too late when I remembered that I could have mitigated the temperature by dumping a cup of hot coffee."

"Mimí, didn't you have a GPS in the car?" I inquired trying to ease his tension, but still it was a provocative question.

"I still do not know how to use it. Can you imagine how intense was the pressure in those moments? It should not surprise the reader, if I confess that I tried some short cuts just to arrive on time.

When I reached the presupposed destination, I searched for the radiology office, but I could not find it. It was getting late. The clock was ticking and, so, was my heart. The traffic was moving smoothly at the bifurcation site and I looked like a lost sparrow. Suddenly, I veered to the left in a parking lot and parked the car. I entered in the office of what appeared to be a glass company's building. With a deep sense of relief, the secretary gently indicated that the place I was looking for was two doors down. I got irritated for the inaccurate directions that the nurse had given me, but I also acknowledged that I had to postpone the time for complaints. But, I could not deny that in all that mess, I felt being the perfect candidate for any illness.

I camouflaged well my feelings and hurried to the X-rays office. It is routine for secretaries to ask for the patient's name. I told her and sat on the first chair available. I straightened my head up and I noticed that she was staring at me. In a well mannered, soft tone, she said, 'You are late! You have lost your appointment. You should have been here fifteen minutes earlier." I tried to explain to her the misinformation that the nurse gave me. She noticed my disappointment and asked again my last name. She smiled and said, "Let me see what I can do for you." She conferred with the therapist and, soon, after, she related to me that she forgave me for that time. I gave out a deep sigh. She laughed and said, "Do not worry. Everything will be OK." Then, she went on by saying how many times she dreamed of visiting Italy. I asked for her last name and she said, 'Cardarelli.' I made a gesture of surprise. Cardarelli was a renowned Neapolitan doctor. After his death, the city government decided to name the main hospital in his honor. She did not blink an eye at the news, and smiling for the first time, she replied, "Those are my relatives." I did not know what to make of it anymore. I was getting from one negative surprise to another positive one in less than one hour. I explained to her that I would be organizing a trip to Italy the following year and that if she were interested, she could join my group. She showed a broad smile, this time, picked her personal card from the desk and handed it to me. The therapist appeared at the door of the corridor and I understood that it was time to follow him.

We arrived at a big room where the therapist abruptly asked me to undress and put on a white cape. As soon as I was ready, he told me to lie down on a machine and warned me that any minimum body movement would have falsified the results. The entire procedure would have lasted half an hour. At that news, I shivered. I felt the urge to empty the bladder already. Staying there for thirty minutes, I would have blasted the bladder. I had no choice. I was in a very tight situation. My patient reader, how well you that it is not easy to control my bodily needs in sickly conditions. I used to evacuate the bladder every fifteen minutes, and now . . . ? He explained to me that the intent of that session was to cut the prostate in millions of tiny slices. That was not gratifying information at all, but I stood there immobile praying all the time. More than ever, I made an effort to use prayer to achieve a double objective: to receive heavenly help during a period of unbearable distress and to deceive time by not thinking about it. Towards the end, I could not take it anymore and me on the verge of collapse. I was unable to function physically or mentally. The human body and mind have their limits too! In that precise moment I heard a noise. My hopes suddenly surged. The lights went on and the shadow of the therapist appeared on the wall. I did not wait for him to inform me that the therapy was over. I jumped on my feet and ran to the bath room. I was enormously relieved and I had no appropriate words to thank God.

On my way out, I renewed my appreciation to Miss. Cardarelli and promised her that I would call her when I would organize the trip to Italy. At home, my wife questioned me, "Who is she?"

DR. MATAMONSTRUO

A week later, I attended the meeting with Dr. Matamonstruos with great trepidation and fear. He looked very young to me, maybe thirty five or forty. He was of medium stature and brown complexion, like a native of India. The eyes were brown and his hair was peach black with a proclivity of turning sparse in the crown area. Anyone who met him for the first time would agree with me that he was quite energetic which inspired assurance and knowledge.

My kind reader will probably remember that Dr. Thorny, my new urologist, prior to the departure from his office, handed to me a brochure on cancer. At first, I was so discouraged that I refused to read it. After a second thought, I tried to gain some understanding of what to expect out of this traumatic experience. At the end of the reading, I gathered a gloomy picture. I will not report the literature because my forehead gets sweaty just at the thought of it. I felt I was in Dante's company in his Inferno. I was in a totally strange environment. I had no knowledge whatsoever of the machines, the time I had to spend under them, what I had to drink or eat, the consequences in which I would eventually incur and the final results. I was walking in a world of fog. May the Lord help me to depict everything with serenity and fairness so that others may learn from my experience to sustain better these times of trial. I could stretch my book for about ten more pages by citing people and events, unfortunately, my mind is numbed and I cannot recall more that what I know.

Dr. Matamonstruos was extremely direct and factual, but spread also positive feelings. He explained the three options that I have already explained at length. I also reported my telephone conversation with a gentleman from Bridgeport, who had opted for the 'seeds.' Well, by the time I met the oncologist I had my mind set for the same procedure. As the doctor continued on the preliminaries, I started to change my mind and I asked him the same question that I had posed to the urologist, 'If you were in place, or if it were your son, your father or grandfather which procedure would you suggest?'

He opened his arms and said, "It is entirely up to you."

I had written down a list of questions and he noticed that and said, "Shoot."

"Doctor, my daughter-in-law's uncle is over eighty years of age and had the 'seeds' implanted ten year ago and he is doing well. This young man from Bridgeport had you for the same procedure and assured me that he is doing extremely well. Nonetheless, it does not mean that I would do the same. Everyone is different."

"Mr. O' Fabuloso, you are absolutely right, but the overwhelming majority does well."

"Doctor, my brother had the prostate removed, but he had a rough time."

"Listen! There are many variables involved here. We take in consideration the age of the patient, his attitude, his physical condition and the stage at which cancer develops."

"In terms of side effects, which procedure promises better results, surgery or radiation?

"Radiation is better. With surgery, you may still have incontinence." Encouraged by that statement, I continued, "What are the side effects of radiation?" As a consumed professional, he replied, "You may have some bowel disturbance during the procedure. You may feel a bit nauseated or weak, but, as you go along, they will disappear."

"And after . . ."

"Absolutely, nothing!"

"Do I have to follow a specific diet?"

"Nothing"

"Do I curtail my activities?"

Like an automated machine, he gave the same answer, "Nothing!"

I was hesitating in asking an additional question. He caught my thoughts and said, "I had a patient last year who used to run.

He complained that during the sessions his time in running had increased six seconds. Imagine, six seconds!"

"Sexual activities."

"The same! For the post procedure period, I will give you some medicine that will help you for one year to continue every week your activities.

"How long do I stay in the radiation room?"

"From ten to fifteen minutes . . ." He looked at me and said, "Mr. O' Fabuloso, I give you from 95 to 98 chances of success. Your tumor happens to be in the initial stage and it is slow, although it is spreading to other areas. You have just made it on time. It is up to you to decide. Either one of the three procedures will take you to the same destination. It is a question of preference now. If you wish to remove it surgically, I will send you to another specialist who will remove it by the means of a robot."

By the end of the session, I had made up my mind. I opted for radiation. My mind was no longer an incubator of hypotheses, dubious expectations and incoherent information. I plunged into a glacial body of water. I felt the polar frigid temperature running through my veins. My spinal cord was rigid. I could not get colder than that. The medical environment was sucking me into it and I began thinking like doctors with their rigorous and clinical approach.

I, either, negated or defused fear. I relived the scene of a navy captain. During a tempest, the passengers panicked and ran to him for assurance. He looked straight ahead in the wind and water buffeting the boat. When, finally, the sun reappeared, he was still looking at the sun with the same passivity and serenity as before.

As the time went on, I became even more confident at the possibility of killing the 'dragon.' At that point, I (Chris) objected to O' Fabuloso, "Don't get the reader confused by changing names. First, you called it 'monster' and now you label it 'dragon,'"

"No, the reader knows very well that the two words are synonyms. I do not need to make any useless explanation. Two added to three is five and three added to two is still five. Now, if you do not mind it, let me go back to the reader, otherwise, he will definitely get astray.

The doctor left me all alone in his office and alerted me to watch a television clip. Actually, it was a self-promoting medical advertisement with his picture on the front page of a national magazine. His research on prostate cancer was extensively promoted. But, they reported also other medical studies, none of which I remember. No one should blame someone who, other than being intelligent, is also self-assertive and adventurous.

When the TV clip was over, the oncologist reappeared and asked me if I had any further comment or question. I got bold and said, 'Doctor, what position will I assume during the radiation?'

"You will be in a sleeping position."

'My brother was placed with the abdomen down.'

"How long ago was it?"

'Approximately, ten years . . .'

"In ten years, medical science has made tremendous progress,' he assured me. He put on another clip and left me to watch it. It contained a national television spot on his work. I could add that it was more or less a documentary on his medical feats intended to calm down us patients. In reality, my mind was absorbed in other thoughts and I did not follow through with whatever they were saying. The doctor knew the duration of the program and came immediately after it ended. He asked me if I had any further question. I shook my head in a gesture of denial. He said that during the therapy sessions, he would see me on a weekly basis. We shook hands and I hurried to my car, somewhat content with the preparatory session.

I was restless at home. I felt an impellent desire to call my eldest brother to relate to him my encounter with the oncologist. It was eleven thirty at night there. I pretended a false self-control and apologized for calling at that late hour. My brother perceived my uneasiness and assured me that it did not matter for he goes to bed late. He stood there listening for a while without interrupting me. Only when I informed him that the oncologist gave me a very high percentage of success, he began to speak on a soft tone. In the past, he strongly favored surgery. After listening to what I had to say, he vacillated. It took a few minutes of exchanging information before he agreed that the therapy was, perhaps, better; however, his tone changed dramatically when I told him that I would be in the radiation room from ten to fifteen minutes. "That doctor is a dog! Get rid of him! Nobody stays that much time under radiation. You cannot take it," he thundered. It was not easy to quell down his apprehension.

He lessened his criticism when I insisted that American technology stands supreme in the world and the procedure is different. Unlike him, who was placed with the abdomen down, I was going to lie in a sleeping position. I think this was the tip of the iceberg. He was surprised to hear about a different therapeutic typology, but he still alerted me to be cautious and hopeful.

My telephone bill, just for Italy, was skyrocketing. My wife never objected each time I picked up the phone. She knew that I needed someone to relate my anxiety. I did not want my brothers and sisters to call me and see their telephone bill increase substantially. I know that they were in apprehension too.

The following day, I called my sister in Rome. Lately, she had been battling thyroid difficulties that required radiation herself. She was a strong advocate of radiation. "Don't worry about it at all! You will not feel anything. I have been going through it. The only thing that I recommend to you is to stay calm."

"How can I? You know how my situation is."

"No, no, don't pay attention to that person. Go someplace else. You cannot afford getting stressed up during this period. It would be counterproductive to stay there and argue. You have a big garden. Besides rest, you need to drink plenty of water. It serves to wash out the radiation residuals. At least, you have to drink seven liters of water per day. Now, listen to me! Everything will be fine. I know it. I can guess by looking at the palm of the hand."

When I heard that, I exploded into a sonorous laughter, "Don't tell me these stupidities?"

She laughed, "Really, I can vision the future. When I have something clear in my mind, it will occur and I see a smooth and successful radiation therapy. Don't even think about it! You will do fine."

A few tears clogged my eyes and I instantly dropped the phone on the receiver.

In the afternoon, I went to work as a volunteer at San Ennius Nursing Home. I was reading the paper in the lounge room. Actually, my eyes were on it, but I was not reading it. My mind was flooded with negative thoughts that were being pushed on me, like clouds driven by the fierce and icy wind of fear. Suddenly, I heard my name. It was Sweety, the religious coordinator and pastor or her church.

My position on woman priest has been clear for years. I disdained even to hear a nun delivering the Sunday sermon during the mass. I may be wrong and, so, the Catholic Church, but it is a position taken on biblical grounds and not on personal taste. When Rome speaks, the world listens.

Sweety asked me if she could join me at the table. Hardly, any woman has ever asked for the same thing in my life. The difference was that we met before each other many times in the hall, but never conversed. Indeed, at the beginning, I didn't even greet her. As the time went by, we started to exchange the ritual 'hello.' She dressed always with long light vests and was very active. I saw her getting involved in activities which were not part of her professional work. She was thin, like a string bean, with dark eyes and a tiny nose. Her hair was also dark and barely reached the upper part of the shoulders. Her demeanor was impeccably gentle. She walked very fast. I wondered, at times, if she did it to save time or because it was a way to keep her weight under control. I could never refuse anyone to sit at my table, especially if it were a religious representative or someone who was seeking a favor.

As she sat, she recounted how she had heard about my unfortunate situation, "I understand that you are sick." I did not respond immediately. My eyes were getting watery and my voice was trembling. As she stared at me more intensely, I felt more emotional. She was waiting patiently. Finally, I gained my composure and said, "I have been diagnosed with prostate cancer. It has been dragging on over a twenty-year time span and I am exhausted. I would have been better if I took care of it when I was younger."

She took my hands into hers and said, "Let's pray!"

I did not pray. She did it all. At the end, she looked straight into my eyes and added, "I know how you feel. I do not want you to get worried, although to worry is human. From now on, I will keep you in my prayers. God has not abandoned you. I have been searching all over for you. I am not going to stop praying until you are healed."

I remained sitting for another twenty minutes with my head between my hands. The newspaper did not exist. The residents around me did not catch my attention. Their words were sounds like dust in a desert storm. When I got up, I stumbled against the table and was off balance for a couple of seconds. The hall was full of nurses, employees and residents. I tried to take a short cut to the corridor, but I noticed this time that their attention was focused on me. I picked up the newspaper and disappeared.

The following Sunday, I attended the morning Mass at my church. Everything appeared to be cloudy in front of me. The same nun delivered the homily. It was rumored that the pastor was very sick and submitted to her will. I did not appreciate it and I hardly understood a word. I did not participate in the liturgical function. The only thing that I did was to go to the altar for Communion.

It is common for the priest to wait at the end of the hall after Mass to wish the parishioners a good day. I waited for the crowd to leave and I approached the priest with whom I was a good friend and revealed to him what I was diagnosed with and I asked him if he could remember me in his prayers. He responded very complacently and asked me to remind him on the following Sunday. I never did.

THE THERAPY

The radiology building was located downtown in Syracuse, a few blocks away from the university and hospital city. It was not accessible by bus or train. My house is located on a little hill in Cicero that overlooks the whole city. The lake lay down a mile below at the feet of Carousel like a pond in the midst of immense vegetation. The university dome raises its head from the farthest air point that the vision can reach. It is not difficult to locate the approximate location of the urology compound. To get there, it is relatively easy. From my house, I turn to route 81 south and I get out downtown at Teal Ave exit. At the traffic light, I take the left and when I reach Erie Boulevard, I turn left again. A mile and a half down the road was my destination. The whole trip takes, approximately, fifteen minutes by car.

The physical structure was not known for its artistic beauty although there was construction going on to extend the premises and nobody knew to what extent it would change its physiognomy. An ample glass window constituted the façade of the therapy section. At the one corner, another section stretched out too far and that precluded the visual communication between the interior and the exterior, except for the entrance. A small area, immediately after, was reserved for check-up and blood tests.

The therapy waiting room was, in reality, a big hall with a bath on one end and the secretary window directly across from the entrance. Above the bathroom door, hang a big TV screen and on the left two coffee pots, one for regular coffee and another for decaf. Adjacent to them, one could see an abundant supply of small boxes of fruit juice and cheese crackers. Initially, I ignored them all because I am not a coffee or juice drinker. Later, I realized their enormous importance, as we shall see in a short while. At least, at that time, this was the appearance of the building.

My wife is a coffee addict. Each time we arrived at the therapy building, she would ask for a cup of coffee. I did not tell her that I was pouring decaf instead of regular coffee. As the days went by, she increased her demand. She requested a second cup of coffee because she complained that I did not fill the cup to the brim. Later, she urged me to get something to eat, like cheese crackers and so on. Whenever they were available, I picked not one, but two. Her face changed color when I did that. The puppy, of course, was waiting for her share. Due to Phoenix' wish, I got involved in another occupation. I became a waiter each time we arrived at the premises.

As I went along, I realized that the limited food and beverages provided served a good purpose. Patients' relatives were able to enjoy a cup of coffee while they were waiting. A second reason was very practical. Patients, who experienced stomach pranks due to radiation, could assuage the uneasy condition by eating something.

The third and last reason was utterly important. Not many patients were lucky enough to bear the full bladder for a long time. We were supposed to drink a big glass of water one hour prior to the actual therapy. Some of us patients found it out late. Most of the time, we had the urge to go to the bathroom prior to radiation. The patient ahead of me, more than once wetted the machine and I could not rush for therapy because I had to give them time to clean the machine. That waste of time caused pains in me and others. At times, we felt like 'exploding.'

'Dry' situations were not uncommon due to different variables. I mean that some days the bladder was not sufficiently up to the required level and we had to skip our appointment time. I found it out for the first time when one patient went to the therapy room and came right back. When I questioned him on it, he explained to me that he did not have a full bladder. Usually, I was one who was overpowered by the bladder and was forced to evacuate a bit, not much, prior to the therapy session. Nonetheless, one day, I found myself in the middle of a riddle. I was the awkward condition of not having enough water. That was very dangerous! I refused to go back home and I disliked the water from the fountain because of its extreme frigidity. I could not drink a glass of water at that temperature. It would have slowed down the blood circulation and affected my stomach. The doctor knew all about it and made sure that the secretaries provided enough supplies of small juice boxes. I drank coffee and juice in great quantity and still the water level was unsatisfying. Aside from the additional juice, I did some exercises to promote a state of urgency.

The hall resembled a big dining room. Not everyone was visible to each other. Only those sitting against the large window could see those opposite to them. The one who sat back to back in the center could not. In a corner, close to the secretary window, there was a machine. When we came in, we had to pass an ID card through it. I never did it, either because the secretary advised me to ignore it or I did not know how to go about it. I suppose that whoever was there got a good glimpse of me from the first day and marked my presence.

Every patient received a card with the written appointment on it. The therapists were nice enough to feel free to choose our time. In the event, either one of us had a problem; we were flexible enough to rearrange the time schedule according to our new needs. One of the most fundamental rules was to arrive a few minutes earlier. Most of the time, Miguel, the only male therapist, gave the instructions to the patients and accompanied them in and out of the therapy room. One interesting aspect of the whole operation was that, upon entering the foyer, we were required to leave the shoes nearby and follow the therapist.

The therapy room appeared desolate, except for the huge machine, looking like the lunar rover. It was a chilly welcome. It made a sudden, brutal impact that disappeared as the time went on. A closet contained clean sheets and pillows, while plastic blankets filled with air served as a support to the legs. The patient was expected to lie in a dormant position with the back down and the legs on the cushion between two furrows. The plastic cushions were identifiable by the patient's name. The sheet, which they changed for each patient before he or she laid down, did not carry any identification. The cushion just below it did carry our names. It was imperative to remain in an immobile position during the whole therapy time, at least with the lower part of the body. One is free to move the upper body, but any movement from the top becomes dangerous. It can affect the stability of the lower part of the body thwarting a positive continuity and putting the bladder adjacent area at risk of radiation. The therapy time is usually around ten minutes, but every oncologist has his own view of what is the best time. They even differ on the number of sessions. All other people I talked to told me that they had thirty six sessions. We had forty-three.

Prior to the entrance to the therapy room, on the left side, a girl therapist controlled the therapy machine through various computers. I am not sure if Miguel contributed anything to that work. Along the foyer, there was a bathroom and across from it two medical offices used by doctor Matamonstruos for his weekly patient's check-up.

To complete this picture of the interior, I should add that against the wall, next to the doctor's office, there was a scale. We had to check the weight prior to seeing the doctor. I checked myself every day to see if I lost weight dramatically because I understood that there was concern about those who lost a lot of weight.

Miguel and the girl therapists were all very professional, kind and accomodable. Miguel was tall and handsome. He dressed casually, but always sharp. He was also very friendly and displayed an innate, impeccable personality. The girls were rather of medium stature and very attractive. Although they performed an extremely serious task, they always found the time for humor. They dressed in different uniforms, but I preferred the one who dressed in white. She looked like a real professional. A smile on their face made always a difference.

THE THERAPY BEGINS-MAY 19

Every patient received one clear and incontrovertible order: "Drink sixteen ounces of water prior to your scheduled therapy." That also inferred to renounce the use of the bathroom during that time. Later, I realized the reason behind that prescription. If the bladder is empty or half empty, the radiation may destroy far more good tissues than expected in the adjacent area. In my case, the thorny issue was not drinking a big glass of water at a particular time and holding it for one hour, but the frequency with which I used the bathroom every single day. There were times when I emptied the bladder every ten or fifteen minutes. Can you, reader, imagine holding it for a bit more than one hour? I have no knowledge of how others were doing in this respect. Maybe, they were not affected as much, or, maybe, they were the same or worse. I do remember of a couple of patients who had problems and I will come back to them later.

I was supposed to start on May 2, but it was delayed due to my urologist's other commitments. I complained to my oncologist's office and the secretaries arranged a different schedule. I was told that a patient cannot start the therapy immediately after the biopsy. He has to wait two weeks; however, the urologist's office had postponed it to three or four weeks. I was so tired and depressed that I wanted to go through hell as soon as possible. My position was simple. I preferred to spend the whole summer with radiation therapy rather than arrive at the end of August when I started my part-time work. In addition to that, I had to take my wife to the doctors for her ailments, at times, on a weekly basis. This contributed to the worsening of my humor. I hardly had any patience left by the time I started the therapy.

In my earlier visit to the oncologist, I asked him if I could run, and go to the gymnasium. He recommended me to continue doing whatever I was engaged with and not to interrupt my regular life activities. He recounted a case whereby a patient complained that it took him six seconds more in his last race compared to that of the previous year. His position conflicted with those of other doctors who emphasized a rather cautious approach. Resting most of the time would give the body more strength to react to radiation. If this is an accurate assessment of the patient's behavior pre and post radiation, then, the latest clinical analyses clearly shatter it. The results indicate that exercises help women during the radiation therapy. The doctor's advice in so far as running was concerned had one drawback. I realized it much after I finished the therapies. My brother's doctor in Italy warned him to stay away from the sun. How could I stay away from the sun if I had to run, at least, three or four times a week? Neither, he told me to beware of the sun. But, he said to another friend of mine who is currently under therapy!

As for other private questions, the doctor said that he would prescribe me a medicine that enhanced certain activities for a short period until I functioned adequately well.

The first day, May 20, 2009, I repressed my urge as much as I could. While traveling to the doctor's office, I tried to distract myself by turning the music on or by singing. By the time I parked the car in front of the building, I was convinced that I could never make it. My appointment was scheduled for 6:28 P.M. We are all aware that a doctor's time can vary very easily. My fear was the delay of other patients, mechanical failures or other unpredictable events.

The morning began with an ominous event. The urinary tract was unusually restricted.

My neighbor was a widower and was also undergoing cancer treatment for another part of the body deeply sensitive. He offered his assistance in driving me to the location, but I courteously and proudly refused to acknowledge any need.

My wife asked me if I wanted her to keep me company. I refused because I did not believe that the therapy would impair my vision or mental state. For a week, I went alone, then, she insisted to come along and I did not oppose any resistance. In a way, it helped me, because we brought the puppy which provided me with a lot of warmth. She would lick my hands as if she felt the trauma I was living or rest on my legs glancing at me from time to time.

The therapist opened the door and called my name. I got up and followed him. He briefed me up on a couple routine requirements and one of them dealt with taking off the shoes and placing them underneath of the chair. From then on, for convenience, I wore a pair of sandals or house slippers to get rid of them quickly. In reality, I did not dress elegantly either. I felt that doctors' offices are a nest of germs and I had enough of my own. I wore casual pants and shirt easy to pull down or up according to the demands of the therapist. My wife rebuked me more than once on my habiliments, but I did not budge on my suspicions. Only in a couple of occasions I dressed up, but it was for some important engagements that I had to honor either prior or after the therapy.

I was already acquainted with the therapy's huge room. I had visited it for my preliminary x-rays, but this time was the prelude to a series of sessions which would eventually determine my future.

The two therapists, Miguel and a girl explained to me the various phases of the operation. The first priority on the agenda was the room preparation. They ascertained that a clean sheet would be laid on the machine for each patient and its stiffness. I had to remain immobile on the rubber cushion. The machine would rotate on 360 degrees around the prostate and pinpoint accurately the cancerous spot. One therapist from the computer room would guide the radioactive machine. I asked them if the radioactive material would remain in me at the end of the therapy and they responded, "Absolutely, not! The radiation, unlike chemo, is external, and stops when the cycle of the machine finishes." I felt much better with those assurances.

Prior to the actual commencement of the therapy, they requested I lower my pants to the pubic area. If the height was unsatisfactory, they did the rest. I felt so humiliated that my mind is unable to find the proper words to describe it. For a few moments, I lost consciousness of my immediate reality. I descended into a subhuman stage. As I gained more control of my surrounding, I reminisced over the inhumane treatments of the prisoners in concentration camps. How we humans deprive ourselves of our sense of decency, moderation and moral responsibility in certain historical times is hard to 'swallow'.

The therapists left. I was so stiff that in more than one occasion I was on the brink of losing my composure and expose my other parts of the body to destructive radiation. To offset this intolerable position, I had an intuition. I started to pray the Rosary. I realized that by the end of the first Decade, the machine stopped. It was not always the case. More than once, the therapy lasted for about two Decades. Usually, I felt a sense of relief when I reached the 'Glory to the Father.'

I was lying like a telephone pole on the back of a steal carriage. Around me, there was the most absolute silence; I was all alone with my God. Many thoughts passed through my mind, but my eagerness to get it done and go home overpowered them. I was not aware whether the radiation process began instantly with the closure of the door or I had to wait for a mechanical activity. Suddenly, the three eye machine vibrated, made an unusual noise and started a slow movement. I did not feel any pain or discomfort at all. One eye stopped to overlook the accurate position. It grumbled as if something needed adjustment. It shifted on the side and a second one took the upward position. This too leaned sideways after looking at me for a while. The third eye arrived with delay, but it stared at me the longest. My immediate impression was that the silent ordeal was over. I was wrong. The machine jolted again and spinned, making a rapid revolution. At the end of it, it slowed down while I could not sustain anymore the oppressive pressure of the bladder. I closed my eyes to pray. The machine was still communicating with its harsh language. The reappearance of the lights in the room and the noise of the shoes on the floor indicated the presence of the therapist and the end of my agony

I did not wait for his instructions. I handed him the plastic ring that I held during the session; I pulled my pants up, buttoned them and jumped on the floor. I can still see the therapist's astonishing face. "Vow," he said "You are an athlete."

"We will discuss this matter the next time. Right now, I have to run to the bathroom, otherwise I will blow up." I said to him.

I, literally, ran out of the therapy room, picked up my slippers and rushed directly to the bathroom to empty the bladder. For the first time, I became aware of the side effects. The urinary tract was restricted. I made pressures. Drops of sweat appeared on my forehead and I got nervous. On the other hand, I felt satisfied because I was able to release water and, that, for me was extremely important. The doctor had warned me that I would experience some urinary tract difficulties followed by discomfort during the bowel movement. He also cautioned me to be aware of some occasional light dizziness.

Miguel and he were more realistic. He explained to me that, generally, patients get weak in the last few weeks, but it depends from the physical make up of the individual. Radiation is not a candy and can leave its marks if one is not careful.

At home, my wife was reading a book. I grabbed the phone and called my brother. I told him that I did not feel any negative impact from radiations. He was happy to hear the good news, but suggested me not to raise my expectations. "In the third week, you start to feel the brunt of radiation. Stay away from the sun, fried food and, above all, stay calm." The last recommendation sounded the alarm. I could not promise to follow his suggestion. He was surprised to hear that each radiation treatment lasted approximately six minutes. He restated his previous remark, "If your doctor made you stay ten minutes, as I said it before, he is a dog. I would change him!"

"Perhaps, he wanted to prepare me psychologically," I objected.

"That's silly! You get burned staying ten or fifteen minutes under that machine."

The rumor of my cancer spread like a flame on fire. At the university, some of my colleagues surmised from my look that something was wrong. One of them assured me that she would remember me in her prayers. The news did not surprise a Jewish friend. Indeed, she made a gesture of indifference. She said, "That's nothing! My ex-husband had it too."

"How did he get rid of it?" I inquired.

"He used preventative medicine."

"What is that?"

"Before he reached the 'point of no return,' the urologist prescribed him a medicine that prevented him to get cancer."

I did not reply. Could it be possible that within the medical field there are occult forces that work against the good of humanity? Two months earlier, I checked the internet and I found out that they have discovered a vaccine against prostate cancer. This vaccine, supposedly, blocks the tumor and leaves it in a freezing state. To this date, it is under the FDA investigation. I wanted to hear the urologist's reaction. It came immediately after with a gloomy response, "Yes, there is, but it is not good for you." My friend reader, think about it! Did they ever inform you that a vaccine against prostate cancer is available to those who do not have cancer yet?

A friend of mine, who passed away, last year had prostate troubles, but the doctor kept him on with medicine and never suggested to him a biopsy even though the PSA was relatively high. Likewise, another friend, also in the seventies, takes pills to control his high PSA, but his urologist has never mentioned doing the biopsy up to now.

During the summer, a doctor from Columbia University came to Syracuse to deliver his message on prostate cancer. The hall was packed with both genders. He has conducted many studies on organic herbal medicine and made pills, available at the store for thirty dollars a bottle. He insisted that the best. At the end of the lecture, he was surrounded by people eager to snatch the slightest information that could raise their hopes. I managed to approach him and queried about the validity of vitamin E. He said, "Take vitamin E 250 with selenium 200. A 2008 clinical study concluded that vitamin E and selenium were ineffective against prostate cancer. The same results were obtained in studying the effectiveness of Saw Palmetto. Incidentally, I read various reports on the efficacy of blueberries for their high antitoxic properties in fighting prostate cancer. I have been eating blueberries ever since, winter and summer, and I still became a victim. I suppose that more than variable acts in favor or against prostate health.

I am sure the reader will draw his own conclusions when he finishes reading this book. I am not a medical doctor, but someone who tried them all! Like Dante, I went to hell and came back by the grace of God to tell you what I experienced. Remember that every one of us is different and what works for me may not produce the same results for you. However, we are dealing with a dysfunctional hormone or, better yet, a protein that affects one man out of three (and even more!). This frequency is equivalent to women's breast cancer. If the source of the cure could be identifiable in one single pill or type food, the discoverer would become an instant billionaire. The spontaneous and logical question is this, "Would the pharmaceutical companies allow it? Are they interested in putting on the market palliatives rather than vaccines?" Well, I am not in a position to allay those apprehensions. I can only offer you my experience. I caution you not to be negative with the pharmaceutical companies. They study and work hard every day to discover something new for the benefit of society.

An old man was able to ask him a couple of quick questions, "doctor, I read ten years ago that an English doctor, working in a lab, made new teeth grow in mice. The newspaper did not indicate if he used a seed, used the bone marrow or whatever, but he did predict that by the year 2010 even people would see new teeth grow without implants."

"I did not hear about that."

"I have a last question."

"Shoot!"

"Four months ago, I read that they discovered a new gel that, applied on the gums or teeth, would prevent cavities and by now the dentists would say 'by-by' to the drill."

"Have you talked to your dentist?"

"The other day when I went to his office for a filling replacement . . ."

"What was his response?"

"The drill is still here."

"Again, look at the positive side of the pharmaceutical companies. They are here to make money, but, at the same time, they do it by putting on the market better medicine to reduce human suffering.

Think about the millions of people who would have died if we did not have the medical researchers."

"They could do more, though . . ."

"I agree with you, but at least, let's be happy with what we have."

FIRST WEEK

I opted for radiation and placed myself in the hands of God. I must admit that at this point I felt almost enthusiastic. Maybe I was pretending to camouflage my inner feelings. I wil never know where the real truth lay. I wanted to 'plunge' into the frigid temperature and get it done with it. The doctor did his part by assuring me that I could continue with my current activities

In the week preceding the actual therapy sessions, I attended a two-day workshop at SU. I marveled at the capacity to sustain a three-hour long session without interruption. I mean I did not feel the urge to go to the lav. I tried to give a rationale to that resistance, but I realized that distraction helped me to keep the bladder calm.

With this framework, I started the therapy. I brought two bottles of wine to the therapists on duty that day. In the successive weeks, I found out that whenever I brought them chocolates or pastries, they shared them with the remaining staff. I have always been of the opinion that kindness is cheap. In reality, it contributed to a better socialization. We had good feelings and this allowed us to keep a happy relationship. It took the best humor out of all of us and we did not waste the time to use it. I suppose that this friendship contributed to elevate my morale and forget about the radiations.

Second Week

May 21

I finished the first week without a scratch, but the second was the most terrible, as far as urination was concerned.

This morning was absolutely terrible. The urinary tract got so restricted that I had to make tremendous efforts to release water. For the first time I began to worry. The road ahead looked tortuous and long. I tried to keep up a good morale, but it was not easy. Each time I went to empty the bladder, it was an uphill battle. With the passing hours, I felt a burning sensation, yet the urine was clear. I remembered my onions. At least, I did not fail on that.

In the afternoon, the condition ameliorated to a certain extent. As I realized later, it was a transient feeling, like a sun's ray in an overcast sky. I performed moderately well, but the fear was looming in the background and kept me apprehensive.

The doctor had warned me that I would discharge a couple times a day. I don't think it would have been bad. The fact of the matter was that I went four times. I was apprehensive, but at the same time, I felt assured by the doctor's premonitions. These doctors know what they are talking about. They produce an almost accurate succession of the events. As long as the frequent discharges do not cause pain or unnecessary discomfort that causes alarm, there is no need for concern. With this positive attitude I was determined to fight 'til the end.

At 5:18, one hour exactly before my scheduled therapy, I drank the ritual sixteen ounces of water. There is no way one can control the bladder during this space of time. Although I developed some techniques in the course of the procedure to offset the urge, I was not successful all the time. Indeed, either I failed or I was distressed at times.

I drove to the radiology building and sat in the waiting room. Some days, I found three or four patients waiting for their call. I did not hear much conversation going on. Everyone seemed to be absorbed in profound reflections. There were moments in which a spontaneous exchange occurred and focused primarily on the therapists' ability to respect the time schedule. For patients who came from afar, their urge must have been horrible. From the few people I ventured to talk to, I learned that a couple of them came from Canastota and one from Albany. Each day, he drove six hours round trip! I could not gather more information in this regard because at the completion of the therapy, each one of us either ran to the bathroom or to the car where a wife, most likely was waiting. That evening, the therapist informed me that the doctor was available for me in his office after the session. When it was over, I could not hold it anymore and ran to the lavatory. Soon after, I saw the oncologist and I exposed to him my urinary problems. He opened the drawer of his desk and pulled out two flasks of Flomax and directed me to take one pill every day after dinner. Its purpose was to relax the prostate nerves and allow the urine to flow through. I would quit taking them after two months. When I queried him about the side effects, he replied that I would not start noticing them after the second week. His assurance coincided, more or less, with the one that my brother gave me.

For him, the troubles began on the third week. Up to that time, my only problem was confined to the poor urination. I had to exert myself behind belief just to let some drops go by. By nature, I dislike passionately medicine. It should not come as a surprise, therefore, that the mere sight of the pills agitated me. I was not prepared to take them for two months, but it was no time to refuse the doctor's order. He assured me that Flomax was tolerable. I did not dispute his position and did not bother to read the label to get acquainted with the side effects. I did absolutely nothing to prevent a catastrophe! Later, I decided to navigate the internet which I considered a reliable source of information. Upon reading some literature on the above medicine, I realized with horror the devastating side effect that it can cause. I am not imagining creating a false scenario. It is written on the box! Not that other pills are candies, but the label generated in me a defense mechanism and an outright aversion to medicine in general.

MAY 22

I took Flomax with the inner fear that something insidious lay beneath its consequences. A sinister premonition accompanied me from dawn to dusk. I should recognize that, in between, emerged a brief period when I cast doubts on my original perception. I thought that it was distorted and without foundation. I quickly realized that it was an illusion, merely an illusion. Nothing else!

At 9:00 a.m. I read the directions and took the first pill. Shortly after, the urge to empty the bladder became pressing and I had to rush to the lav. What a relief! I felt like being a different man. The flow was torrential and free from any discomfort or pain. I was ready to call the pill 'a miracle drug'. The change of opinion was like night and day. I completely changed my attitude from worse to better on a 360 degree. My optimism proved to be of temporary duration. With the passing minutes, I started my neck began to contract. The nerves twisted and the blood flow to the brains decreased. Gradually, the pain intensified and by evening I could not bear it anymore. I was unable to think rationally, to move around, to rest, to sleep. I regained some consciousness and strength and I called the doctor. He was unavailable, but the secretary assured me that I could expose my problem to the nurse the following morning.

MAY 23

The nurse called me early in the morning to ascertain that my condition was not deteriorating. She stated that the headache was not the result of Flomax, but of the radiations. I doubted it. I did not know what course of action take. We debated for a few minutes on the value of the pills. She did not recall any patient who had problems in the past with that medicine. Toward the end of the conversation, she appeared to have lost her self-assurance on the matter and suggested me to take for one more day. If the same side effects repeated on an equal scale, I should stop it and take bioprophane, one in the morning and one at night.

The urinary flow was excellent and I, too, wanted to give a second chance to Flomax. After all, it eliminated the only difficulties that

I was experiencing. Could the headache originate from a different source, such as high blood pressure, mental exhaustion, excessive reading or hypertension? I got bold and plunged once again into the unknown with uncertainty and hope. There was no question in mind that if the same symptoms appeared the next day, it had to be debited to the pills. I fell in depressive and disconcerted mood.

Phoenix was taking the sun on the terrace and hollered, "Honey, bring me a big glass of water with ice and lemon!"

I wanted to take off and never come back again. Sweet Princess came to me and licked my hands. I picked her up and held close to my chest. She looked at me with her beautiful deep blue eyes. She moved her mouth. She wanted to talk to me, to console me, but she could not. She laid her head on the side and kept on staring at me. After a while, we both fell asleep.

MAY 24

I got up with a headache almost similar to the previous day. It lasted all day. I conferred with a friend pharmacist and he indicated that the headache was definitely retraceable to Flomax. I called back the nurse and expressed my concern. Once again, she restated very clearly that the headache had no correlation with Flomax. Two medical professionals differed in their opinion and I was caught in the middle of it without a doctor and without knowledge.

To shrug off all the uncertainties and to forget my problems, I went to the gym to exercise on a limited scale. I cannot give a rational explanation of how I was able to carry one those light activities. I had the sensation of being in another world.

In the afternoon, I slept a couple of hours on and off. I fell asleep again later on. I move sluggishly and perform the least possible menial jobs. I am terribly afraid of being inactive. Inactivity, for me, is synonymous of slow death. Around me, there was silence, a deep, frightening silence.

May is the month that the Church dedicated to the Blessed Mother. I said to myself, "Where is she? How come I do not see her? How come I do not hear her?"

A voice behind me said," That is because you Catholics put too much emphasis on her and when she does not answer your prayers, you are deeply disappointed. Listen to me! Lay off of her. She is not listening to you. If she is an intermediary, as you claim, she is too busy with more important things. I tell you all the time. You are alone in this world. If you are lucky, OK, if not, you have to accept reality."

I wanted to answer, but I realized that I did not have the strength neither the will to augment my stress level.

MAY 28

Two days went by since I took the second pill. My mind felt relatively calm. I took advantage of it and I exercised and watched soccer games throughout the morning. The doctor had received the news.

I was lying on my back in the radiology room. My mind was getting prepared for the prayers. The noise of a hard banging interrupted my thoughts. From the corner of the wall, I detected Dr. Matamonstruos' profile. Evidently, he banged the door and was rushing toward me. I expected a reproach or a bad news. "Stop immediately Flomex. Instead, take two hiboprophine a day, one in the morning and one in the evening after supper. I did a gesture of assent with my head and he disappeared as fast as he appeared.

The change was remarkable. The urine flow returned to normal and I did not feel any urge to go to the lav. The new medicine, innocuous as it seems, did wonders for me. The general belief is that hyboprophin is used for arthritis. It does not just alleviate muscular or bone pains, but it relaxes the prostate as well, so that, the urinary tract widens. Other than reactivating the regular urinary flow, it does not carry side effects.

Around noon, I felt slightly weak and I asked for food. It was an external weakness. After eating and taking the multiple vitamins, I felt stronger.

At the beginning of the program, the doctor suggested me to take multiple vitamins. I hardly dealt with them in the past. The only one I used to take was vitamin E. I followed the doctor's suggestion and went to the pharmacy. I was more confused than ever. I bought one kind I thought it was good and returned home. I took the vitamins for a few days until I asked the doctor, "There are so many types of vitamins. How am I supposed to know which is the best for me."

"Take 'Centrum,' he said.

I shook my head in disbelief. Why didn't he tell me at the beginning? More I thought about Dr. Maria from California, more I believed in her values.

JUNE 5.

We skipped a few days because the doctor was on vacation or assisting at conferences.

Today, I got up with a terrible headache very similar to the one I suffered with the Flomex pill. I did not know what to make of it. Did that powerful medicine leave its mark on me or the therapy was getting harsher to sustain? I felt dizzy. To make my condition worse, I started to feel heavy pressure on the stomach, like hunger pangs. Incidentally, the stomach had been bothering me on a routine basis. This time, however, was joined by a state of dizziness. The only techniques that really assuage the turmoil were massages. I massaged two or three times the stomach clockwise and counterclockwise and, immediately after, it disappeared.

By mid-afternoon, I revived. I remembered that I relied heavily on massages and now I ignored them. I put both hands on the ears and began to massage that area. Then, I followed up with the face, throat and shoulders. I leaned with my back against the corner of the cellar door and I tested which muscle or nerve hurt me the most. After massaging for a couple of minutes the back and the spine, I felt a gradual relief. When the clock hit six o' clock, the headache was virtually gone.

In the course of the years, I made repetitious attempts to teach the value of massaging to my family and relatives. Unfortunately, the seeds fell on rocky areas. Phoenix was the main opposition to my ideas. She claimed that I appealed too much on my imagination

JUNE 6

Each time I talked to my brother and sister, I assured them that my life was running smoothly. On this date, I was running in rough waters. At nine o'clock, my head felt like being in a fog. I could not hear and

I lacked the will power to engage in any conversation with anyone. My body was weak, weak even to make the routine errands. The multivitamin, which supposedly, had to energize me, was ineffective; at least, I did not feel any boost. My brother's warning that the initial optimism was going to turn into tough reality was approaching.

In the garage, I sat on a lounge chair and sank into it. I lacked a reactive energy. I looked like a boxer who had been knocked down and was unable to get up. I opened and closed the eyes in a mechanical way. For three hours I stayed there. As soon as my mind began to clear up, I got up and tried to walk, but I was wobbling. The puppy came at my feet and stared at me. I looked at her cute, little nose. A mysterious warm feeling invaded my whole body. I picked her up and held her against my chest. I returned to the chair. Next time I got up, the headache was gone.

Phoenix was skeptical as usual. She accused me of practicing shamanism.

JUNE 7

I was walking toward my car, when a patient's wife approached me and handed me a small box. "This is for you. I won't be able to see you anymore. My husband has been removed from the afternoon schedule and has to report in the morning." I stood there speechless for a minute. She kept on looking at me. I was surprised by her nobility of soul and concerned about her husband. My silence almost embarrassed me. It seemed eternal. I wanted to reciprocate, but how? The lady, with her sad face, had touched the chords of my heart. Finally, I took courage and responded in broken monosyllabic words, "Do not lose hope. The Lord will be walking with both of you in the midst of your ordeal." She looked at me once again with a soft smile and thanked me. I turned around with tears in my eyes. What did I do to deserve that recognition, that gentle act, that show of love? A woman, a wife, a lady whom I hardly knew, except for the few ideas we exchanged in the waiting room taught the great significance of love. May the Lord bless that gentle soul and her family and may He help her husband to full recovery.

I gave the box to my wife. She opened it and found sweets. The puppy was jumping at that opportunity and I grabbed her before she could get at them.

JUNE 8

I followed scrupulously the routine drank the sixteen ounces of water at ten after five and I was convinced that I would pass the endurance test with flying colors. How many times shall I make mistakes before I learn once and for all not to exceed in my exuberance? Continuous disappointments are terrible. They are conducive to depression and auto-destruction.

Ten minutes passed by and I already felt the urge of emptying the bladder. Nonetheless, I stood firm trying to postpone the evacuation. My intent was not to concede too much to the weak bladder; otherwise it was going to become a norm. This strategy produced some positive results in the sense that I was able to sustain the stimulus until the completion of the radiation process.

Miguel, the therapist, asked me to step on the scale. That was a procedure that we had to observe prior to Dr. Matamonstruos' weekly check up. I weighed one-hundred and seventy nine pounds. Of course, I blamed the sweets I had devoured during the day. I had to find a culprit for the weight increase. I suppose that an excessive weight loss or vice versa could be an indicator that the cancerous cells are not being destroyed.

In the radiology room, the young girl therapist asked me if the weight had changed. I responded that I had been slim all my life. It was an athletic condition that began in my early years of life when I used to compete with my friends in foot races and soccer games.

I must admit that I was baffled when she asked me about my marital status. I really did not understand the logic behind it. I was sixty-eight and my face was the mirror of an eighty-five year old man, even though and without vanity, the rest of the body looked very young. She pursued the matter and asked me if my wife shared my same hobbies. I responded that for years I tried to engage my wife in sport activities, but she shunned the invitation claiming that her heel hurt. I had my doubts about it; however, she was right only as far as the last two years are concerned during which she developed serious problems on her right heel and next week she will be operated.

In the meantime, the doctor was talking to someone, while I was waiting in his office. Five minutes passed by and he came in smiling. He sat and thanked me for the chocolates. I noticed certain restlessness in him and I queried about it. He admitted that he was curious to know my country of birth. When he heard that I came from Italy, he became even more disconcerted. "How come you teach Spanish and how come you bought Czechoslovakian chocolates?" I laughed, but did not reply.

The conversation shifted quickly on another topic. He gave a glance to the computer, scrolled down one page until he found information related to me. "Everything looks good here," he said.

"That's what I like to hear, doctor."

Before leaving the office, I questioned him about the stomach pains that I felt in the course of the day. He could not offer any rational explanation. I also told him about some headaches. He did not seem concerned and I revealed a peculiar way that I used to get rid of it. He shook his head with incredulity and added, "Keep on doing the massages."

As I stepped outside, Phoenix asked me, "Go get another cup of coffee. Bring also a few cheese crackers for Sweet Princess."

"I brought you one before."

"Get another one. It is hot. I need coffee to stimulate me."

In the evening, I decided to visit a couple of friends who were in the hospital. The lady had been recovered for the past three weeks for cardiac problems. Her health worsened when she contracted a severe case of an unknown infection; consequently, the visitors, for precautionary health reasons, had to wear a special hospital garment before having access to the room. I stopped at the door and greeted her, "How are you? Listen, I am not coming in because I have been experiencing an allergic reaction or cold. I know that it is contagious and, considering your debilitated health condition, I do not wish to worsen it."

"It is fine. I feel better now. I am exhausted."

"That is what the medicine does."

No, it is not that. I have received many visitors all day long and I can't take it anymore."

"I understand. You need rest."

I left and visited a male friend. He was alone and felt dejected. There was a long masking tape on his chest. I looked at his left leg. It was heavily bandaged. I asked him, "What happened to your leg?

"It is not my leg. It is my heart."

"You mean . . ."

"Yes, I had an open heart surgery."

"Miguel', I said, "I don't see anybody here. How long have you been here?"

"Two weeks. If everything goes well, I will be discharged in three days."

"Has the lawyer come to visit you? You know what I mean."

"He is not my lawyer. Nobody comes here, except my ex-son-in law.

I did not and could not say anything else and I told him that I would keep him in my prayers.

JUNE 9

Incredible! Upon arrival to the therapy office, I did not have any urgency to relieve the bladder. That posed a risk. If the bladder is full, it acts as a shield to the radioactive rays.

Conversely, if it is empty, radiation can burn the adjacent tissues, as I have had the space to mention it much earlier in this book. I had an obsession to adhere rigidly to the medical prescriptions. I was supposed to drink sixteen ounces of water one hour and ten minutes before the therapy and I looked at the clock constantly when the time was approaching. In the event I missed it, I feared serious repercussions. The doctor's orders were law. Luckily, I remembered the words of another patient who incurred in previous urinary obstructions. He said, "From now on I drink more. If I cannot bear the burden, before I enter the radiation room, I will discharge some. That is all."

In the waiting room, there was a fountain against the south wall next to the entrance. I grabbed a glass and filled it half way with the frigid water. I could not drink it! I poured a bit of hot coffee into it to mitigate the temperature. I hardly drink any coffee, but under those circumstances I made a strenuous effort. Unfortunately, it did not reach the desired effects.

My turn came and I was audacious enough to refuse to go. No one offered any advice. I looked around the coffee pot and I noticed small juice boxes with straws. I drank two of them. After five minutes I did not see any sign of progress. I was getting disgruntled. The therapist came back and I firmly passed again. I had never found myself in that situation. I drank more juice, I walked up and down the hall, I did some exercises to promote the urgency of evacuation and on the third call I decided to go in.

At the end of the therapy, Miguel praised me for the precautions I took. He warned me against undergoing radiology without having a full bladder. He added that in some instances he had to stop the therapy because he found out through the computer that the patient's bladder did not contain enough water.

In my case, I ascribed my unusual condition to the fact that I ran in the morning hot weather and the body got dehydrated. That served me as a lesson for the upcoming weeks.

JUNE 12

Bowel turbulence continued and the stomach complained occasionally. While with the stomach, I had found almost a panacea by massaging it; with the other disturbance I had no alternative. Doctors assured me that it was not being caused by the therapy. The family doctor could express himself on a matter he knew only marginally and I was there a victim of doctors' inability to give me a satisfying answer or some medicine that could cure it. I passed some nights sleepless. I was in the middle of a tempest and I had to insist on heading forward or else was going to be the end of it. Many times, I was on the verge of a psychological collapse. I felt hopeless to go on in this way. Too many question marks crowded the sky in front of me. I wanted to let everything go. At the same time, I knew that it was a Christian approach and I reproached myself for not being strong enough in my weak moments.

More than once, I broke into tears while I was talking with my sisters or brother-in-law. They believed that my faith would make me untouchable. At the contrary, I was more vulnerable than others. The fact that I was in that predicament, it showed, most likely, that my faith was too weak to withstand the brunt of the enemy. He was always lurking in the background ready to strike at any moment. I do not want to make things difficult for the reader. I wish to say that not even faith can save you from physical demise because human condition is made to suffer. For most of us, suffering is a mystery. For those who hold a deep faith, it gives real meaning to our existence and a 'sine qua non' to have access to the kingdom of heaven.

JUNE 13

I got up at six o'clock this morning. I wake up early. What can I do in bed? Dwell on my groaning and pains? I defy the monster by exercising. I forget. I forget more when I run with the puppy. Can you imagine, my friend reader, spending forty five or fifty minutes jogging on the grass around the reservoir with a puppy? He is my loyal companion. He is ready to follow me wherever I go. He is especially happy when he runs in the open air. In the cellar, he has all sorts of obstructions. Outside, he acts like a bird. He does not have the wings to fly, but fast feet to run. I look at her when the morning breeze raises her hair over the collar. It does not seem that she touches the ground. She is so light and fast. I cannot keep up with her.

On the opposite side of the reservoir, a man was holding a gigantic dog. He growled and made an attempt to attack the puppy. She came close to me. I picked her up and held her against me. The big dog barked a couple of times, while his owner dragged him away.

I was climbing the eastern side of the reservoir and I held the puppy by the leash. Suddenly, a big black dog appeared from nowhere right on my back. The puppy withdrew back from me and started screaming. I pulled it toward me and tried to lift her up, but she screamed even more. Finally, I squatted and grabbed her. Only, then, on my chest, she felt safe. I chased away the big dog.

Since then, when I take her running with me, I always check around if there are other animals. What bothered me the most was the free attitude of some dog owners who kept their dogs unleashed even at the sight of a puppy. I got tired and in one occasion I complained to the local authorities.

JUNE 14

The puppy was a sun's ray in my frigid heart. I do not recall the times I held him tight in my arms. Her big blue eyes spoke words of understanding and love. She was my refuge. I took her out and played with her even when I felt depressed. Depression lurked in my background, always available to fill in empty space. I tried to deny it that opportunity as much as I could. In the deepest of my soul, I saw a light. I felt that the Lord would not abandon me, after all.

In the waiting room, I saw a lady accompanied by three people. The lady was in her seventies, had her hair over bleached and her face heavily covered with make-up. She looked tired and seemed to depend on her entourage for moral support. I do not know if the man were her son, He could have been forty years old and dressed in a unique way. The suit and the tie looked as if they had just been ironed and the shirt was white. His hair was combed straight backward. They looked lustrous. I am not sure if he used some kind of cream or if it was his natural color. I heard him confabulating with the lady in an unpolished Italian, but I did not intervene in the conversation. It is a matter of fact that we never exchanged a word in the week I met them. He was so self attracted that, each time he made a comment, he looked around to ascertain that all of us would be listening to his words of wisdom.

The lady finished the therapy and arrived at the waiting room. Her escort quickly surrounded her and showered her with compliments. They used all sort of good manners to let her feel their love.

JUNE 15

I arrived at the waiting room and I noticed a sort of turmoil going on. The lady had just signed the book of the "graduated." That scene was quite unusual. At least, I had never seen anything like that. One by one, the people of her entourage, which had increased from the previous week, gave her a gift. A happy atmosphere engulfed every one of them. I was watching with curiosity. The lady did not unpack the gifts. She was enjoying the moment.

She said in a marked foreign accent, "I am all done. Finished!" All of us applauded. The man with the polished suit proudly stated that graduation produces a feeling of elation and that they would consider that date as a festive day to be commemorated every year. He looked around a couple of times to ascertain that everybody was listening to him and proudly took the lady under his arms and led her triumphantly out with the escort. She was gleaming with joy while she was leaving the room.

The patients and their family members in the waiting room got involved emotionally with the lady and, although, they did not understand Italian, were fascinated by the happiness that evaporated from the lady's pores. One of them said, "I hope I will graduate too someday."

JUNE 16

I decided to spend a few hours at the hospice where I volunteered. I did not want to show up on Friday when I had other commitments. Maybe, the sight of friendly faces would draw my attention elsewhere. I could make some private visits and get involved in simple conversations. Whatever distracted me from my condition was worth it.

I arrived very tired. I passed moments of drowsiness during which I could only sink on a sofa and wait that the storm passed by. My eyes were glassy like. Candace, the lady-priest was kind enough to stop and queried about health. I thanked her and proceeded elsewhere.

The elevator was slow and I lacked patience. Four old ladies in wheelchairs were also waiting. Finally, it arrived and we were able to go to the third floor. I dragged myself to a room where an old acquaintance stayed and I sat next to the window. She welcomed me with a smile. I greeted her and positioned myself against the sun's rays. She must have read my mind and did not question me. The sun inundated me with its heat and I enjoyed it all the way. I must have slept for an hour.

Virginia welcomed me back to the real world. I opened my eyes and she started talking. Not to estrange myself from the conversation, I spelled out a word at uneven intervals. I remember absolutely nothing of her stories. I only know that I made a supreme effort to get up at the time of my departure. My mind was still cloudy and I wobbled all the way to the entrance.

On the way down in the elevator, I thought about how worthless I was. I could not bear that punishment and I left.

At home, my wife prepared a big pot of soup. That was and is my favorite dish because it warms me up, especially in winter. It seems that even the mind feels better when you enjoy a certain food. I ate abundantly, maybe, because I was restless. I lay down on the sofa. I was devoid of energy. The puppy came and licked my chin. I hugged her and I fell asleep again.

JUNE 17

The air was fresh and on the hills the breeze was very inviting. I felt in a different mood and wanted to shrug off the lethargy that clanged on me from past days. I regained my original willpower and the mobility desire was quickly set in motion.

Most of my garden is downhill and to cut the grass in that area is an ordeal. The lawnmower is heavy to maneuver and dangerous to hold. When it leans on one side, the oil rushes all the way in that direction, and, when it tilts on the other side, the oil flows there. This continuous extreme movement dries up the carburetor and causes smoke to rise. On an uneven and treacherous terrain, it is even difficult to stand up. I had to hold on the fence to avoid many falls. On the wet grass, it was dangerous to cut the grass.

My brother had warned me not to exert myself or expose to the sun. I was stubborn because I love the sun. In my late years, I learned that my relationship with this planet has been a strange one; a love manifested by one, but not corresponded by the other. And, so, even too much sun can burn and destroy. In short, I loved the sun, but the sun did not love me. My dear reader, did you ever love a woman, but she did not reciprocate?

Two black dots appeared on my nose. They expanded and contracted. I did not know what to think of it until I decided to let a specialist check it. The surgeon was not sure. He suggested me to do a biopsy and the result came positive. As if I did not have enough problems, another plague afflicted my existence. I was determined to act and with speed. I made an appointment to remove it surgically as soon as possible.

The preparation resulted more painful that the actual surgery. The surgeon injected a needle to anaesthetize the area below the nasal septum. He drove it deep enough to shake my brains. It was horrifying.

The surgery itself did not bother me. I saw the doctor cutting and giving some tissues to the assistant who sent it for analysis. The whole procedure did not last too long. At the end of it, I gathered all my strength and managed to get home. I cannot tell, friend reader, the prayers that I recited in the clinic.

A week later, the nurse called me and informed that the response of the biopsy was positive. I was astonished. I could not comprehend how a well known surgeon could have failed to eliminate the entire tumor. With all the scarce patience I had, I waited six weeks before I could go for the second attempt on my nose.

At the designated date, I was back again in the surgeon's office for the same ritual. I resigned myself to the case and went ahead for the second removal. The injection of the needle was again horrifying. I started praying, so that, the time passed by fast. During the operation, I noticed that the doctor removed some tissues from one side of the nose and placed them on the opposite side to balance the nasal unevenness. This was a good relief because I always was self-conscious about it. .

On the following Friday, The nurse informed me that the response to the biopsy was negative. I had overcome another hurdle.

Last year, I noticed a small circular crust on my left leg. Gradually, it protruded out like volcanic lava. On some days, it appeared that it was decreasing in bulging.

The enigmatic alternation lasted three weeks until I decided to apply antiseptic soap. I squeezed it to see if the pus would leave the area. All my efforts to quell sown the anomalous condition failed miserably and I had no alternative but to make an appointment with the doctor. At that stage, I was too apprehensive to let it go on any longer without medical attention.

A nurse practitioner guessed that it was a deer bacteria or a squirm. I was dissatisfied with the diagnosis. She charged me for the doctor's fee even though she gave a different version to my wife.

I switched to a dermatologist. She explained to me that the best course to take was the biopsy. She also suggested seeing Dr. Falcone to get a second opinion. The blood flushed through my brains in an unparalleled race toward a stroke. The fear that the tumor would travel all over the body was, per se, destabilizing mentally speaking. The surgeon told me that it was caused by the sun. The biopsy, as the reader may infer, came back positive, and I needed another surgical intervention. The successive biopsy resulted negative, but I have never seen anything like this. Six months later, a black spot still covered the area. It took a year before the darkness disappeared.

The reader may wonder why I relate all these separated events. Well, doctors, want to scrutinize your past to be able to make better predictions and correlations, but what still bothers me is that, all of a sudden, every problem stems from the sun.

Dr. Matamonstruos was aware of the devastating effects of the sun's ultraviolet rays, but refused to correlate it to cancer. For him, sun and radiology were and are two 'distinct animals.' Consequently, he chose a bold position, too bold to consider it completely reliable. It is not surprising that he never warned me about the danger that comes from the ozone layer.

Miguel, his assistant, shared the doctor's view only to a certain extent. "The sun," he said does not hurt you because it increases the radiological potential side effects, but it may hurt you separately. The rays beamed on your body," he explained, "by the machine are external. Once it stops, the beaming also terminates."

In Italy, the medical field has a different vision. According to a therapist, who shared with my brother their knowledge, the exposure to the sun contributes to the deterioration of one's conditions.

I believe that the answer to the two opposing medical positions lies in the middle. Only there the equilibrium can be reached. I still ponder over Dr. Matamonstuos' additional position that refuses to get involved in the controversy by insisting that the worst enemy of the rehabilitation process is fear.

JUNE 20

It was a warm day, but how could I have enjoyed it if every fifteen minutes I had to evacuate the bladder. I was obsessed by the stimulus in the hour proceeding the therapy session. The bladder made the demands, but the body could not control it.

I asked questioned to anyone who had gone through the same ordeal to learn how to cope with it. I saw Vincent in the street and I inquired about his health. He had the prostate removed years ago. He was very composed when he recounted in simple terms that he got through surgery with flying colors.

A few weeks later he was already jumping in bed. I do not understand why he chose the bed to jump when there is a trampoline in the Youth Center. I did not pursue the matter and his remarks are open to any rational interpretation.

Like, Vincent, other people displayed an enthusiastic reaction to their prostate condition. My brother-in-law claims that he never encountered any difficulty during or after the surgery. Conversely, my brother asserted his incapacity to react to the post period surgery. Indeed, he stated that he almost died were it not for the assistance of Tina.

All these memories were reverberating in my mind while I was in the garage. That made me very irritable. I was unsure on whether to be optimistic or pessimistic. Even the presence of my relatives began to annoy me. "Why me?" I kept on repeating numerous times. That was the question that only fools pose to themselves. I realized that I was being egocentric and envious. A more serene reflection made me aware that all humans are subject to health problems and if it were God's will, I had to accept it. I hope I have learned that lesson.

JUNE 21

I was supposed to confer with the oncologist, but he did not show up. A lady doctor welcomed me in her office. The sole thought that she was going to check me, gave me a sense of embarrassment. My eyes turned counterclockwise. I made an attempt to mask my uncomfortable appearance, but without success. She perceived my state of mind and issued a comforting statement, "I am not going to check you." It was very gratifying to see that she was trying to appease my nervousness. I gave a sigh of relief. She smiled and sat in front of the computer. Without turning around, she asked me the same questions heard from other doctors.

I did not pay much attention to them, instead I was scrutinizing her from the back her physical make up. She had an olive color skin and her accent identified her Spanish heritage. She was petite and pretty. Her hair was dark brown. Circular gold earrings dangled from her two small ears. She must have enjoyed that kind of scrutiny because she quit the research and sat in silence for a couple of minutes.

I forgot about the urge. The doctor, in a slow motion, turned toward me and looked straight in my eyes. I did not know how to interpret that move. She helped me to overcome my indecision by querying, "Are you an artist? You are Italian aren't you? I am a little dubious about your intentions. Setting aside the prostate topic, I am wondering if you may be sick someplace else."

I was stunned by those remarks and I did not respond promptly. Obviously, she interpreted my silence as an acceptance of her thought s, but I instantly woke up from my torpor and replied, "Flowers have to be admired." She smiled and said, Mr. O'Fabuloso, I am glad for you. This is one way you can ignore your monster. And, now, you may go."

Other patients were in line in the hallway. I looked back and I caught her watching me. She looked down the papers and called on the next name. I rushed to the bathroom. The urge was great. I was hesitant. It was my turn to get the therapy. I emptied a bit of the bladder and ran into the room where Miguel was waiting impatiently for me.

On my way out, a middle age woman, half disheveled, approached me and asked if I could spare a cup of coffee. I pointed the entrance of the building to her, but she turned around and went to another street where she stopped besides a stop sign.

My wife was watching the scene from inside the car. When I got next to her, she seemed to be in bad humor. Without any explanation, she scolded me for having talked to the stranger.

JUNE 22

I met another nurse at the radiology center. She was short and brunette and displayed an ostentatious array of ornaments: necklace, bracelet, earrings, a ring for every finger and gold chains around her ankles.

I queried about her living quarters and she told me that she came from Lakeland, approximately, two miles from Solvay. The geographical area of her origin uplifted somehow my morale. A nurse, who was responsible for my well being, lived near me. If emotions play a significant role in the fight against an invisible enemy, then, I felt much better when she reminded me that she was a Solvay High School graduate. She was much younger to have seen my sons in the classrooms.

By this time, I became more familiar with coffee and juice practices and, I must confess, that I went behind the social mores. My wife always recommended me to bring her a hot cup of coffee, wheat crackers and redouble the request once she finished them. Of course, she had to take care of the puppy, which was eager to jump at every opportunity for extra food. My wife felt uneasy and she ended up sharing whatever I supplied her. The meager consumption served also to appease her stomach pranks which were caused by the numerous pills she took on a daily basis. I disliked passionately bringing food and beverage outside of the physical compound. I do not think that the secretary appreciated my behavior, even though she never objected to it. But, I also used a lot of precaution. Before making the move, I assured that she was not looking or going somewhere.

Back in the radiation room, the robotic machine stopped snoring and I jumped like a feline off the bed and stood on my feet. My pants were still hanging down. I pulled them up instantly and was ready to leave. Suddenly, I noticed the nurse's face wide open and her eyes rolled up. "Please, do not do that again!" She warned me. I remained petrified. I did not know the reason for being reprimanded. She seemed to understand my perplexity and added, "You almost hit the metal bar with your head! You do not need to hurry! You scared me!" I apologized. Once again, I realized that "the ball of fire" in my character had not been extinguished by maturity. It was the same impulsive trait that caused an infinite number of problems throughout my existence. Maybe, in my subconscious, I wanted to defy medicine, radiology, cancer and whatever other malefic force hiding in me. I looked in the mirror of my imagination and I saw a bullfighter, who, although wounded, stands proudly in front of the animal with all his defiance and arrogance. Ironically, this is hardly the case in a medical context when a patient feels impotent and devoid of energy and hope. The matador can always outsmart the bull even in times of danger, but a helpless patient feels devastated by his condition and the medical limitations and his reactions, like mine, can only be pretentious in scope.

JUNE 23

I saw the same lady roaming around the building. I called the secretary's attention. She explained to me that the anonymous wanderer had entered into the premises in previous occasions and the security guard was alerted to chase her out.

Upon entering the waiting room, I heard the television anchorman announce that a false priest had been discovered carrying on priestly duties such as confessions and celebrating mass. A girl came out of the confessional booth visibly upset. She reported her experience to the ecclesiastic authorities and the 'clergyman' was apprehended by the police. A woman, who was accompanying her husband for therapies, commented, "Wouldn't that be nice if doctors would identify all these potential enemies from our bodies and eject them with a simple stroke of an injection?

Needless to say, the atmosphere in the visitors' room was somber. At times, dialogs or exchange of information were carried on almost imperceptibly. Oddly enough, as soon as the secretary left temporarily her post, the voices gained momentum and were more audible. A lady, whose name had been unfamiliar to me until that instance, was unleashing venomous attacks to the government, guilty for not allocating enough money for the discovery of the cancer. Another woman directed her criticism to the voracious pharmaceutical companies from either opposing vaccines or slowing down the new medical advances. She reminded her absent minded audience of the new method to cure blood clot in the artery, to avoid strokes and other heart ailments. She swore to have seen it on TV. The hosts were Howard Hughes and Dr. Johnson. They were claiming that a new revolutionary approach would reduce high blood pressure by sixty per cent. They also outlined a series of vaccines that would be preventative in nature against cancer. The woman ended up her argument by reminding us that the government does not do anything to protect the sick.

JUNE 26

I sank in the labyrinth of my thoughts in a deeply curved chair in the garage. The puppy was staring at me. I felt a bit envious of her. It is true that was, and is, an animal, but she, at least, she was healthy. Her compassionate eyes made me change my thoughts. I picked her up and tightened her to my chest. I felt her warmth and her companionship. In those moments, my pains were alleviated. She did not move from my grip. I could hold on her forever for I felt loved, cared, understood. I made an attempt to enter into a secret of God. Why did he create animals? Why didn't He give them the gift of talking? Why aren't they part of the redemptive process? I quickly realized that it was a sisiphic struggle and I gave up with the same speed as I started,

In the street, familiar faces passed by. They did not even look toward me.

It was a dormant day. Nature appeared at standstill. The blackbirds were not flying over my house. Their shrieking sound did not even wake up the dogs with their bodies spread on the asphalt of the driveways. The leaves on the tree branches did not bend back and forth as usual. There wasn't a breath of wind around.

Within this sleepy atmosphere, I departed in the afternoon for the ritual radiology treatment. I was going to go back to a place full of incognitos. Nobody knew for sure about the outcome. We lived with hope and fear.

In the waiting room, a disheveled woman was sitting next to the bathroom entrance. She must have been a new patient. She had a young assistant, probably her niece, and her daughter who attended to her. After the preliminaries, I inquired about the nature of her illness. The lady had collected a few extra pounds on her body in the past years. Her frequent pauses to catch breath were quite plausible.

Her husband joined her shortly after. He was of a medium stature, bold and with crooked teeth. He showed signs of nervousness by pulling constantly the knuckles. His wife laughed and said, "Look, he is nervous and I am sick."

"You want to be here," he responded.

"Listen to him! What a jerk you are! Ask these people who wants to come to this dungeon."

The other patients with their relatives turned their attention to the newcomers, but did not make any comment.

The lady's husband said, "You don't want to drink wine and that's why you get sick."

"You are a dumbbell! If I don't like it why should I drink it?"

"Look at me! I drink it and I am not sick."

"That is because you get drunk all the time and you don't even realize what you are saying."

"I just take a sip at meal time."

"And, how long does that sip last?"

The patients and their relatives were beginning to enjoy the improvised theater. The lady continued, "Who told you to come here?" responded his wife with her heavy voice. "You follow me wherever I go."

"Stay home the next time! I am already sick of being here. I do not need any more aggravation from you." The tension was increasing between the two. The secretary was listening from behind the glass window, but, unlike the audience, she did not enjoy the scene. I inquired to the lady about the reason for being there. She replied, "This is a very naïve question."

I apologized and changed my question, "Really, I was querying about the nature of your illness."

"You ought to know, whoever you are," she responded in a loud voice, "Anyone who passes through these gates enters in the sorrowful city. What you see here and everywhere is a false image. These doctors are all for money!" A veil of sadness fell on the other patients' faces. No one made any comment.

Fortunately, the nurse opened the door and called on the lady's name. "Do I have to go through this ordeal again?" the lady asked.

"Which ordeal, the one with your husband . . . ?"

"That too" responded the lady.

A man in the audience chuckled, "You made our day a bit brighter. You don't want to go to the hospital where there is suffering and death."

A lady added, "You are fortunate that he came to assist you here rather than at the funeral home."

"You are not kidding! In the way I feel . . ." She responded quickly while she was trying to get up with some efforts and without the use of the cane. "I went for the cauterization of the artery for the second time," she added "And I almost left my skin there."

Her daughter helped her to stand up and she made a few steps down the hall, but stopped. She pointed the cane to her husband and said to the nurse, "Always the wrong people get sick. He should be in my place. He claims that wine is the cure for all diseases. I would like to know if the drunkards are healthy." This time, she got mixed reactions from the audience. That irritated her even more and said,

"Evidently, there are some baboons here too." I heard some spicy comments on the tips of the lips but the nurse cautioned her not to offend anyone and accompanied her to the radiology room. From far away, we heard some loud words, "Too bad if they did not like it!"

JUNE 28

This morning, I had to run, run, and run. The night was not propitious. I woke up three times. I felt like going victimized by superior forces and I was unable to oppose any resistance. I went back to bed trying to regain some lost sleep. It was just impossible! I moved to the kitchen making my way in the darkness by moving my hands left and right. I avoided any unnecessary noise so not to wake up my wife or the puppy.

I looked outside through the main window and I could see the city lights in the distance that shed radiance all around them. I positioned myself against the windows and I began to do some exercises that did not require much effort. I would follow up with the heavier ones outside at dawn. In other circumstances, I would have engaged in such an activity, but the reader should remember that my primary objective was to be active. I had to push my body not to let the mind collapse. After all, if I did not condition myself to the optimum physical level, the therapies could have devastating consequences on me. I was fully aware of it and I fought with teeth and nails. In the meantime, the minutes, the hours, my entire existence was flying away and I was living in constant fear.

To keep my sanity, I would take a walk or a ride. During a trip, I found a marvelous statue in cement of the Blessed Mother. It was about three feet tall and twenty inches wide. Her head leaned slightly to the left as if she were turning her sight away from me. The facial countenance resembled that of Michelangelo's Pieta'. There was no Christ in her arms, but she seemed to be withdrawn from this world and was immersed in a mysterious contemplation. As the days passed by, I realized that I could not have found a Blessed Mother with such an expressive mood. Nonetheless, each time I looked at her, I felt a feeling of rejection, of worthlessness. I came to the conclusion that I was no longer worth of the divine mercy so deeply was the impact that the face made on me.

Although I nurtured the notion that I was no longer part of her army, I could not stand her unpainted. I set it for the time being in the back yard. I planned to flank her on the wall with other saints. One day, I decided to remove her from there indefinitely. She could not affect anybody's life there; therefore, I brought on the front lawn where people passed by all day. My readers could not imagine the negative comments that followed after I painted the statue. I heard that Jesus' Mother appeared only in light blue clothes.

My first objective was to place it on a pedestal. I took three solid blocks and I placed on it a piece of marble that my neighbor offered me. I made some painting retouches with blue and light blue hues on the clothes; I used other colors for minor parts of the body.

By the afternoon, I was exhausted. Fortunately, the therapy session passed by unnoticed and I felt somewhat relieved by that burden. Back home, when I saw the Blessed Mother in colorful garments, I was inundated by an immense feeling of joy.

JUNE 29

The sun was emerging from the East early in the morning among an array of dark clouds that looked more like lazy sheep who would prefer the heat to the pasture. I could hardly hold on the view that I began to feel drowsy. The stomach was making unnecessary demands on me. It was a strange sensation that I felt only in times of intestinal viruses. With the minutes going by, the pangs kept on the pressure on the digestive organs. I could no longer stand the uncomfortable condition and I was expecting the worst. I realized the benefit of the massage and I started to rotate my right hand in a clockwise and later in a counterclockwise movement on my stomach. A couple of burps followed and the normality was reestablished.

It was warm and I decided to go out and breathe some fresh air. My wife had planted two roses and various types of yellow and red flowers around the statue. They looked pretty. Much more needed to be done to make the surrounding area more attractive.

I raised my eyes and met the same face of Mary. I looked at her with a mixture of disenchantment and hope. I cannot explain it, but there was distance between us. It was not a question of faith anymore. Could it have t been the cause of monster's visitation? In other words, I blamed sin for my misery. The reverberations of sin can be ramified in different sectors. It may have critical consequences socially, physically or psychologically. It can tear apart an individual by causing tension, pressure and distress. The weaker we are the more vulnerable we are. After much debate, I concluded that God has a plan for each one of us and this should suffice to keep our heart at rest.

While I was entertaining the above thoughts, I ran to the store and bought about six rose plants. When the job was over, I got inspired to do something of which I would be proud for the rest of my life. I went on the empty lot loaded two wheelbarrows with flat rocks and dumped in front of the statue. Now, I needed a pump and I had to dig a pool with pick and shovel. This latest job was the hardest. The dirt was not soft and it took me a couple of days to complete it. I am not going to disclose the number of times I visited the store for additional explanations on how to install the electrical gadgets. I also purchased eight solar lights that I fixed around the heart shaped water fall.

I cannot define the extent of my happiness. I felt so proud of my accomplishment that my physical conditions played a secondary role. The solar lights illuminated my heart and the whole area surrounding the statue. Even the deer came to my lawn not to pay a visit to the Blessed Mother, or pray, but to prey on the roses. And so, the plants, to my chagrin, hardly gave out any bud and slowly faded away. It makes me wonder at times how these animals are able to chew the thorns around the stems.

JUNE 30

The puppy barked earlier than usual to wake us up. My mind was an active volcano all night. The plight of that woman from the previous day did not help me. The bath room became almost synonymous of the bedroom. The stomach was in turmoil and I had to recur to the ritual massages to alleviate the pain. To fall asleep was impossible. The only alternative left was to close my eyes for a couple of hours just to give them a chance to repose.

Noon was always a time when the nerves would flare up more than usual. I started to despise food. I would skip it if it were not for my precarious health conditions. So, I grabbed a tomato and sliced it; I took an onion and did the same; I dumped a bit of oregano and olive oil and solved the meal problem.

With the completion of the water fall, I took the habit of sitting in front of the statue and recite the Rosary. Other times, I sat there to watch the water movement and the music that generated from it. I was fascinated by the endless flowing of the water and I could have stayed for hours if I did not have to attend other family needs. During that time, I closed my eyes and fell into contemplation. I knew that I was not supposed to expose my face to the sun's rays. The dermatologist had warned me to stay away from it. I was already operated twice on the nose for two black dots that appeared from nowhere. Even my brother had cautioned me to beware of the sun, but I grew wary of the warnings. I was no longer afraid of them. The truth is that the sun became soon an instrument of reaching the other Son. I illuminated myself in it. I got dissolved in it. I lost, for the time being, my own identity. Once I realized the benefit of that contemplation, I returned to it frequently.

Around two o' clock, the same lady stopped again to admire my artistic production of the water fall. I invited her to sit and she did. Without initiating the conversation, she began to tell me how assiduous she was with the morning Mass, confessions and other religious commitments. She was not too much fond of the charismatic movement and did not show any particular attachment to the Healing Mass that the new Pastor started at our church. But, she did participate with a group of ladies to a Novena on the first Monday of each month. She was in her sixties and because of a health problem she took early retirement from General Hospital where she worked as an administrator. She went on revealing her inner turmoil. She had been diagnosed with a very serious malignant disease that tormented her day and night.

Her husband was a scientist, and to assist her, he too, retired as the company allowed him. Certainly, he did not share his wife's religious proclivity, but did not hinder her from carrying on her faith in all its ramifications. Occasionally, he joined her for the Sunday Mass or Healing Mass just to please her. He did the same with the waterfall. He acknowledged its presence, but never cared to appreciate the artistic beauty of it.

His wife spoke for about an hour to me. In the course of our conversation, she decided to speak about her grave illness with surgical precision of the details. Her physician had explained to her that it was a rare case of neurogical malformation that developed around her heart. He was also very candid about the chances that the surgery would fail within a range of fifty per cent. Not content with her words, she took a pen and a paper and drew a picture of the heart to explain to me in anatomical terms the risks involved in a three hour operation. Once before, she canceled the appointment and, even now, she made it clear to the doctor that she may change her mind because she was not entirely ready for it.

The reader may understand how I received that news. I was fighting for my own survival and now I had to fall into a deeper depression with that quasi negative news. Despite my stomach spells, I could not let Spirita down and let her download all her feelings. It was a matter of humanity more than gentility. In a couple of occasions, she broke down in tears and I did not have the strength to console her, neither did I know how. I needed someone to comfort me, to make me laugh, to make me forget, and there I was weeping along with her. This went on for a couple of minutes during which I wiped the tears with my hands. Her ordeal was overwhelming and, up to now, I have not been able to shake it off my mind.

At the radiology session, I could not even hear the noise of the machines. I was too absorbed in other thoughts.

JULY 1.

It was around ten o'clock when I finally sat in my usual spot on the lawn. I turned my head to the right and I noticed Spirituelle walking slowly toward me. Truly, I was in no mood to cry again and I hoped that she would continue her strolling. Instead, she walked toward me. I covered my face with both hands. She was not sure how to interpret my gesture and queried whether I minded her company. "At the contrary," I replied. "Your presence is an honor for me. It is also a pleasure to converse with a woman of high moral and spiritual values." She felt assured by my words and asked if she could join me in the recital of the Rosary. The request took me off balance. Of course I replied, "I could not desire anything better than this."

The neighbors were scrutinizing every move we made and their negative comments did not delay to come. "What are they going to do when the cold weather comes?" "Who is going to entertain who inside?" "It does not look good to pray on the lawn." And, finally, "There is too much noise in this area." This is just another straw fire. It will not last too long." Those comments incited us to pursue our objective with major vigor and agreed to form a prayer group. Our aspiration was not to gain proselytes, but if others wished to join us, we would welcome them.

Subsequent to our resolve, Spirituelle seemed more comfortable and began to spread the news. For the moment, our prayer group consisted of three subjects: she, the puppy, and I.

In our preparatory time, which is, before we began the Rosary, Spirituelle startled me with her political convictions. It was not that she was on the wrong course, but that she would speak so freely about politics. Soon, I realized that she was a fervent anti-abortionist and accused with passion President Obama of heinous crimes. "He is a monster who has been allowing thousands of unborn children to die. With his mellow policy toward abortion, he has allowed countless of women to make tragic decisions." Surely, she could have continued her inflammatory remarks if I did not invite her to our reality. I suggested her not to be antagonistic, but to pray for him. My suggestion had a balsamic effect on her position. She said, "Good, from now on I will pray for Obama."

I also benefited from her company. For an hour or so, I was able to distract myself from my ordeal. When I went to the radiology building, my mind sank again into a sad mood. Nobody talked at my arrival. It gave me the impression of being at a funeral Mass. The only difference was that the priest was the TV commentator. I had just sat that the opened door. The nurse called my name and I followed her up to next room. I took off my slippers and I placed them behind the door and not at a more distant location. Upon the termination of the session, I did not wish to stay there one second longer.

JULY 2

Today, my daughter brought me a dish of cookies. I brought them to the nurses who enjoyed every bit of them. I had just sat down in the waiting room when the fat lady arrived with her entourage, seven in all. Her wheelchair was surrounded by colorful balloons. Everyone in the group was dressed as a clown and, instantly, the patients' attention shifted on them. The lady was euphoric. She picked up a bunch of candies from a bag and began to distribute them. As the distribution wound down, one of her assistants handed to her a bronze pail with a ball bottom piston. The pail had water in it. The lady grabbed the internal part of the pail and sprinkled the water on the audience. There followed a lot of commotion among the crowd. Some of them took cover in the bathroom, others ran outside. The dispersion of the water was accompanied by a blessing, "I ordain you ministers of this place and I transmit on you my gift of dispelling evil spirits. By the way, if someone doubts this consolidated truth, I will crack my knuckles on his pepperoni nose." The people were still wiping their faces with paper towels provided by the secretary, who was annoyed with that improvised, pretentious, self proclaimed religious authority. One of the patients, however, got up and exclaimed, "Madame fat lady, may you spare us with the miraculous water and save for yourself the blessings. We do not wish to be ministers of your insanity church or whatever you think you have."

One of the lady's assistants did not appreciate the language and was ready to strike him. The fat lady held back his hand and said, "Don't bother! I am not going to waste my time to convert them on my birthday. No wonder they are sick. I got out of the dungeon, but you are going to stay in forever." She turned to her group and said, "Take me out of here before I squash them like little balloons." The chief nurse was advised to intervene. By the time she appeared on the scene, the fat lady had disappeared.

JULY 5

The radiology center was closed for the national holiday.

I was collecting my thoughts in front of the statue of the Blessed Mother in a sunny day.

Spirituelle showed up with her son and told me that she was expecting a miracle. I looked at her with compassion and a pinch of disbelief. I was going to remind her that the time was running out for miracles, but I did not wish to hurt her feelings. She carried a bunch of documents in her hands and began to unravel them, one by one, to demonstrate that the chronology of a saint's events were analogous to her life situations. At one point, she stopped talking and asked me, "Do you believe that a miracle will come to me." Again, I took my time before I answered. She was waiting impatiently for my reply. Finally, I said, "Everything is possible. There are all sorts of miracles that occur in our daily life and we don't even recognize them. Each one of us is called to determine the significance of an event according to his or her religious belief. The type of miracle you are so ardently begging from heaven is very rare. Remember that at Lourdes, since 1858, only sixty-five real miracles have happened, almost one every three years. Medicine and science must recognize behind any reasonable doubt and without any scientific explanation that you are clinically healed, if that happens."

She lowered her head and did not respond. I did not want, by any means to weaken her faith, therefore, I continued, "Miracles take place all around us, but due to our human ignorance, they hide, so to speak. Everything falls into God's hands and follows his plan." I saw a couple of tears falling down her cheeks. I handed her my handkerchief, but she turned around and went back home.

The same afternoon, Spirituelle was in front of the statue just when I was having a real hard time. I was collapsing by heat exhaustion. I was in no mood to recite the Rosary. I would have preferred to say it later when the heat subsided. I could see it on her face. The woman was languishing internally and I did not want to deprive her joy and the solace of encountering Christ. I did not want to act like an alien indifferent to her pain. Surely, I was living an earthly hell and the flame of my sanity was getting dimmer; yet, I tried to collect all of my strength and follow her. She smiled and said, "I am ready."

The reader cannot imagine how miserable I felt. That treasure of a human being had come also to keep me company, to alleviate my agony, to cry out to the Blessed Mother with me, to come and rescue me from loneliness and depression. So, I sank into the folding chair made of cloth and took the Rosary from my pants pocket. To my surprise, instead of starting the prayers, she recounted once again, step by step her vicissitudes. She rever berated her hope for a miracle. She was quite sure that she was going to be the recipient of that miracle, so that, with the second miracle the nun was going to be sanctified. Somehow she was absolutely determined that she was going to make a difference. I made an attempt to explain to her that only God makes miracles, but she bent her head down without replying. I kept on looking at her in silence. I asked myself over and over again how God could be so far away from a woman who felt so close to Him. Suddenly, she broke down in tears. I remained speechless. Suddenly, she stopped as fast as she had started.

The quick change of mood made me wonder about the next step. I did not forget my plight, but I did the best I could to cope with it. She must have noticed my suffering and shifted her thoughts. "You won't believe it!"

"Believe what?" I responded with poise.

"You can ask my husband here. He is a protestant."

"Ask him what?" I begged her.

"Last spring, we were in the kitchen. We were praying when in the sky the sun opened up a passage through a jungle of clouds and its rays came straight on us. The phenomenon lasted a couple of minutes. During that brief time, we lost consciousness and became clouds in the splendor of that light."

"This supports what I have been saying all along that somebody loves you from up there."

She laughed and like a little child she shouted, "I want a miracle! I want a miracle! I want . . ."

"My fair lady," I said in a convincing way, "If you don't get it, I do not know who else should deserve it."

She was overjoyed with my comment and urged me to start the Rosary.

At the radiology department, I was absent minded. I felt like I was doped up. I did not see anyone. I did not hear anyone. I did not feel anything. Phoenix was interested in her coffee and cheese crackers.

JULY 7

Each time I talked about to my brother or sister, I assured them of living a normal life. In reality, I would not go as far as labeling the minutest problems that radiology was causing to me. At nine o' clock, my head was like in a fog. I was unable to hear or to talk to anyone. I felt week, too weak to carry on even the most basic needs. Gradually, my brother's warning about radiology was becoming reality. I sank into the cloth chair I keep in the garage, but I did not sleep. My mind was traveling at light speed between fantasy and reality. I resembled a boxer, who after a knockdown has no strength to get up. I opened and closed my eyes vicariously.

Three hours later, I attempted to stand up. I wobbled and fell on the same chair. More than once, I tried to raise myself on my feet. The puppy walked slowly toward me with her usual cadence and sat on my side. I paid particular attention to her nose, so cute and so unique. A mysterious feeling of warmth ran through my veins. I picked her up and laid her on my chest. It was at that point that I fell asleep. When I woke up, my mind was clear.

Phoenix said, "Where is your God? You build this shrine, you write religious articles, you go to St, Anthony Novena, just to say a few, but in ultimate analysis, you do you find now that you need help? Nobody! Absolutely nobody! Did you ever see your Lady? Did she ever speak to you as you claim she does with seers of Medjgorie? Be realistic! Don't keep on sleeping! Wake up! You are a living dream. I can't believe it! If you do not help yourself, nobody will. Do you understand it?" Her voice assumed a crescendo that sounded more appropriate in a theater hall than at my house." She got tired and left.

JULY 8

One of the exercises that I do in the morning consists in lying on the back and keeping my feet high for about five minutes. The next step is to bend even more backward until my feet almost reach the floor. The reader may very well surmise why I am unable to make the contact. One more minute and I return to my initial position. I repeat this exercise three times. The descent from a high to a low trajectory, while being on a back position makes the older folks very vulnerable to back injuries. A fast landing may cause vertebral distortions. Not to mention neck and back muscle spasms. The objective of this exercise is to give additional elasticity to the body and to postpone the consequences of past injuries or the age impact. Many years ago, Dr. Toma suggested I have back surgery. I am glad I refused it. No doubt, at this point, my main concern is to slow down the damage of the radioactivity.

Prior to the clinical ascertainment of the prostate cancer, I experienced light pains and abnormal warm feeling in the tale bone area. I brought it to the urologist's attention, but he dismissed it as a temporary symptom of vitamin deficiency and did not have any correlation with the prostate. Despite his assurance, my suspicions increased. At the completion of the sessions, the same fastidious condition persisted in an alternating movement, like the waves of the sea. I used many techniques to overcome the problem. I placed the feet high on another chair while I was lying with my back down, produced intermittent relief. These were times when the discomfort would be incessant for weeks. Of course, I got apprehensive. The pain spread internally and I feared that something more serious was at the bottom of it. The doctor had dismissed any legacy with the prostate. The only comfort came from my family doctor who claimed that my kidneys' function was normal.

I reported the problem to my eldest sister, who had always an advice to offer at any time for any inconvenience. She suggested I wrap in a cloth a hot brick. I tried to explain to her that I was well aware of that remedy, but she insisted that such an application would undoubtedly bring me benefits. In reality, I lacked the willpower to pursue that objective.

In the gym, I laid for fifteen minutes in hot water to alleviate the pressure at the lower section of my back. It was there the origin of the bowels irritability. I was very convinced of it. Unfortunately, the Jacuzzi did not provide any relief, so, I concluded that radiation was the real culprit. But, in all those vicissitudes, I learned that each time I laid down, the fastidious condition would disappear. Standing up became symptomatic of a gloomy omen.

JULY 9

THE EPILOGUE

And, so, after forty three sessions of radiology, I came at the end of my horrifying experience.

A friend of mine told me many years ago that her doctor assured her that having a bowel movement two or three times a day was healthy. Believe me, friend reader, I dislike wholeheartedly this low language, but it is part of our human condition and my objective is to help other sick people.

In the months preceding the therapies, I ascribed the bowel pains to the unhealthy prostate. The urologist excluded that association, but he did not offer any explanation either. I did not urge him to expend the issue because the waiting room was overcrowded.

During the day, I did my best to ignore the pains or I pretended that I was feeling well. I tried to be active as much as I could. The problems began when I sat down on a chair or couch. Depression suddenly inundated me, behind any imaginational level.

I visited the rest room from three to four times a day. The doctor appeared unconcerned, but I was! He would never allow anything unusual to be associated to the therapy, not even the food. Well, he did not convince me. My diet relies heavily on fruits and vegetables. I knew that it had to be something else.

At night, I noticed a drop in my foot temperature. My feet are cold. I have to use heavy socks, otherwise, I am restless. It was very distressful! I had been a soccer player and I still ran six months a year from May to October. Of course, I could not understand my state of frigidity. I feared that I was a recipient of a heart attack. The blood circulation was utterly low the body's extremities and rendered my nights sleepless. In the past, my feet were abundantly warm. The shift was too abnormal to accept it. In a few instances, I thought that it would have been also the presence of stigmata, but I scuffled quickly that idea and called myself 'ignorant.'

As I mentioned earlier, I was forced to wear socks at night and I, almost, resumed sleeping on a regular basis for the few hours I could. Subsequent to radiology, my blood condition ameliorated and I could do without them in warm days. In winter, the circulation suffers more, but I have to wait and see.

The oncologist's office had a conflict with the urologist's staff on who had to see me first after the completion of the radiation sessions. The oncologist made his secretary call the other office and cleared the misunderstanding. I went for a blood test prior to my final visitation with Dr. Matamonstruos. Again, it was a tortuous experience. I ended up with an amateur nurse, who was learning how to use the needle. He did not want to admit it, but wanted to spread the impression that he was a pro at it. He checked the arms and asked which vein was the most suitable for drawing the blood. Precious time passed by without doing anything. Finally, he pierced the skin with the syringe, but poked at the vein. He repeated it three times until he succeeded. I felt much relief when he asked me to hold on the gauze for he was going to secure it with a piece of adhesive.

A week later, I arrived at the radiology center five minutes earlier. The nurse led me to Dr. Matamonstruos office and asked to sit. The doctor would come right back. As we all know, doctors are never on time. No doubt about it, his delay caused me a lot of irritation. My blood pressure increased and I started to display overt symptoms of nervousness.

I checked my watch. The doctor was twenty minutes late. When he finally showed up, he had a glove in his right hand. He asked me to pull down my pants for the rectal. I almost died. It seemed that a stone entered my body. I was about to scream, but, at the last moment, I was able to suppress the pain. I endured the last seconds of that trial. The doctor had used a coarse glove much thicker than the usual ones that made me sweat. Dr. Matamonstruos did not proffer a word. He unfolded the glove from his hand and threw it in the trash. Then, he sat on the chair in front of the computer and pulled out my file.

As soon as I pulled up my pants and regained my composure, he asked me, "Does the water trickle when you pass water?"

"No, doctor, I don't think so."

"Do you feel any pain?"

Upon my negative reply, he said, "Your PSA lowered from 6.7 to 1.2, the lowest it can be. I expected to go as low as 5."

I was jubilant! I did not know how to express my joy. I was immensely relieved. God had finally showed me his presence.

He asked me, "Don't you have anything to add?"

"Well, I am a bit curious to know how my wife's cousin from Cleveland had lowered his PSA to 0.08."

"That is because he had the prostate surgically removed."

"Doctor, excuse me! Can the PSA go up again?"

"No, it will eventually go down even more." And, he accompanied the words with the movement of his hands.

"Doctor, he claims that he doesn't visit the rest room with frequency anymore and he will see his urologist every three months for the next two years. He also has to take some additional medicine to counterattack the tumor resurgence."

The doctor did not discompose himself. "His case is more serious."

I knew that I would not see him anymore, therefore, I added, "Doctor, my cousin in Toronto had a similar condition, but he underwent only 36 sessions, instead of the forty three I had. Moreover, he has to see the urologist every three months to have a hormone shot in his belly. This procedure will last two years. Six months have gone by and he feels terrific."

"As for the hormone shot," he responded, "I must caution you that we are talking about different cases. Don't put yourself on the same level of others."

I had exhausted my questions. The doctor looked at me and said, "Are you still running?"

"Most certainly! Two weeks ago, I ran a mini marathon and I came second in my group."

He was startled and, stretching his right hand added, "Go! You have won the greatest race of your life."

Phoenix' Tragedy

Toward the end of Mimi's therapy, Phoenix went to the pharmacy. She had been having an unusual pain for the past two months at the lower abdominal region. She wanted to scout the pharmacist's opinion first. She stopped at the local pharmacy and talked with the first one she encountered. He was about thirty years of age, tall with a moustache a la Clark Cable. He showed a few extra pounds on his belly, but not to be considered obese. He smiled and greeted her, "Hi, how can I help a tasty girl like you?"

"A quite adventurist language for a professional like you, won't you agree with me?"

"I am out of service at this moment. In fact, I am on my lunch break."

"I see . . ." responded Phoenix with a smirk. "This means that I can't ask you a question anymore," she added.

"No, no, indeed, you can ask me any question you wish," he insisted with gentleness.

"Never mind . . . Some other time."

A short distance away, but in the same aisle, two friends of Phoenix were observing the scene with particular interest. They pretended to get some items from the shelves, but, in reality, they were looking at Phoenix' direction with the corner of their eye.

Phoenix did not make any inquiry, neither she was able to buy any medicine. At least temporarily, the pharmacist was more interested in her that in anything else. Phoenix could not be bothered and moved to the bakery section of the store. An old high school acquaintance recognized her and kissed her on the cheeks, "How, how are you, stranger? I haven't seen you for a decade."

'Tempus fugit' said the Romans.

"Vow! You still remember the mottoes of that noble and ancient language. I marvel at your memory voluminosity."

"Don't exaggerate! Until Rome lives, Latin will never die."

"That's for sure, like your beauty."

"Take it easy."

"I mean it. By the way, how is the family?"

"We have been going through some tough times. My husband was diagnosed with prostate cancer,"

"Sorry to hear that. How are you going to cope with that?"

"In what sense?"

"I mean you are young and full of joy, while he won't be able to meet your expectations. Can I invite you for a lunch tomorrow?"

"You may, but I can't accept it." The tone turned serious and she said, "Listen, young Casanova. I never betrayed my husband. Why should I betray him now when he needs me the most? Shop around. You may find a lost ship."

Her friend remained astonished. He did not have the strength to bid 'good-bye' to her. Her statement was so powerful that shook him off his boots.

The two ladies, in the meantime, abandoned their plan for the shopping list and threw occasional glances to Phoenix. Evidently, they compiled a long line of gossip because upon returning home, they made their top priority to invite some neighbors for a coffee hour. We saw Phoenix at the pharmacy engaging in a romantic conversation with a pharmacist. You should have seen the glare on their face," said one of them.

"Another young man kissed her," added the second one.

A guest made a provocative statement, "Lately, she has been displaying an eccentric demeanor. Maybe, her husband is no longer interested in her."

A third guest interjected, "You mean that she is not interested in him anymore. Remember that he has just finished radiation therapies?"

The coffee hour ended, but the gossip continued in the neighborhood.

Phoenix' health deteriorated. She became progressively irritable and refused to see a doctor. It took her family's pressure to make an appointment with a gastrointestinal specialist.

The surgeon was in the fifties, short with spectacle and a prominent belly. He was a charismatic character and, most of the time, in good humor. It was without doubt that his gentle personality played an important role in allaying the patience's fear, but it was mostly due to his nature rather than trying to use it as a technique. Phoenix had no difficulty in conversing with him amicably from the first meeting.

"Good morning, doctor."

"Good morning, my darling. For those eyes, I would kiss the stars and for those cheeks, I would go to the end of the world."

"Easy, easy, doctor!" interrupted him the nurse. Don't get carried away. You have the waiting room full of patients . . ."

"With this nurse around me, I feel constricted even in my movements," joked the doctor. Then, I am going to sing an aria Puccini's Tosca. I have the voice of a tenor, not like Caruso, of course, but . . ."

The nurse giggled. The doctor realized that he could not convince her, and changed tune, "My dear Phoenix, what seems to bother you?"

"I have been suffering from abdominal pains for a while. Lately, they have increased in intensity. I do not know what causes them. I do not smoke and I do not drink wine. Once in a while, a glass, you know . . . , but the problem persists."

"Very well," responded the eminent oncologist. "First of all, let us talk about the symptoms. Do you have irregular menstruation?"

"At times."

"Are you havng diarrhea?"

"Doctor, there are days when I go four or five times. I can't control it."

"Do you have constipation?"

"Like anybody else. Every month, I have to drink prune juice. If it does not suffice, I have to recur to suppose*

"Do you experience internal bleeding? Do you know what I mean?"

"Perfectly! Yes, I do, occasionally."

The doctor took a stick and pointed to the picture of a human body hanging on the wall. "I have a pretty good idea of what it may be, but let us proceed cautiously. We can do two things in order to determine the culprit and its location. We can do either a pelvic test or a physical test. Now, any tumor, or anything out of the ordinary, will eventually surface and we will identify it."

"What do you think it may be, doctor?" Phoenix implored him with apprehension.

"As I said, we have to conduct some tests to ascertain my theory. I do not wish to speculate, but I can tell you that most likely we are dealing with ovarian cancer."

"Oh, doctor, that is not possible," cried out Phoenix and covered her face with both hands.

"Well, let us hope that is not the scenario I depicted. It was good that you came now because early detection is crucial for most cancers. We do not know for sure what causes ovarian cancer, but we have a pretty good idea. The prevailing theory on ovarian cancer points infections that are sexually transmitted."

"But, doctor," said Phoenix in tears, "I have only known my husband,"

"I don't doubt it. The second medical theory is that the disease is caused by many sexual partners or by premature sexual activities."

Phoenix closed her eyes, "Please, do not repeat that again, doctor. I don't consider myself a religious woman, but I can attest on my pre-matrimonial chastity and post matrimonial fidelity to my husband."

The doctor tried to switch a bit the questions even though they were on the same subject, "Are you a smoker?"

"Not really . . . I quit a long time ago. I think I mentioned it earlier."

The doctor looked straight in her eyes and said, "Listen carefully, once again. We are not completely sure what causes ovarian cancer. We have an ocean of theories, but no facts. However, you may consider yourself safe if you do not fall in one of those categories that I have enumerated."

"Doctor, I am a strong willed person and I can assure you that I never gave in to any demand of any young man courting me."

"I believe you. I just want you to understand that we have many suspect elements. For instance, do you have many children?"

"Yes, only two."

"Did you take birth control pills for years?"

"I had no need for them."

"Did you ever do a colonoscopy?"

"No doctor ever suggested me to do it."

"The last obstacle is the deficiency of the immune system. And for this reason you have to undergo a test. The nurse will schedule an appointment for a screening. As soon as the results will be available, she will call you to come and see me."

"At this point, what am I supposed to do?"

"Relax."

Phoenix followed the nurse and made all the necessary arrangements. In one single morning, she completed the test and waited for the call.

Two days later, Phoenix received an urgent call from the doctor's secretary. She had to report immediately to his office. Phoenix got in the car and rushed to the office. She even went through a few yellow lights. A police car spotted her and observed her on the next traffic light. She was lucky that the light was green. Mimi' was oblivious of his wife's drama. He attempted to find out what was going on, but she changed the subject.

The surgeon was sitting behind his desk. He took off the spectacles and placed them between his hands. He greeted her and asked her to sit. He was not smiling. He looked at her and in a low voice said, "The test results are here. I am sorry to inform you that my suspicion was confirmed."

"Which it means that I have ovary cancer," asked her with intense trepidation.

The oncologist twisted his lips and answered, "I am afraid that it is so." And, put back the eyeglasses if you want to read the statement. Phoenix began to sob and the nurse did her best to calm her down.

She asked her if she wished to call her husband, but she refused. She reiterated her position that under no circumstances he was supposed to know it.

When Phoenix stopped sobbing, the nurse handed a box of facial tissues to her and she wiped her face. The doctor waited for her to get recomposed and asked her, "What is your wish?"

"We can do two things to determine the culprit. There are two main tests available:

One is pelvic and another is physical. Both check the presence of cancer or abnormal cell assemblage. Unless you undergo one of those tests, there is no way for me to ascertain what is going on for sure."

"OK," responded Phoenix with apprehension. "On a list from 0 to 10, how do you rate the success of either treatment?"

"My dear, "said the doctor with the outmost patience. "I must be honest with you. It depends how far gone is the cancer and how the is the patient's health. How you respond is fundamental. In your case, the cancerous cells have been travelling at an abnormal speed and I cannot offer any plausible explanation. In other circumstances, I would give you many hopes because it is treatable. And, lastly, do not forget the condition of the immune system. We could start either with a laser cell killer or hysterectomy. You may opt for surgery and radiation . . . . It is entirely up to you. If we can arrest it, it would be a miracle."

Phoenix lowered her head in a sign of defeat. From the look, the doctor and the nurse evinced an internal drama. The oncologist stood there silent waiting for an answer that appeared never to come. In the waiting room, patients were getting restless. Phoenix' visit was taking far too long than expected. They were getting impatient. The atmosphere was somber, funereal. The doctor decided that it was time to break the ice, "You have to decide on which course of action to take, my dear. Maybe, you should consult with your husband."

"How can I give this horrific news to him when he has been going through hell himself in recent months?"

"I understand your dilemma. On one hand, it would be advisable to inform him, but that would throw him in a depressive mood and undermine his rehabilitation process or even jeopardize it. Not to mention the children who would suffer a staggering psychological impact. The second suggestion would be to abstain from revealing the seriousness or the advanced stage of the disease."

Phoenix raised her head as a proud soldier and stated, "Doctor, I will take my chance."

"What is it?" inquired the doctor with anxiety.

"I will take the second option."

"Very well," replied the doctor with a sense of satisfaction. "And, as for the treatment, have you reached a decision?"

"Yes, it is my desire to wait. Once my husband has recuperated, then, I will face the inevitable."

"I do not blame you. If there is time," responded the doctor with aplomb.

"If there is still time," repeated Phoenix.

"One last suggestion, before you leave . . . When you are out of this office, try to act as you have always been. Be yourself."

Phoenix jumped on her feet like a feline. "I will do that, doctor. Thank you for your advice."

THREE MONTHS LATER

After three months, the bowl situation was unchanged. One day, I visited the bathroom eight times. Either I caught a virus or I was in a regressive stage. During the night, I started shivering. I was almost sure that it was symptomatic of the flu. I must confess that I felt relieved. It is not that I like having the flu, but, at least, I knew what I had. I received confirmation the following day when my conditions returned to normal. I still see lights and shadows on the frequent visitations to the rest room. I force myself to believe that it is due to the high amount of fruit and vegetables that I eat on a daily basis.

During the week, Dr. Hei's office called me to remind me that I had a scheduled colonoscopy the following day. I was not enthused at all. I inquired with the nurse why I was due to a second one after four years. Other people tell me that it is given every ten years. She informed me that the last time, the doctor found a polyp that could have grown into a tumor and he cleaned it. Now, he wanted to make ascertain that id did not grow back.

At the right time, I was at Community General. I could not refrain from contemplating how the world is changing. The first time I had colonoscopy it was about fifteen years ago and I had it done without anesthesia. In forty minutes, I went home.

This time, I was asked to go one hour earlier, fill out papers, sign the, dress up in hospital garments, take the blood pressure, and, I don't remember what else. Worse of all, I got an injection that put me to sleep. Before that moment, the nurse asked me if I were ready. My reply was simple and direct, "I have the Blessed Mother with me. What else do I need? Let's go!" My friend reader, I passed out instantly into the world of nothingness, of non-existence. Although I was still breathing, I was unconscious. I was like dead. When I woke up I asked the nurse if it was over. She nodded.

In the aftermath, I pondered for a while, and still do on the inescapable reality of death and on our ignorance to prepare ourselves for the inevitable. We have the tendency to procrastinate our responsibilities with the final moments and, sometimes, it is too late to "reshuffle the cards."

The doctor showed up before my departure and he put the thumb up and said, "Everything is clean. I will see you in four or five years." The news shrugged off a heavy load from my mind, but I could not repel the protest, "Why I have to go through it in four or five years and not ten? Well, I let the reader draw his/her conclusions.

In the last few months, I have been drinking a special super antioxidant juice. It is very expensive. The jar does not even last a week between my wife and me. I should add that we drink half of a small glass each. Through some researches, I found out that the juice I drink is good for the colon. At this point, I can only ascribe to it the colon's health.

Colonoscopy revealed also a negative truth. According to the doctor, the bottom is red and it is caused by radiation. He said, "If the hemorrhoids bleed, come here and I will cauterize them. No big deal!"
"It is no big deal for him, not for me!"

I had hoped that my fight with the monster was over, but not yet. I looked in the mirror and I saw that my face and hands were bloody. I had just sustained the bloodiest fight of my life. I looked like a gladiator, who, at the end of a brutal fight with his rival, was about to fall down from exhaustion and mortal wounds. His survival depended on the extent of lacerations and wounds inflicted upon him by his enemy. The only one capable of emitting a verdict of life and death was the emperor. In my case, it was the doctor. Yes, the verdict was in my favor, but I was extremely cautious. Many times, during my life time, I was considered myself being on a winner streak, only to be disappointed later. My last check with the urologist, everything seemed right. The machine did not reveal anything abnormal and neither the rectal examination. The biopsy threw everything and everybody off balance! Since then, I learned that a battle is not over until the referee declares it ended.

The Dragon and
the Exorcist

One day, I (Chris) asked Mimi', "Can you visualize the monster?"

"I will describe it to you in many details the Dragon."

"Don't change the name," the reader gets confused. "The beast is the general name we identify an animal. A monster is terrifying animal. At times, we apply that name to a person in a positive or negative way. A dragon is a specific beast."

"For me, they all have the same connotation, but if you, as an author, think that for reading purpose I have to make such a distinction, I will. All in all, I do not think that the readers mind it if I use them synonymously. The most preponderant part of this book is the message that has to seep through the veins and arteries, until it reaches the aorta.

I apologize to the reader if the author interrupted me before. What I wanted to say was that I could not see the dragon. I could only visualize it not in my imagination, but in a way that seemed to be real. It was an image that one sees on the computer or TV screen. That vision cannot be tested by tactile senses. It is caused by the reason's eyes. I could feel, though, the tentacles on the organ of my body that he was brutally attacking, slowly, like a snake, but savagely. Not content to have gained possession of this prey under his curved long nails, the dragon was poised to spread his poisonous hairy roots to the whole body.

One night, I saw the dragon under a different profile. The snake had multiple heads. The central head acted like a computer, or brain, or main office. Each head acted autonomously, each having a different authority operating under the supreme supervision of the "central office." The first head breathed in me and my body swallowed up till it achieved the shape of the earth. The second head withdrew a sword from her brains and sliced the clouds on the Caspian Sea that flooded the adjacent area and killed all its inhabitants. The third head hurled a rock on Mount Vesuvius that caused a huge crater and the magna flowed down the mountain and buried the entire house along the way.

I will not go on describing the horrific rest of the heads, but it suffices to ay that each time one of them struck a geographical area of the earth one organ of my body felt unbearable pains. As I mentioned previously, the epicenter was the main head of the dragon. It had made the bottom section of the earth the base from which it would launch its attacks. It appeared evident that the final goal was the total subjugation of the planet earth.

To conclude on the dragon, a fourth head spiffed fire from its furnace, the brains, and hit some galaxies. These fell on an area of Israel (that represented my head) and devoured millions of acre of land, which lay waste now and it is called Negev Desert. The stench emanated by the animal carcasses was so offensive that killed every form of living thing in a one hundred mile radius. I started to sweat profusely and screamed to the mountains, "Come on down and give rest to this vacillating body. Oh, God, where are You? Are You blind to the destructive force of the dragon? Are you deaf to the tears and suffering of Your creation? Are You insensitive to the plight of the human race? Why are you so insensitive? Why do You distance Yourself so much from the most perfect part of Your creation, man.

You created him in Your image and likeness and now You abandon him? He is the only one who can love You; the only one You entered into an alliance and the only one for whom Your Son died for on the cross. He has no more value for You? You have emarginated from us. You have abandoned us. If this is true, I do not wish to be part of the human race.

Right at that moment, the Archangel Gabriel descended from heaven and engaged in a fierce battle with the beast that lasted forty three days. Before, the dragon withdrew in defeat; he slapped me with its tail. The smack was so powerful that I fell unconscious with my face flat on the floor. When I, finally and slowly gained knowledge of the surrounding, I realized that I could move the mandibles and my vocal chords where no longer functioning. I made an attempt to wake up Phoenix, but I was unable due to the loss of my voice. For forty three days I was mute. I was drenched in sweat and barely managed to take a shower while I was still in a state of confusion.

To carry on a conversation, I had to resort to writing or to gestures. Most of the time, I was alone in my room. I stared at the wall, but it was mute like me. When the time elapsed, I began to enunciate a few syllables, like a baby. The process of vocal recuperation was a slow process, but, at the end, I regained the precious gift of the tongue.

Everybody knows that Brazilians are very Catholics and I followed my parents in their faith. I was never an observant Catholic. In fact, I hardly attended the Mass on Sunday. I went on Christmas and Easter. Contrary to the Brazilian soccer players who make an ostentatious display of their religiosity by touching the grass and making the sign of the cross as they enter the field, I felt no necessity for it. By the time I was well into marriage, I lost every trace of it.

The reader could ask me what I expected from God. And, I would reply, "Nothing except an act of reciprocity." I felt like a wanderer, stranded in the middle of a desert without hope of being rescued.

Here finished Mimi's monologue. From now on, Chris will narrate for us the last episodes of Mimi's and Phoenix story.

Phoenix did not wish to interrupt her husband. As soon as he finished, she said, "I can no longer hold my patience. I do not identify myself with any denomination anymore. The Catholic Church only now is recognizing the urgency of cleaning up her acts with the priestly abuses. Priestly vocation is languishing. What does it tell you? The church does not serve anymore the spiritual needs of the people. This is not to say that other religious groups are doing better. They are smelling blood and go after the agonizing patient, but they are no better. I would rather spend my free time at the casino."

Mimi' did not continue the conversation. Perhaps, he had talked enough on that subject. His final days at the radiotherapy were brutal. Without the religious faith behind him to support him, he had no other place to turn to for moral encouragement, he fell into a deep depression debilitating even more his body and mind's resistance. There were times during the day when he was completely out of reality. His body was dwindling. He had to hold on the chairs before he fell on the couch as a dead corpse. His stomach was constantly in turmoil and was ready to give up the fight, "I can't take it anymore."

But his sister kept on prodding him, "You are at the last of the tour de force. You can't quit. You got to do it for your children, for yourself. Never give up!" On the way back to the kitchen, he stumbled against three or four pair of shoes that his wife left in the hallway. He looked on the table, but Phoenix had not prepared the lunch. She was sunbathing on the terrace.

In the meantime, the legal process for the separation had reached the final stage. In a few days the lawyers of both spouses would present them some documents, explain the obligations and rights of each one of them and sign the papers. At the last moment, and in a surprise move, the judge opted for a "cushion period" or "grace period" during which the litigants could still find a peaceful solution to their ongoing matrimonial disputes or incomprehensions. The judge had taken this decision based on the health of one of the parties. He also ordered the spouses to attend marriage counseling sessions to smooth out their differences.

For Mimi' it was another blow to his psycho-somatic instability. Phoenix, instead, showed disinterest to her marital plight, "If that is what my husband wants, he can have it, but he has to remember that he will not see his children anymore during birthdays, school events, holidays . . . Someone suggested that I showed contempt for the judge's report. Actually, I have no qualms about it. I suppose he used wisdom." Suddenly, the atmosphere changed. She grabbed a statute of Jesus and threw it at him. Mimi' barely dodged it. "Are you crazy!" he said in an enraged voice, "Take it! Go with Him! Nobody wants you anymore, anyhow. Not even the dog."

"You follow Him! I am disassociated from Him already."

"I go to my lady fortune. She is my goddess."

"That is why she brought you and me to bankruptcy? If I did not open that business downtown, you would have sent me begging."

"That is not true and you know it."

"If you wish to stay in this house you have to learn a responsible lady."

"Quit abusing me, do you hear? You expect too much from me. You never show any interest in restaurants, casino or any other entertainment."

"You have no shame," replied her irate husband. He withdrew to his room and showed up about an hour later.

Mimi', by his nature, was extremely skeptical of the doctors. On July 6, 2011, the local newspaper printed a long article on robotic surgery. After reading it, Mimi' almost exploded with sarcasm, "Look here!" he said, pointing at one paragraph. An administrator admitted that some outcomes have been favorable while others have been unfavorable, and that some hospitals have been dishonest. It took years before someone within the hospital spoke objectively about it. The Da Vinci robot is used to perform mainly minimally invasive removal of prostate gland or for heart surgery and makes an incision as big as a dime versus the opening of a wide area in the abdomen or art region.

Mimi' recurred to other sources to confirm, at times, his own experience. When he was seventeen he went to see a dentist to fill in a tooth cavity. He was terrified. The dentist numbed the gum around the toot. A minute later, Mimi' walked out of the dentist's office enraged. He had pulled his tooth.

In America, two different dentists followed the same pattern and pulled two teeth when they could be saved. Finally, I got bold the next time and ordered the dentist not to touch any tooth. He went there to fix them, not to pull them. Today, he still has those teeth for standing up to his rights. One day, while in conversation with his friends about dental health, he exclaimed, "some dentists are dogs! They are criminals. They should serve a few years in jail! In the name of the almighty dollar, they trample on their professional duty and on the patients debility and ignorance. They betray their medical oath. And, many still do! They are unscrupulous managers of others' health. Don't they realize the human suffering and discomfort they cause? How many problems they create for poor people!"

Dr. Matamonstruos never described the post-therapy scenario to Mimi'. His last words were rather reassuring; "You won the greatest race of your life!" From then on, he was no longer going to report to him, but to the previous urologist.

Three months went by and Mimi' returned to Dr. Spilorch office to follow up on the radiation therapies. Mimi' thought that his ordeal was over, instead, he started all over again to deal with the same urologist. For some reasons, either for doctors' shortage or for the heavy clientele, nowadays, there are many nurse practitioners who do the same medical functions as a doctor. So, even though Mimi' disliked immensely to be visited by one of them, inevitably a female doctor doing the check up.

In one occasion, Mimi' even complained," I feel uncomfortable with a female doctor. My insurance pays for a doctor not for a practitioner." His protest was to no avail. The office justified the practice by pointing out that no many students are studying medicine. Mimi' responded, "Before there was a shortage of priestly vocation and many churches have been closed. I don't buy it. The truth is the peoples' attendance has diminished dramatically. Now, they claim that there is a shortage in doctors. What is the next shortage about?"

Chris advised him, "Mimi, if I were you, I would assume a more cautious attitude toward the medical field. There are outstanding doctors in the hospitals."

"Good Heavens!" exclaimed Mimi' losing a bit of his normal poise. In every profession or trade you find some conscientious, responsible, successful human beings. Each one of us owes them a tremendous respect for their dedication, honest y and superior knowledge, but the bed ones have discredited a noble and humanitarian profession. Their avidity is a disavowal of their oath."

"How can you prove it?" challenged him Chris.

"What more proof do you expect me to offer," responded an impatient Mimi'. "If my personal experience is unconvincing to you, I am going to resort to a third party to confirm my position. Last Sunday, I went to walk to raise money for a health cause at Beaver's Lake. Along the rural trail I was approached by a young lady who was a nurse. Among the various subjects we discussed, she revealed to me that she had been fired by a doctor who claimed that she was not making enough money for him."

"That is an intriguing case. I would like to find out the real reason, though, behind the dispute and final dismissal," interjected Chris, once again.

"I just told you! She was honest and advised patients not to get involved in unnecessary health expenditures." The doctor would not accept that practice and told her that her job was terminated."

Mimi' quit talking. He excused himself and came back a couple of minutes later with two big glasses of cranberry juice with ice. Chris appreciated the cold drink in a sultry day although he had been practically a listener for the entire narration. Mimi' felt that he needed a short recess because his throat was getting dry. Suddenly, a lady's voice shrieked in the air. It came from the terrace and it was his wife. She had been sunbathing for quite a while. "Honey, bring me a glass of juice to me too."

"Can' you get up and get it yourself. Don't you see that we are engaged in a serious matter? We are busy."

"You are busy talking, but I am busy taking care of my health."

Mimi' frowned and shook his head. Chris attempted to reduce the dispute by asking Mimi'; "You did not finish talking about the urologist."

"Oh, he is a dog! I wanted to quit him so many times . . . I cannot stand his rough mannerism."

Phoenix was ready to revamp the conflict with her husband, but Chris was quick to prevent her, "What makes you think he is ill mannered?"

"Imagine an urologist using a thick glove for a rectal. I had never seen before that type of painful glove. It causes discomfort and pain. His lack of sensitiveness prompted me to take a drastic decision. I was not going to schedule another appointment in less than six months. On my way out, I looked at the card. I was fainting. She gave me an appointment in three months.

The time flew and Mimi' was back at the urologist office. The good news was that the PSA had receded to 0.6. He was overwhelmed, but that did not prevent him from complaining over the use of the rough glove. "We have this method of testing now, "the doctor tried to justify himself.

"Yes, but what happened to the thin glove?" insisted Mimi'.

"The doctor gave in, "O.K. I will use that the next time."

The nurse knocked on the door and entered. The urine test showed traces of blood in it. Mimi' became livid. He wanted to wreck the office. The doctor ignored him. He turned his attention to the file on the desk and ordered Mimi' to go downtown, to the radiotherapy office and scan the whole abdominal section. On the way back, he would send a probe in Mimi's bladder to ascertain that it was not the origin of the problem . . .

For unknown reasons, the doctor left without any explanation. Mimi' got ventured to ask the nurse, "What is the cause of the blood in the urine?"

"Most likely, the radiotherapies," she replied. "In fact, that is it."

"And, why, do you inform me now?"

"In reality, the problem began when you terminated the therapy sessions. Usually, after a while, that malfunction disappears. In your case it persists."

On his way home, Mimi' was a bundle of nerves. In the car, he yelled, "God, where are You? Can You tell me? Forget it! It is a waste of time! Wherever You are, if You are, you are not interested in me. I definitely close my book with You."

In her pajama attire, Phoenix was searching for her lucky charm. She had even ordered a local artist to paint her proudly showing the object. I am not going to ask to the supposedly Controller of the universe whose adobe could be trillions of light miles from here, to find it for me. It would be futile. My prayers always fall on deaf ears. I should implore my Lady Fortune, Mother of all destinies, to help me in this endeavor. She has been very gracious to me many times in the past.

Right at that moment, Mimi' pressed a few numbers on the cellular and the door opened. He did not say a word. Phoenix said, "What happened? Did you lose your voice? Are you in bad humor again?"

"How can I be in good humor? Each time I go to the office of this dog doctor, he finds me with something wrong. I have no more faith in anyone.

Phoenix made a gesture of disinterest, "I lost it long time ago," she said. "You believed in someone being dead. I do not believe in dead gods."

"Why did you go to church when you were a young girl," asked Mimi' without looking at her.

She yawned. When she finished, she shook her head and said, "I did it to please my parents."

"Just to please others, eh?" replied her husband with a touch of irony.

"Now that I am an adult, I use my mind. I have my own goddess, but she won't help me unless I find my amulet."

Mimi' was climbing the stairs that led to his bedroom. He woke up at noon of the following day.

On the due date, Mimi' went through the abdominal scanning. The nurse injected a substance in his right arm and ordered him to lie down on the machine. He hated to undergo another radioactive test. He wanted to run away, but he had no choice if he wanted to ascertain the cause of his problem. As soon as the test was over, he pulled up his pants, brought down the shirt and ran to the street where he kicked a garbage can.

Once in the car, he called the nurse again, "Listen! If you do not find a trace of blood in the urine on my next visit to your office, do I have to go through the procedure with the probe?"

"Not at all!" she assured him.

The day of the truth finally arrived and Mimi' took the urine test. The doctor did not give him the results right away. He made the technical preparations for the probe to test the bladder without anesthesia. The insertion of the probe without Vaseline caused excruciating pains to Mimi'. He called on all sorts of help. He was heard saying," Jesus! Blessed Mother." But the pain intensified to the level, where he could no longer bear it. He began to shake, to rattle, to agonize.

The doctor shouted, "Mr. O' Fab . . . or whatever it is, you are making a disservice to yourself! Stop it, otherwise I will be compelled to terminate the test ahead of time and, therefore, annul it." A few seconds elapsed and he added, "I will not repeat this test again." Mimi' received that news with special with special joy, but he was too frail to reply.

To assist the doctor, there were two nurses. The younger tried to console me by passing her hand over my forehead. Mimi' made an effort, "Thank you so much for being very kind to me." A few tears streamed down his cheeks. She took her personal handkerchief and wiped his face.

The urologist did not see anything. He was careful in reassembling the tools. At the end, he gave his final report, "All the tests are negative. There is no trace of the blood in the urine. Nonetheless, you have a couple of cysts on the kidneys. In October, we will run other tests to find out if they have grown or not. If there is no growth, you are all set."

The results were extraordinarily positive for Mimi', especially, if the future test will not show any increase in the size of the cysts. He was weak. The doctor and the older nurse left. The young nurse helped Mimi' to dress up. She made him sit for a few minutes until he recomposed himself and gained some confidence. In the meanwhile, she placed the furniture in order, but did not stop giving occasional glances to him. He was breathing heavily and began to sweat profusely. She stopped working and wiped his face once again and held him tight to her body. He took her hand in his and whispered to her, "I shall never forget you. If, as they say, there are a few angels on the face of this earth, you are certainly one of them. I would . . . . , but, I can't." She smiled and muttered, "Good-bye."

At home, Mimi' felt notably perturbed. The young nurse had touched the strings of his heart. At the same time, he was confronted with another terrible experience. He went to the lavatory and noticed some drops of blood. He got scared. Immediately, he called the doctor's office and the older nurse explained to him that it was a common occurrence. The discomfort would gradually disappear and so would the presence of the blood. She suggested drinking a gallon of water a day to alleviate the glands inflammation.

Chris visited Mimi' soon after. The air was somber. The mailman had just delivered two letters, one to Mimi' and the other to his wife. Their attorneys had brought the separation papers were to the final stage. They only needed their signatures. Neither one said a word. Phoenix appeared to be embedded in a strange meditation. She was sitting on the couch with both legs encroached, her eyes closed and her hands united as in the act of a prayer. Mimi', instead, kept on pulling the fingers of his hands. At the end of a stubborn silence, Mimi' broke the ice and said in a very low voice, "I have to sign up the separation paper."

Phoenix jumped on her feet with a feline agility. She opened her letter and read it. She refrained from making any comment. She withdrew to her private room and knelt before the painting of the Lady Fortune, she took a piece of paper and a pen and began writing, "My dear goddess, you are my only source of pride and successs. Help me to endure this tempting period. In case of success, I will build you a monument in front of my mansion. Since I lost my amulet, I lost my happiness and my fortune. Rehabilitate me; purify me; take me to new heights; let me fly like an eagle. I will glorify you every moment of my life. I am going to the casino right now to see if you keep your word. So, do not disappoint me. I need your help in these difficult moments of my life. My victory will be your victory."
She folded the paper and pinned it on her chest.

Phoenix was not a scary person. She had played football with boys in her younger age. Now, she was going to test herself. She united her hands and fixed her eyes on the Lady Fortune waiting for an answer. She was so intensely staring at the picture that she began to sweat. She was in deep meditation again. A raucous noise interrupted her thoughts. She woke up like from a dream. The painting started to crack. Blood from the brains seeped through the cracks and reached the prayer paper. The blood covered it and sponged it. A second noise, like an explosion wracked the rooms. The innumerable parts of the painting began to fall down at Phoenix feet. She withdrew terrified. Her eyes were vitreous, her hands stony, and her legs like trunks of trees. She made an effort to avoid the waves of blood, but she realized that she had lost mobility. The nerves were paralyzed. The Lady Fortune turned into a monster, whose tentacles were encircling her whole body. A cry, coming from Phoenix, lacerated the air. It was heard all over the mansion and its vicinity. The children were taking a walk with the assistant.

Mimi' and Chris heard the shout and ran to Phoenix room. Upon opening the door, they found a horrible spectacle before their eyes. The painting of Lady Fortune was no longer in the room, but Phoenix was a mask of blood. Mimi' made an attempt to revive her. Chris yelled, "Don't touch her! It is the blood of a monster."

Mimi' pulled back in horror. A minute or so passed by. Mimi' took courage, "Well, what do we do now?" he implored him.

"I surmise that you are not going to like my suggestion."

"What is it?" pressed Mimi, all excited.

"I see it as the only alternative in this shameful scenario."

Mimi' was listening attentively. When the answer did not come, he begged the author, "Speak up! Have you lost your tongue?"

Chris yawned, then, he said, "Only the Blessed Mother can bring peace to this house."

"What do you mean?"

"You have to call a priest."

"A priest? That is the last person I would like to see. Spare me from that agony, please," responded Mimi' in a desperate tone.

"If you want to restore order in your heart, there is no other alternative."

"What can he do for us? My wife is dying in the other room and instead of calling an ambulance, you expect me to call a prelate." Mimi' did not know what to do anymore. Finally, he took a decision, "You call him for me."

Don Valentin was an exorcist with a long experience behind his seventy years of age. He had driven the evil spirits out of the bodies of two thousand people. In more than one occasion he was the object of scorn and physical abuse during the rite, but he proceeded undaunted facing dangers for the sake of the man possessed by the devil. The most notable aspect of his work was his ability to score always success.

For this reason, a lady neighbor, alerted by the noise, inquired with Chris about the happening. The author, disturbed by the sight of the blood and all other abnormal events, left the premises temporarily to get some fresh air. The woman quickly suggested calling on the famous priest, which was done without Mimi's consent.

Phoenix was still lying on the floor in a sea of blood and breathing heavily. The presence of the exorcist changed her behavior. She launched profane epithets toward him. He stood there immobile sprinkling holy water on her body. Suddenly, she grabbed a tablet hanging on the wall and hurled it at her husband. It was the tablet of the Ten Commandments. The Tablet hit Mimi' right on the forehead and caused a heavy laceration. Surprisingly enough, no blood gashed out. He hit the wall with his back and slowly slid down resting in a sitting position on the floor. Many of the onlookers were frightened at that point. Phoenix took a chair and broke it on the exorcist's head. He fell unconscious with the chest over a chair. A muscular young man came to his aid and helped to revive.

As soon as he was able to resume his activity, the exorcist exclaimed, "Resurrectio Domini."

Phoenix responded angrily, "what do you want to know? It is all false. It is a story fabricated by your dirty clergymen."

"Don't spread lies anymore, you dirty pig!" The foam was coming out of her mouth like lava from a volcano.

The exorcist kept up the tempo, "In nomine Christi," he shouted and sprinkled the holy water on the woman. His face was a mask of sweat and intense involvement. "Son of the living God, "he shouted again. "Abandon this human abode!"

The evil spirit spat from the mouth of Phoenix and spread all over the exorcist's face. "Go away, man of God! Why have you come here to disturb me?"

The priest quickly wetted his handkerchief in the holy water and washed his face. He, then, brought it outside and put it on fire. Once again in the room, the exorcist demanded that the demons leave without delay, "I command you, in the name of Jesus, to run away from your prey and join your acolytes in hell."

The evil spirit growled, "Stop mentioning that name!"

Phoenix body rattled once, then, twice. It suspended itself in the air for about a minute and slammed against the bystanders. Many of them fell on top of each other and some got injured. A group of old women, with the rosaries in their hands decided to pray, but when they heard new threats from the demon, they kept themselves at a distance. In the meantime, Mimi' with his bewildered looks stood without moving his mouth. He looked petrified. Chris, unable to write notes in those circumstances, used a tape recorder and an iPod to consult at a later time.

The news spread rapidly, and a huge crowd gathered around the mansion. Somebody, among them, alerted the police that arrived with the sirens on and tried to bring order.

Don Valentin was being abused verbally with all sort of slur language. Chris will not report it because it is beneath his dignity to make such degrading references. The evil spirit shouted at one point, Phoenix' mandible made a move that sounded like a crack. The neck snapped backward and, then, twisted around. Fire rose from her head and along with it, a horrible stench that made everybody cover his mouth with a cloth. The smoke exited through the window. An explosion occurred. Phoenix head resumed the proper position and she began to breathe normally. The sweat got mixed with the blood and ran all over her debilitated body.

The exorcist took out the handkerchief from his pocket and wiped his brow, "Glory be to God through Jesus Christ now and forever!" The crowd responded, "Amen,"

No one dared to approach Phoenix. They were still afraid. A stout young man tried, but he received a punch from nowhere and flung through the window. When he got up with the help of his friends, his face was a dark mask with hematomas over and under the eyes. He never returned inside the mansion.

The exorcist did three times the sign of the cross and showered, once again, Phoenix body with holy water. He looked toward the heaven and exclaimed, "Gratia Tibi Domine." He had just finished God's praise that he heard a gnashing of the teeth and a loud sound.

Phoenix' body slid into a resting position. As in a constant change of moods, the onlookers' attention shifted outside. A bunch of dark clouds gathered in the atmosphere and formed a circle while the setting sun was still spraying with golden dust the horizon's entire background. Instantly, a light shone through the black clouds and turned them into an indescribable rosy color. The mysterious light danced for a few seconds. The exorcist opened his arms toward the heavens. The light rested on the window of Mimi's house. A Lady with a crown of twelve diadems appeared through the light. Under her feet, there was a dead, gigantic monster. She stretched her right arm toward Mimi' and Phoenix in a blessing gesture. The crowd was spellbound by the vision and fell on its knees and, so, did the police. The rare and mystifying event lasted for two minutes.

Someone quickly alerted the media who rushed into the area by helicopter. Cameramen and reporters descended a bit clumsy and started to interview the spectators. Inside, Mimi' and his wife were unable to speak. The vision had transcended their human understanding. Phoenix was still in a kneeling position. Her mouth was wide open. After the ball of light disappeared from the sky, the exorcist invited Phoenix to get up and wash up. She showed stains of blood all over her body. Someone tried to help her, but he prevented him from doing so. According to the prelate, no one should have touched her until after the ablution.

Mimi', too, was quite shaken by the event. For forty three minutes, he could not emit a sound. He felt in a state of mental dormancy. When the fog from his brains began to dissipate, he slowly made sense of reality, but he was still shaken by the vision. Outside, among the crowd, some of them were reciting the rosary, others were singing religious hymns.

The media surrounded the exorcist and pressed him questions. His religious garments were drenched with sweat and he had hard time wiping his face. Mimi' and Phoenix, finally arrived, surrounded by improvised bodyguards. The exorcist exclaimed, "As you have witnessed, the power of God is among us."
"They responded, "Amen! Hallelujah! Hallelujah!"

One of the reporters provoked him, "How come your first statement was, "Resurrectio Domini?"

"Satan is terribly afraid of Jesus' Resurrection."

"That is for the believers," insisted the reporter.

"For the non believers too, it is erroneous to interpret the Resurrection as a mystical exaltation."

"But Christians can approach it by faith."

"Not even," responded the exorcist. "It is based, instead, on the eye witnessing of people, for that reason, it is historical. In the year '54, St. Paul reminds us that he found it out from the twelve apostles."

"Another reporter, who arrived late at the scene, contested his version, "I am an atheist and fully believe that man is the owner of his destiny. It was Phoenix and her self-assertive willpower that allowed her to regain her sanity and identity."

The exorcist reflected briefly on the answer and replied, "Man is not the Alpha or Omega, as reported by the Catholic Catechesis. This means that he is not the origin or the end, but only a participant in the continuous flux of existence. He is not the essence or the existence. He does not possess any power, except that of loving. It is true that among the creation, he stands out as the most perfect machine, created in the image and likeness of God. He is the only one that entered into an alliance with the Creator and the only one who is able to love Him. Man is only a component in the process of the macroscopic existentialism."

A female cameraman raised her hand, "I do not see how creation points to a creator . . . What happened here could be the result of self-destructive imagination."

"Let me answer this last question before I go back to the rectory," responded the exorcist.

"When you look at a famous painting, you praise the content. By inference, you praise also the author of that work of art. By analogy, if there exists a relationship between art and the artist, then there is also a relationship between creation and Creator. The whole universe is an orchestra of different sounds that in unison manifest the glory of its director. The sun does it by giving light, energy and life to earth. The birds do it by their chirping. The flowers show it with their mosaic of wonderful colors, and so on, and so on . . . Now, the demons can stand neither the Resurrection nor the glorification of nature to God.

They cannot bear the intense light that the Supreme Master lets it shine on the universe. Everything is so simple! By using me in the eviction of the evil spirit from Phoenix body, He has shown us a glimpse of His power."

A carpenter was quickly summoned to fix the shattered window. It was dark when the bulk of the crowd streamed out of the area. The neighbors formed small circles and kept on commenting the event of the day. The lights were on the whole night at the mansion.

It took about a couple of weeks before the fumes of the exorcism started to evaporate. Mimi' and Phoenix secluded themselves for the time being. Neither one of them left the house. It was rumored that they self imposed a period of meditation. Chris did not even bother calling them during that span of time. At the end, he visited them on a Monday. He found both of them in the living room sitting around the big table. Chris was surprised to see the separation documents in front of them. He asked them, "What are you going to do about it?"

No one replied. Phoenix was staring out of the window. Her eyes were like two balls of bewildered fire. She vicariously picked up the pen and drew a heavy line. Then, she dropped the pen and slowly put in motion her hand over a portion of the document pulling it over her side. Mimi' laid his left hand on his side of the documents and pulled it toward him. Both hands ended up superimposing each other. The document was ripped on both sides.

Mimi' took the floor, "I cannot lower the curtain without sharing with my friend reader one last memory. Last Sunday, I found a paper near the computer that made me reflect a lot on it. I did not pay much attention to it, but moved by curiosity I opened it. To my great surprise, I found, attached to it, a necklace of the Madonna of the Miraculous Medallions. On one side I read,

"Immaculate Virgin Mary,
Mother of our Lord Jesus, we have

confidence in your powerful and
never-failing intercession,
manifested often through the
Miraculous Medal. We, your loving
and trustful children, seek your loving
and trustful children, seek you to
obtain for us the graces and favors.
We ask during the novena if they
will be for the glory of God and
the salvation of souls. You know,
O Mary, how often our souls have
been the sanctuaries of your Son
Who hates iniquity? Obtain for us,
then, a deep hatred of sin and that
purity of heart which will attach us
to God alone so that our every
thought, word and deed may tend
to his greater glory. Amen."

I pulled the necklace from the paper and hung it on my neck. The following day, I repeated the urine test at the doctor's office, and, as I testified earlier, the results were clear."

Phoenix' face was glowing with euphoria, with a mysterious radiant light. Tears streamed down her cheeks. "Why, my darling, I did not realize all the disrespect I showed to you? Why I did not know how to truly love you from the beginning? It could have been a catastrophe. Forgive me for all the hard time I gave you."

Mimi' covered her lips with the left hand and, with the right one; he took the handkerchief and wiped her tears.

"We owe everything to Our Lady," remarked Mimi'.

Phoenix shook her head and exclaimed with a touch of remorse, "Think! I was going after the wrong lady . . ." Then, she gave order to the maid to destroy anything related to it.

Phoenix' friends did not make much of the event. They were not around and declared that the apparition was the fruit of the peoples' imagination. "They are too gullible!" they stated. So, in the succeeding days, they invited Phoenix every night to go to the casino. She refused. They did not give up that easily, and, so, they insisted that August was the month that brought them luck. Phoenix was inflexible. With aplomb, she responded, "I am no longer the lady that you know for many years. I died in the past days."

"You are still alive!" responding one of them without understanding the real meaning of the sentence.

"My past is history. The present is what counts. Tomorrow is hope." Another friend stated, "Phoenix is truly gone insane."

It was the fifteenth of August, feast of the Assumption. Mimi' and Phoenix were sitting in the last pew. A great statue of the Blessed Mother was placed laterally to the main altar. After Mass, the priest and the parishioners would take her out for the traditional procession. The musical band was on the front, followed by two lines of children dressed as angels. A stout man bore a heavy and high banner right behind the statue. The priest and the parishioners were next.

Upon a panoramic view of the statue, Phoenix got startled. There was a dead dragon under her feet! Was she the one who appeared to them? Phoenix was struggling with those thought, when Mimi' whispered in her ear, "Doesn't she resemble the . . ." He was unable to finish. Both got inundated with a warm feeling that made them vibrate internally and externally. When it disappeared, they looked at each other speechless.

The bell rang to announce the beginning of the Mass. The priest said, "Dominus Vobiscum." A loud voice rose in unison under the vault of the temple, "Et cum spiritu tuo."

"I would like to extend my warmest welcome to any new parishioner."

Phoenix got closer to her husband. Both blushed. It had been a long time since Mimi' had stepped in a church. For Phoenix, who belonged to another Christian denomination, it was the only time. She leaned over him and said, "Are those words intended for us?"

"I hope not. I would feel embarrassed. I think he uses that language before every Mass. There is nothing personal. I guarantee it to you."

During the collection, Phoenix' eyes fixated on the statue. Mimi' leaned over her, "I still do not understand one thing," he queried in a serious tone. "Why did not she intercede for us before?"

"But, she did for you, my dear. As for the time element, we will never know it. One plausible explanation is that she does not appreciate people who seek immediate gratification."

The homily was rather short. The priest capitalized on the separation between God and man. "There is a widespread feeling among Christians and not Christians that God does not care about us anymore. He distanced himself from us. He abandoned us to our destiny."

Mimi' whispered to his wife, "I don't believe it! Those are the exact words of my past complaints. How does he know that?"

"Beats me!"

"My dear friends," the priest continued, "God left us not out of lack of love, but because he tired of our ignominious sins. Look! There are monsters ready to attack you!"

The audience went into hysterics. They turned around, jumping over the pews and seeking the exit in panic. The priest shouted, "Where are you going? Stop! Come back! You are missing the point. I was alluding at the invisible beast."

The latest remarks alleviated their fears, but they were not particularly clear. The ushers had to work hard to convince the people to return to their seat. Once, calm was restored, the prelate concluded, "My dear ones, the monster lodges in us. We must reform!"

Not too many people went for communion. The reason was evident at the completion of the religious celebration. The congregation wasted no time in the most extravagant comments. A lady exclaimed, "Now, I know why I have been rushing to the bathroom too many times!"

Another old man shook his head and said, "Maybe, I have been taking too many pills."

And a middle man stated, "At night, I hear something bubbling in my stomach."

At home, Mimi' and Phoenix could not believe the peoples' reactions. "They almost caused a pandemonium," said Mimi'.

Phoenix responded, "People need to be educated."

"I agree wholeheartedly with you on that," replied Mimi'. "And, now, we can close the curtains, "he added.

"Not yet," responded his wife.

Suddenly, a light shone through the window. A Woman appeared in a state of expectation. On her head, she had a crown with twelve diadems, under her feet, a slain dragon. She had deep blue eyes and her long, black and wavy hair flowed down her shoulders. She wore a white gown that reached her feet. Her head was covered by a white veil. Mimi' and Phoenix could not stand the light radiance and covered their eyes. The color of their faces turned pale and their mouths were blubbering. They fell on their knees and were engulfed, in what appeared to be, a mystical experience; however, that phenomenon lasted briefly. When they regained their consciousness, they tried to talk, but the voice was suffocated in their throat. Initially, the Lady did not utter a single word. She stood there watching both of them. Then, she directed her attention to Mimi', "You have won the greatest race of your life."

Staggered by the light intensity and by the surprise statement, Mimi' felt petrified. Soon, he regained some strength and turned to his wife, "Those are the exact words that the oncologist told me at the end of my ordeal. I can't believe it!"

"Believe it," replied his wife pronouncing each word in syllables, while she was completely absorbed in the Lady's vision.

The Lady smiled again and disappeared in a cloud of lights. Mimi' and Phoenix followed the incandescent luminary as far as they could. Suddenly, she felt a strange, internal peaceful feeling. She could not explain it. Gradually, she reached the cellular and contacted the doctor's office to schedule an appointment. The nurse announced to the doctor that Phoenix had reached a final decision and wanted to talk to him.

Mimi' did not know what to make of it, "Why did you call the doctor's office, honey?"

"There is something going on in my body. I can't explain it."

"What do you mean by that," responded her husband more curious than ever.

"I have been fighting a fierce battle with a savage enemy in the last few years without knowing it."

"I do not understand," insisted her husband.

Phoenix walked around the room as to loosen up her leg muscles. Mimi' kept on following her with his eyes in every step, too, had a monster in me."

"What is wrong?" asked her husband anxiously.

"I have been diagnosed with ovarian cancer and I do not have much time to live, according to the doctor."

"And, you kept me in the dark from all your pains?" pressed her Mimi'.

"I could not. I would have undermined your chances of recuperating."

"Is there anything they can do?" kept up the pressure Mimi'.

With an uncommon poise, she said, "There are a couple of treatments available, but the cancer is so advanced . . . And, this is no success story, my dear. Basically, there is hardly any hope."

"Oh, no!" cried out her husband.

Phoenix tried to console him, "On the other hand, after the light apparition, I felt a change in myself. I picked up the phone, as you saw me, and I set up an appointment with the doctor to verify if my imagination has gone astray or if the condition deteriorated behind any control."

Mimi' abandoned himself on the couch in a mood of despair. Outside, it got windy, chilly wind. As for Phoenix, it was not easy to schedule a second test even from a financial perspective. The insurance would not cover it. She had undergone one a few weeks earlier. Nevertheless, she decided to go through it again at her own expenses. After all, she had stopped going to the casino and her husband was a success story in the new business downtown. The doctor, upon the news, commented, "How can a woman be so stubborn! . . . Unless she has a magic band . . ."

THE SLAYING OF THE MONSTER

Phoenix went through the routine test and waited a few days for the results. In fact, the secretary called her and invited her to show up early in the morning at nine o' clock.

The doctor took off his eye glasses and wiped the brows. He waited patiently for about five minutes. He took a spray bottle and began to clean his glasses. A knock at the door interrupted his work. The nurse announced Phoenix arrival. "Let her in," responded the oncologist in a firm voice.

"Good morning, doctor! How are you?"

He did not respond to the greetings. Instead, he raised his head and said, "I notice a different mood in you. May I ask you what or who prompted you to request a second test in such a short period of time?"

"I do not know it. It is a question of feelings and feelings are unexplainable. I wanted to have a confirmation of my feelings," she said in a serene tone of voice.

"I fully agree with you on that, but may I ask you if you remember when such feelings started??"

"It is a long story, doctor. Why are you asking that question anyhow? Are you some sort of agnostic?"

"No, but medicine is science. It seeks hard facts. In your case, it cannot explain the phenomenon."

Eager to find out the truth, she inquired, "Which one?"

"You are no longer affected by any disease. It is gone! Gone! Do you hear?"

Phoenix screamed with joy. She became ecstatic and started to hug the doctor and the nurse. "Hugs and kisses are welcome early in the morning," exclaimed the doctor in the nurse's direction.

"Don't be facetious!" replied the nurse.

The doctor turned around to say something to Phoenix, but she run out of office like a tennis player who runs to the middle of the court after winning a tennis tournament. The nurse attempted to call her back because she had to sign some documents. In the waiting room, the patients did not know what to make of that high commotion. One of them suspected that Phoenix had gone insane.

At home, Mimi' waited for his wife's call, but she did not. When she arrived, the first question was related to the results. She suppressed her happiness and led him to the site of the apparition. Mimi' was waiting for the news, but she kept her lips tight. A ray of light filtered through the window. Phoenix leaned on her husband's side and closed her eyes. She whispered to him, "Mimi', the monster is dead."

The ray of light withdrew. Mimi' caught up with the meaning and asked her, euphorically, "You mean that you are clear from the monster?"

Phoenix nodded. Mimi' rushed for more questions, but she closed his lips with her fingers. It is over for both of us," she said. "Let us thank this ray of light from heaven." She opened her eyes, but the ray of light had disappeared.

Seven day passed by and Mimi' was at the Mass with his wife. Both were kneeling prayer after many long years. After a couple minutes of meditation, Mimi' whispered to his wife, "I killed my monster."

Phoenix smiled at him and answered, "I killed my monster, too."

They were about to return to a sitting position when they stretched their eyes to a statue across from them, almost hidden behind a pillar. They moved a bit more to the right and had had a full view of a Lady standing on a dead dragon under her feet. Of course, Phoenix had no knowledge of it, while Mimi' could not recall ever seeing it.

The two looked at each other with incredulity. The silence lasted for a while. Neither one of them had the strength or the courage to talk. Finally, Phoenix said, "I have the premonition that we mortals are in tune with the sinister forces of nature. We think we are indestructible. We pretend of being in full command of our destiny and become arrogant and unapproachable on a human level, to say the least. We are oblivious of the fact that man is only a component in the cosmic scenario of human existence. The human race breeds contempt in a constant vortex of conflicts, manipulations, distortions, Machiavellian schemes and Sisyphean delusions. When man finally decides to bend his knee in a state of humility, it is the death of an illusion and the birth of the real person.

The following Sunday evening, Mimi' prepared a great party at his house. None of his friends or relatives was invited. People came from every corner of the world that lived in the U.S. Some of them were distinctly recognizable for their somatic features or the color of their skin. They were Chinese, Japanese, Africans, Russians, Indians, and so on. The guests gathered in the large hall that served as a movie theater in the huge cellar. They raised the glasses, overflowing of champagne to cheering both hosts, but also to Chris who mingled with them to hear their reactions.

At one point, the lights slowly dimmed. Everybody was asked to sit. A young lady lowered the screen on the stage. Chris was sitting among the spectators. A man, from the back of the hall, clicked a key on the desktop of a computer and the first scenes of the movie began to appear. After about an hour, three raging monsters rushed toward the audience. The spectators shouted, "The monster! The monster! Kill the monster!" Their terror turned into a profound relief when an intense light from the space suddenly struck the beasts dead. Their feelings were at a rest when the word "End" slowly showed up on the screen and the curtains closed in. The lights were turned on in the hall and an excited guest yelled, "Where is the monster?"

A short lady answered, "He got killed!" The hall fell in a funereal silence.

Mimi', suddenly, jumped on the stage. His wife followed him. He looked intensely at the audience and said, "My friends, I have come to the end of my journey."

His wife got close to him. She put her arms around him and said. "This is the end of an agony. Of my agony. I, too, have seen the light through my suffering."

Chris was listening. He seemed to be immersed in deep thoughts. Mimi' invited him to join them. He walked slowly to their location and addressed the audience, "My hearty appreciation to all of you and to those in the future who will join us in our journey. Until the next time, this is Chris Lesaca. Bye, bye."

The spectators were still commenting on Chris words when the electricity went off. The crowd began to get uneasy. "We can't see!" yelled someone. "It is dark here!" followed another. Chris rushed to side wall and pushed a button. A large window opened and a mysterious light flooded the stage. The audience jumped on its feet. The spectators shouted in unison, "The light! The light! Finally, we got the light!"

END